sunburn

SUNBURN
First published in 2024 by Verve
Copyright © 2023 by Chloe Michelle Howarth
All rights reserved
First Melville House Printing: May 2025
Distributed by Penguin Random House LLC, 1745 Broadway, New York,
NY 10019 USA. www.penguinrandomhouse.com

Melville House Publishing
46 John Street
Brooklyn, NY 11201

and

Melville House UK
Suite 2000
16/18 Woodford Road
London E7 0HA

mhpbooks.com
@melvillehouse

ISBN: 978-1-68589-211-1
ISBN: 978-1-68589-212-8 (eBook)

Library of Congress Control Number: 2025934187

Printed in the United States of America
10 9 8 7 6 5 4 3 2 1

A catalog record for this book is available from the Library of Congress

The authorized representative in the EU for product safety and
compliance is Easy Access System Europe, Mustamäe tee 50, 10621
Tallinn, Estonia. gpsr.requests@easproject.com

sunburn

A NOVEL

CHLOE MICHELLE HOWARTH

MELVILLE HOUSE
BROOKLYN · LONDON

For Erin

sunburn

1

JUNE 1989

NOW IS THE TIME BETWEEN birth and slaughter. Another Summer has arrived. I spend my days waiting for something to happen. Something glorious, even something tragic. Nothing ever happens.

It's hard in the countryside, when there is nothing to do and nowhere to go. Life in the Summer goes slow, like one long, drawn-out fade of the sun. Doesn't every day in Crossmore feel that way, at this tricky age? Without the structure of school, and without any amenities in the town, there isn't much to do but hang around the village. Mother calls this loitering. She seems to take a stricter dislike to me in the Summer. I can understand that. Between my newfound admiration for drinking, the threat of a blundered attempt at sex, and the incurable frustration I feel, I wouldn't expect her to like me very much. Often, I am just as annoyed with myself as she is. Yes, I am at a very tricky age.

Perhaps when Mother was my age, she was like me. Once she might have felt the same thrill that I do when sharing a cigarette with the girls or coming home late. Perhaps she has forgotten what it is to only get glimpses of independence. Those glimpses are everything to me. Feeling adult is everything to me. It gives me a sense of self, which is important, I think. Recently, I have really wanted to figure out who I am. There must be more to me than being Martin Burke's best friend or one of the girls or the Nolans' daughter. I'm just not sure what that is.

Today Martin and I walked the long and bumpy road into the village together. There is a lot of talk about Martin and me. We are only friends. Although I presume we will end up as something more than that eventually. Truthfully, I don't like thinking about it. I just enjoy his company, that's all. I function far better with him than without. When we were eight, the Burkes withdrew Martin from St Anne's National School to go instead to St Andrew's, twenty minutes away. There was some trouble with his older brother and a teacher which his parents didn't want repeated. Off he went. I didn't think I would even notice his absence. Besides one feverish breakout of kiss chase in the yard, we never really played together in school. I didn't expect there would be anything to miss. But then he was gone, and I missed him every day. I felt so outside of things. It took me a long while to look around and not expect to see Martin smiling back at me. But it's easy to adjust to things when you're young. I got used to the void, it was fine. I was one of the girls after all, even without any girl friends.

On long school days, when I was missing him, I used to daydream that he and I could be married on our Communion Day. His and my school always joined up for the day, as well as the Gaelscoil, and still with the three classes there were only ever thirty of us. I knew that Martin would be at the altar in his suit, and I would be there in my white dress, and so it would just look right. I used to plan it so that when he said 'Amen', I would kiss him, and then we would be married. My most plain and easy dream; I don't even think anybody would have been too upset with me if I had kissed him. It would probably have been funny and well-remembered.

He takes me as far as the chipper, where the girls are all waiting for me. He will bring the boys in later. Our groups were never really separate like this before. But around the time that Maria Kealy became aware of the boys as boys, we split in two. Maria's interests very much influence the interests of the group, and so everybody became somewhat obsessed with the boys. If Martin and I were not magnets to each other, the girls might never speak to them. I am still waiting to find the boys intimidating. Often, I find my own girls more intimidating than them. Until I became the bridge between us all, I thought that I was a shy person, a sort of trembling leaf. Now I know that I am not a leaf, but a strong branch. I connect the blossom to the bark. Thanks to the girls' weak hearts, I have realised my own bravery. Perhaps it's just that I don't give to swooning as easily as the others. These days the girls let themselves crumble when the boys come around. I'm hoping that I'm just late developing, and in a month or two, I'll start to crumble as well. I can't stand being on the outside of what everyone else is feeling.

The windows of the chipper reach from the ceiling to the floor, and they play the same Eurodance CD on loop. I can see the girls inside now. There is Maria. Endlessly lovely Maria, with her tightly curled hair, her pointed nose, her long and straight torso. And there is bright yellow-blonde Eimear, and flaxen lesser-blonde Joan. Bernadette, and her teeth which so desperately need braces, and Patricia, barely visible behind her camouflage of freckles. And Susannah, beautiful sunbeam Susannah, with her coat folded up on the seat that she is saving for me. The walls are lined with white tiles, and there are strips of fluorescent lights in the ceiling which put shadows on their young faces. The bell above the door chimes, announcing me, and they all turn to look. How would they describe me now? Susannah lifts up her coat for me, camel-brown suede, and before I can even say anything about it, she says,

'Vintage.'

I could have guessed. A lot of my clothes could be considered vintage. They have been given to me by older cousins, some even saved from Mother's youth. Somehow my sort of vintage isn't as cool as Susannah's. She is miles ahead of the rest of us, with double ear piercings, her own hi-fi, and a hefty inheritance coming her way.

This food gives us acne, and yet we eat it all the time. Bernadette is not eating because she doesn't want to be seen with a mouth full of chips when the boys arrive. Bernadette doesn't eat around people, I think we were in primary school the last time I saw her put anything in her mouth. She is perched on the end of her seat, sucking her teeth like she thinks they are dirty. Joan, with her oval face having perhaps the worst reaction to puberty of us all, asks a plain question, which starts a fire among us.

'Any news about the Debs?'

This Summer, the Debs has been a greater concern to us than breathing. Before, we would have been interested on the day, with pieces of gossip about dates and dresses leading up to it, but this year it's all we talk about. I really don't know why. Perhaps because it's only a few weeks away, so it's in the air. Perhaps because going to the Debs is becoming less of a fantasy and more of a tangible reality. As girls only approaching Fourth Year, we would never get asked to go, but a girl in Fifth Year could be, and we know plenty of those. Perhaps it's just because we like talking about other people.

With Maria's sister Sorcha now a popular Fifth Year, we have access to an artery of information on the Debs, on the older girls and all their exploits. Gossip just comes out. Even when I don't want to hear it, I hear it, and so I know about the older girls – about who is failing which class, and who has been cheated on, and who is on drugs. Sorcha provides details so secret that we have been told Laragh Donnolley wears a red bra for PE, and she lets the straps fall off her shoulders, hoping someone will notice. My bras are all white and come in a box. They seem both juvenile and geriatric compared to what Laragh is wearing. If the older girls knew how we idolise them, if they knew all the intimate things we have been told about them, I would be so embarrassed I'd have to change schools. But they must expect it, when they see us with our jaws on the floor and our pupils fat in awe as they pass us by. This admiration is the natural order, I'm sure. It has been this way since we were in primary school. A nun would send one of them around to our little yard to do a job, and we would crowd around them like insects surrounding a spill of honey.

There are plenty of other things that we could talk about, but we talk about things like bras, and boys, and the Debs. Even when we have feelings that eat us alive, and which desperately need to be talked about, we talk about things like this. Nobody wants to bring the mood down. Imagining Debs dresses is nicer than airing out our emotions. Those awful, shiny satin dresses in their gaudy colours, the sort of things that keep us from thinking of our troubles, whether that is good or bad. Our dream dresses, and the dresses we would choose for everyone else, and past dresses we have hated. We have pooled the information we have about existing couples, and we dole out the remaining Sixth Year boys among ourselves, as though we have a chance with them. It should be embarrassing to have these fantasies at our big age, but this is a private game for us, so it's sort of alright.

Dates are always the worst part of this collective daydream, because all the good boys are already taken. All it takes is one wrong suggestion to be stuck with a boy forever. Eimear once flippantly said that Bernadette would look nice with Danny O'Neill in the year above us, only because they both have curly hair and freckles. Perhaps what she meant was that they look alike, not that they would look good together. These theoretical couplings can haunt a girl for life. Since Eimear said that, anytime Bernadette mentions a boy, somebody will turn around and say,

'But what about poor Danny?'

And lately, she has started to say,

'Well, yes, obviously there's also Danny.'

She has never liked him, but we all know, and she knows, and he has started to suspect, that when our own Debs finally comes around, they will be going together. There are plenty of these assumed couples, Martin and I are often mentioned as one. To avoid this, I tease Bernadette about Danny.

'Apparently, Niamh Mc has two dates.'

Niamh McNamara, glittering goddess of St Joseph's. I could talk about her all day and not feel silly, it would be a discussion of divinity. More beautiful, more pure than any girl in Crossmore, she is something of an icon among us. Hers are the grades Sorcha cannot tell us about; hers are the bra straps we have never seen; she is so subtle, so dignified. Fully developed, giving, intelligent, saccharine Niamh, with English cousins who have sent her Debs dress over from London. She is only in Fifth Year and already she has the Sixth Year lads fighting over her.

'Two dates? Well for some.'

'Yeah, Séan asked her first of course, but now John is after asking her as well, apparently.'

'Imagine choosing John over Séan!'

Bernadette's eyes are stuck on me while I eat.

'Would you be well?'

'Yeah, well, apparently she did.'

Maria is so cute. Everybody likes her.

'As if anybody would choose anyone over Séan!'

A sigh falls over the table at the thought of Séan O'Sullivan – six foot two, footballer, eldest of three sons.

'Séan could ask me to cross the road with him and I'd die, never mind asking me to the Debs!'

'Stop, he's so cool.'

Susannah says through a bite of her burger, chewing with her mouth open. I watch the meat as it is reduced to mush on her tongue. The girls all laugh. Susannah has connections with older boys, they all know her because of her brothers. She does not disclose the details of these connections, but she knows how to talk to them. She knows how to talk to everybody; somehow she knows exactly what everybody wants to hear.

'Poor old John.'

'Yeah, but would ye listen! Apparently, she said yes to both of them!'

'She could be asked by a third fella yet.'

'She nearly could.'

'I'd nearly ask her.'

I only say it as a joke, but it makes Patricia roll her eyes at me. It seems I cannot say the right thing to her, she is always looking at me like she hates me. It wouldn't bother me much if she does, because she is the least interesting and least pretty of the girls. The others don't like her either, they've all admitted it but they won't stand by it. I think we would get on fine without her. Even before all the misfortune in her life, Patricia wasn't a nice girl, but we have known her so long that she is unshakable. Sometimes knowing someone for a long time is the only reason you'd be friends with them. It isn't much of a bond, and still it is unbreakable. Patricia's father is a lot older than her mother, he is in the early days of dementia. Between her husband and her young twins, Patricia's mother doesn't have much time for her. The younger twin did not have enough oxygen at birth, they were not sure if he would live. He requires a great deal of care now, as does the older twin, as do all five-year-olds. It all means that Patricia lives a very lonely life at home. When she is headed for college, she will feel guilty for leaving her mother with so much, but she won't let it stop her from leaving. Sometimes her father doesn't recognise her. These times are becoming more frequent. Susannah feels a deep sympathy for her; sometimes they spend hours together, just the two of them, talking very seriously about life with half-parents. I only put up with Patricia because she understands a part of Susannah that I do not. I want Susannah to feel understood. Although when Patricia is sitting in the chipper, rolling her eyes at me, I forget to feel sorry for her. It might make me sound callous, but I have no patience left for her. Everyone else laughs at what I said about Niamh, they all know that the chance to spend any time at all with Niamh would be Heaven-sent.

'I'd ask her if I wouldn't look so ugly next to her.'

Joan laughs, and everyone laughs with her, and I just won't look at Patricia anymore today. It's the small punishment she deserves, which she might not even notice. Does that make me an awful person? I don't think her hardships are an excuse for treating me badly. I sometimes wonder if I am the only one who thinks Patricia is a nasty girl or who remembers that she has always been this nasty. All I did was make a joke; everyone has moved on but me. I'll keep my mouth shut a while, in case I say something else stupid. It's nice to get engrossed in the girls' imaginations while they talk about Niamh and her dress, and about how Séan will complement her so well. It's nice to watch them, and hear them, and feel I am one of them.

Although it's comforting, we have had this conversation so many times, and without staying engaged, I find my attention drifting from the table and focusing more plainly on Susannah's mouth. The girls' chatter is only a beehive's buzzing near my ears, but I hear very loudly her teeth cutting through her food. The slap of her tongue off the roof of her mouth. The squelching of her spit raising a hundred decibels with every bite. Must she eat like a dog? My cheeks redden, but I make no moves to conceal this, and in a wild moment of abandonment – something I have never known before – I think, I would be the microbes in the beef that her body seeks and destroys if it meant she would be paying me even the slightest bit of attention. The warmth and the wet of her mouth.

What a thought to think! How suddenly and vehemently I think it. And how hot my cheeks are. It makes perfect sense to want to be inside her mouth, to be torn to pieces by her; until I catch myself wanting it, and I am shocked, I am disgusted. I almost laugh at my own absurdity. That wasn't me at all, just a bad notion that got into my head to make trouble. That wasn't me who thought that. What a weird feeling. Very discreetly, I bless myself and hope to be forgiven, and I hope that I never feel anything so inexplicable or strong again.

'Lucy?'

I look up. They are talking to me.

'John or Séan, I said?'

Blessed be this tired conversation. I could have stopped listening for a year and I would still know what I am supposed to say. It's easy, these are my people, waiting for me to say the words and feed their hungry hearts. I understand these girls, I follow the pattern, it's alright. I give them what they want.

'Séan. Every time.'

They are drowned in a frenzy of giggles, and I let it wash over me, and as I see her mouth hanging open in laughter, I thank every angel in Heaven that Susannah has swallowed her food.

'Oh, don't let Martin hear you say that!'

Patricia winks, and I wish I didn't let her wink at me. I want a second alone to settle myself. But here is Martin now, coming to the door of the chipper with all the boys behind him. He looks at me, not at the other girls. It feels very nice when he looks at me. My heart races, and I keep my eyes on him. It's grounding. The girl behind the counter hates to see the boys coming. Bernadette sits up tall. It begins.

2

WHEN I GET HOME, GRANNY announces me to everyone.

'Here's our changeling, now.'

It's her special joke just for me. I think it's because I have recently gone from child to young woman; perhaps there is more to it, I won't let myself be offended. Mother makes me sit at the table and eat dinner with everyone even though she knows I have already eaten, because I'm not supposed to eat at the chipper.

'Waste of money and waste of appetite.'

Mother says as she heaps boiled vegetables out of the pot and onto my plate. I struggle through the carrots and parsnips while she smirks. My perfect Mother, a sweet and stinging honeybee. When I was a little girl, when I was very young and confused, just a small fruit fly bumbling around her kitchen, I refused to leave her side. Even at my small age, I understood that there were limits to love, and I felt sure that one day people would run out of love for me. I think with Mother, it started when I was in junior infants, when I received three slaps to the palm from Sister Loretta for playing kiss chase in the yard. Mother was always so smug over my good behaviour. Even today, she likes demure and cooperative girls. That day with my ruler marks was the first time she thought I might not be as easy to manage as I seemed. Granny said I must have done something awful to deserve it, because these things don't happen without a good reason. But the truth was, I shouldn't have been slapped, because I didn't even want to play kiss chase that day. Without meaning to, I played the game and got kissed. How was I to explain all that? I couldn't even say the word kiss in front of them, let alone explain the workings of kiss chase. Granny was so frustrated with me that she promised to slap my other palm until they matched, but it was an empty promise.

'Ah, dote, you'll be better before you're married.'

Mother said, like she always did, although for the first time her tone was weary. Besides that, all they did was send me to bed a half an hour early, where I lay on the freshly washed sheets and inhaled the smell of her detergent, and I felt her love in the pillowcase.

We have never been the type of family to argue; we feel things very strongly, but we feel them quietly. Our deepest emotions may be manifested in the lightest of sighs, but not much else. The silence says a lot. All that upset has to go somewhere; I sometimes feel it moving under my skin, waiting to be lanced. One day, Mother will grow tired of me. This isn't a worry or a guess, it is an instinct. Her affection will wane, and so I must absorb all the love she gives me while she is giving it. She was never annoyed by me staying so close to her in the kitchen. Granny used to threaten to put me on the back doorstep if I didn't stop following Mother around. She used to say,

'If we leave you out there for the night, another mammy will come along and take you away. We'd have no trouble then.'

Many times, Granny would open the door and point to the step and slowly count to three, but I was never actually put outside. Mother wouldn't allow it. All I wanted was some company, to be one of the grown-up girls. I never thought I was being a pest until I was made aware I was one. Whenever Granny gave out to me, Mother would scoop me up, and with a little groan, she would sit me on her hip, and she would say,

'Sure, Lucy is my little helper. There's no one helps me as much as this one! Oh, but you're too big to lift up anymore.'

Still she kept lifting me without being asked to, and I guessed that meant that I didn't have to leave her alone. When I was a little girl, it was always like that. I was always welcome around Mother. I might even say we were inseparable. Now that I am getting older, it doesn't matter whether I am right next to her or out of sight, I'm heavy in the air, I am something always on her mind, she cannot be without me, even when she is dying to be. Maybe I deserved it, maybe not.

After dinner, Martin comes over for my Irish lesson. Last year I dropped from the Higher Level class to Ordinary Level, and still I am falling behind. Unable to pay a tutor, Mother has enlisted Martin to come over and help me in the evenings. He does as she tells him. Isn't that insulting? Granny used to try to help me out, but with her temper so short, it only made things worse. Martin is breezing through Higher Level Irish, so my curriculum is nothing to him. In the low and sleepy light, he sits next to me at the kitchen table and kicks me when he sees my attention fade. He is trying harder than usual tonight to keep me interested, as Mother can see us from the living room. She won't look away from *Glenroe* for long enough to catch me daydreaming. He should know that.

Although it's nice that he wants to help, I don't think this is a fair way to teach me. Martin isn't embarrassed about it, he thinks he is being helpful, and he is very happy about that. This deep into the Summer, I just don't see the point in homework. Whatever I learn now will be forgotten by September, I promise. Then I will be back in the classroom, not listening and not learning. I don't know why I need to waste my evenings preparing for that.

After an hour of trying to teach me, he gives in and lets us play hangman in his copybook. It's sweet that Martin wants to help me, it's funny that he thinks he could hold my attention. I like sitting at the table with him, with the evening air coming in the window. He never makes me feel upset or stupid when I can't keep up with schoolwork.

He makes me feel grounded. While I'm trying to work out which letters are missing, he tells me how cool he thinks my new jacket is. I don't bother telling him that the jacket he saw me wearing today was Susannah's and that I was only trying it on. It's the compliment that counts. I don't think he looked much at the jacket, but he definitely saw me admiring myself in it. He is attentive in ways that the girls aren't. I want him to know I appreciate it, but I don't want to have to say anything about it.

When he leaves, I watch from the back door as he disappears down the garden, out onto the dark road, taking the last of today's goodness with him. Then I am left alone with my family. Mother comes downstairs in her dressing gown to take a painkiller. Something about Mother in her nightdress puts me on edge. She tells me to turn off Ciarán's lamp when I am going to bed and leaves me alone again. I hate the quiet of the sleeping house, especially after a day out with my friends. The silence rings. It makes me feel so much more isolated than I really am. I ought to go to bed before I have a chance to do too much thinking. I linger at Granny's door as I pass. When I was young, I would always go in and say goodnight to her. A big part of me wants to go in and do that now. Instead, I go upstairs and convince myself that she is probably asleep. As much as I like getting older, parts of it make me feel guilty and uncomfortable. I brush my teeth and knock a lump of dried toothpaste off the edge of the sink. I don't know if it's me or the mirror, but my face looks too long. It's my hair, it doesn't suit me at this length. I should cut it short again. That was flattering, but that was not very feminine. The girls all have long hair, even the boys have long hair. I want to look like all of them. I could look at myself in the mirror all night. In bed, I hear water run through the pipes. The immersion timer clicks off, and the house exhales. Today is over, and we have a few hours before we must start again.

Although we don't discuss it, the girls had similarly melancholic evenings to me. Patricia went home to a darkened house, just the glow of the television on her parents' worn-out faces to let her know that anybody was there. The volume was very low, their phone might as well be disconnected for all the use it gets. Eimear's house was alive with the choir of her young siblings crying over bath time. Her mother did not notice as she came through the door and trudged up the stairs to her bedroom. As Susannah made her way up the steep driveway of her house, Croft Hall, she saw her father's car gleaming in the evening light, and she heard her mother shouting. When she got inside, Catríona slammed her bedroom door, and Phil threw something heavy at it. He is not a big man, but he uses every ounce of the weight he has. Normally he would only visit when Catríona is not around. The rest of the time he spends with his shining new family in the city. Susannah didn't bother asking him why he was in Crossmore.

'Waste of time! Waste of money!'

He shouted, but softened when he saw Susannah.

'Hi, Daddy.'

Taking her face in his hands he said,

'Did you get something to eat, love? There's no dinner made.'

She nodded, and he told her,

'Great. Go away up to bed, why don't you? We'll go to the garden centre tomorrow before I go.'

He headed to the guest rooms downstairs, and then she was in a silent house, just like me.

This is how the days go, and how the evenings follow. This Summer has been so quiet, surely something explosive is to come. Surely, we won't carry on like this for much longer, gossiping and eating and coming home to disappointing houses. In our separate and sad beds, we all think of each other, and although I don't mean to, I think of

Susannah and her chewing, and I say a prayer that I won't think about it tomorrow.

Like always, my prayer goes unheard, and I struggle through four days of intense focus on her jaw, her incisors, and her amylase. I wish I could explain it.

When, finally, I come to terms with the functions of her mouth, and I think it's over, she thrusts something new and unexpected at me. First it is the reflection of sunlight on the sebum on her forehead, and then it's a blue pedicure, and then a golden crust of pus on her bitten and infected cuticle.

Regrettably, this is not a new fascination. Susannah is the very reason that I did not try to kiss Martin on our Communion Day. Among the flurry of ivory and white and organ music, there was the blinding light of Susannah, who looked as though she had been dipped in bleach. Hers was the only dress not borrowed from a sister or cousin. Suddenly, I could not forget that my own dress had been starched and rehemmed and passed around the family so many times that one wrong move might have unravelled it entirely. I spent half the Mass burning with jealousy over how brilliant she was. How was God going to see me as worthy of Communion, how was he going to see me at all, when she sparkled so beautifully beside me? I remember that day her prayers were said so perfectly, each syllable enunciated properly, as though she understood the words as words, and not just a slew of sounds she had committed to memory like me. Watching her pray was much more captivating than whatever Father McDonagh was doing with the wafer and wine. I could not feel my bony knees on the carpet at the altar rail anymore, I could not feel the draft of the church. She took her eucharist before me, and I quietly apologised to Jesus for the downgrade from her tongue to mine. It was a feeling of deep shame which I still don't understand. Martin was then the last thing on my mind. As was our kiss. As was marriage. My interest in that has never really resurfaced with the same fervour. Sometimes I wish it would.

Afterwards, outside the church, I did not wish Susannah a good day, because my own day was ruined by her poise and beauty, and her terrifying grace. I never knew a person like her, nobody else made me so afraid. Back then, it was easiest just to hate her. I get the very same feeling now, even when it has nothing to do with Martin. I don't know why it makes me feel so badly, or why I felt so guilty on my Communion Day. I don't know why I remember it so well or feel it so strongly. But I am sure that if I can understand these pieces of my past, I will understand my present. And so I allow memories like that to circle, while fascinations like this evolve.

The first weeks of July come and go, and when the day of the Debs arrives, I hardly even notice anyone's dress. I am too enamoured with the hole in Susannah's jeans, her unshaven knee exposed. It's alright, I'm sure in every group there is one friend who is superior to the rest, and everyone admires this friend. I am sure the other girls look up to her the same way.

When September comes, I do not hear any gossip from school. I do not keep up in my Irish class. I only go to school so that I might get another moment of her. With each shortening day, I am reading deeper into her unconscious movements. Perhaps I do not want it explained.

October brings a capsule of fake blood to her mouth, which she bites and lets drip down her chin, laughing as we walk all our young siblings around trick or treating. She tells me I am a good sister, something she doesn't say to the rest of the girls.

December brings her blue lips, after she and Patricia sit talking in the ruins of an old farmhouse for hours, not leaving despite the cold. Afterwards, she tells me everything that they talked about. It all seems very personal. I'm not sure why she trusts me with it, especially when she has already vented to Patricia. Susannah tells me more and more these days. I wonder if it upsets Patricia.

February brings a new tube of frosted lip gloss, Phil's way of saying sorry that he didn't make it home for the weekend. We start spending all of our weekends together so that she doesn't have to be on her own. So that I don't have to spend a moment without her.

I am glad that we have so few classes together. When she is off excelling in Higher Level everything, I am struggling through Ordinary Level and enjoying the small respite from her. I have heard it said that the only reason she tries so hard in school is to try to impress her parents. That's not fair, and it's not true. Susannah is very clever, she doesn't have to try, and her parents are never impressed. It's not nice to admit, because she is my friend, but when she is in class with me, I feel under such pressure to concentrate and be smarter than I am, because I can't think of anything more embarrassing than failing in front of her. It is not made easier when I cannot keep my eyes on the blackboard because they keep drifting to check what she is doing. I check the other girls, to see who they are staring at, and to make sure that I am not the only one falling behind. My grades might benefit from repeating the year in another school, where she is not.

All of Autumn, and into Winter, and now Spring, I have been far too deep in Susannah and her wonderful mouth. A year wasted on watching her. The long light of March is so welcome, I must clean myself in it, I must move on from this. Am I wrong to notice all the things that set her apart from the rest of us? She is better, nicer, prettier, just miles ahead. There's no trespass, it's just a year of watching, and observing, and waiting for the next thing that will make me crumble. There are times when it becomes so much that I can't stand to be around her. But there is something in her attitude that I am drawn to. Perhaps it is the way that she hardly notices my admiration. Or the way that she can bully me or be my best friend and I can hardly tell the difference. Perhaps it is her moods, the glows and shadows of them, as though her heart is made of the changing sky. It's humiliating to wonder if I have ever meant the same things to her as she does to me.

My only solace from all this is Martin. Seven months my senior, and his house just a scattering of fields from mine. The Burkes are the nearest thing to neighbours that we have. Originally, his proximity to us was the only thing that made us friends. It made sense for our mothers to share school runs, and with his siblings about the age of my siblings, the Burkes and the Nolans naturally fell in sync with each other. Now I don't think I could function without him. I've known him too long, he has become a part of me. Since we were young, he has been a carbon copy of his two older brothers. Each of them a pale-eyed, dishwater blond. I can tell by his brothers what Martin will look like in two years' time, and in four years' time. It will not be altogether different from the way he looks now. I wonder if it is reassuring for him, to know that he will always look absolutely fine. The only look into the future I have are a few creased photographs of my mother. I try not to think about how we will grow up. I try to focus as much as I can on the moment that I am in. It makes things easier.

Like now, this evening in March, when Martin is in my garden, and I am throwing a sliotar towards his hurley. This isn't my favourite thing to do, but I know that he likes it. When we were younger, I spent a great deal of time standing in goal for him or catching his handpasses, doing anything I could to get him to hang around with me. I was fascinated by him then. I was fascinated by a lot of the boys. In the last year, I've realised that even when I refuse to play GAA with him, he still likes to hang around together. Whenever I want him, Martin is there. He knows I don't like to play GAA, and so he lets us just sit and talk. Still, I know he likes to play, so I put the effort in whenever he hands me the hurley. He isn't like the rest of the boys; I don't think they would want to have conversations with me. The stickiness of puberty has given us a lot to talk about. When we spend the evenings talking and playing in my garden, I feel so liminal. We are adults and children at once. It's my favourite thing to do. Nobody else really makes me feel this way. With the girls, no matter how comfortable I feel, I am always afraid of being the odd one out. With Martin, there is no fear of that. I am never a loser with him. I never have to try. He just likes me as I am.

For all the long years of our childhood, we have been so closely together. Now that we are growing up, I sometimes feel we will be pulled apart. I am getting further from my family, from my home, from him. The girls and I get closer. Susannah and I get closer, and closer still. No matter how much I want to spend my time with Martin, it seems these days I am always with the girls.

3

MARCH 1990

HERE, THE DAYS DRIP BY as slow as half-melted candle wax. Time is hard and soft at once in Crossmore. It is the meeting place of the old world and the new, I think. Once it was a big and important town, with a train track and a heaving mart, I have heard. There were plenty of young people, plenty of opportunities for them. Grandparents and nuns like to remember it, and they tell stories so well that I remember this version of Crossmore without ever having lived in it. There are two photographs of that old Crossmore in St Joseph's Secondary School, one showing a steaming train with windows full of passengers waving, and the other showing crowds in the centre of the village. That Crossmore is very far away now. I sometimes wonder if the rest of the world even knows that we are still here.

There is no need to come by anymore. The train has stopped running, and the track has been eaten by grass and wildflowers. The mart has been relocated. There are more thorn bushes than people. Soon the sprawling farms around us will be halved and sold, and split between children, and halved and sold again, and the city people will come and buy up that land, and they will build houses to live in during the Summer, when we are worth visiting. They will make Crossmore important again, even with their absences; it's the money that does it, although we will pretend it isn't. Right now we are between uses, and it is very quiet. The last census reported that there are only 335 year-round residents in Crossmore, but as a year-round resident, I can say that number sounds awfully high. It feels like it's the same thirty or forty of us milling around all the time. This is one of the few things Granny and I agree on.

'They must be all hiding.'

She said, and sometimes still I wonder what ditch or ruin they are in, and if they would let me join them.

I suppose it's nice to live somewhere quiet. To me, I think, a city would be an overwhelming melting pot. Dad likes to remind us that there is no chance of a bombing in a place as far away as Crossmore. It's safe. It's airtight. In a place so small, there isn't much room for wild thinking or ambition. That can be a comfort. We may have been born unique, but the village blends us all into one person. We are superstitious, religious, traditional, that's all. The only differences between us are slight. There are Protestants among the Catholics. There are rich among the poor. Those who have children and those who can't.

The only true deviance from normality in Crossmore is Catríona O'Shea, Susannah's mother. She is the stray that we all recoil and marvel at. She lives in the closest thing Crossmore has to a Big House, with no mortgage, and no obvious income, and no husband at home. A rural socialite is a funny thing to be. I wonder how she copes with the attention. Her life has always been scandalous, which makes Susannah's life sadder and more dazzling than the rest of ours could ever hope to be.

'Them O'Sheas are no Catholics.'

Mother says, as though it levels her and Catríona out. When I compare Catríona to Mother, and other women in Crossmore, I don't know which of their lives I should be aiming for. What is worse, to be remarkable or unremarkable? I wish I had never noticed that we girls replace the women, that the boys seamlessly replace the men, and that we all follow a pattern. I ought to follow the pattern, to bask in all the wonderful security it provides. But then I see Catríona, disregarding patterns. Look what that has left her with: a buzzing social life, endless glamour. Something about it is sad to me. If not sad, then certainly scary.

When I was young, I never imagined there might be anything beyond the horizon. This was the only sort of life that ever made sense to me. Now I wonder if I could go somewhere else, somewhere that is busy, without thorn bushes, with functioning train tracks, a place that does more than buzz on the ghost of once being important, as our village does. Imagine a place where I could scream and not be heard, and fail and not be seen. A place where my insignificance would not hurt, because everybody would be insignificant. That is not where I am. Here, every breath is heard, every evil thought is known. It might be beautiful to look at, but it is abysmal to exist in; a sweet, sad dream. And while I could think of a million places that I would rather be, I fear that I will never have the nerve to leave. I fear that Crossmore is too deep in me, and I would not know how to exist elsewhere.

Everybody is frustrated when they are fifteen, I know, but knowing this doesn't ease my frustration. It feels as though I am an island, apart from everybody else. Perhaps we are all islands, apart from each other. Perhaps everyone else feels foreign in their hometown too. Yes, perhaps we are all just islands, as wild and merciless as each other, separated by our countless defects. Perhaps there is no remedy for it, and all we can do is learn which parts of ourselves to deny and which parts to bring into the light.

We have mothers at home and fathers out working, we all have votive candles on the kitchen windowsill and masses of siblings to get lost in. Outwardly, we are all living the same life, but inwardly, I hope, everybody has as many private crises as I do.

My father, like most Crossmore fathers, is on the farm all day and in bed all night. He comes in for his dinner, sparkling with rain and smelling of sweet silage and sweat, his hands swollen and caked with grey dirt even after washing them. While he eats, he listens and mumbles to all we have to tell him from the day, and when we are gone to bed, he speaks quietly with Mother about adult things. There are a few hours on Sundays when he is around, cologned and well-dressed for Mass. We eat our midday dinner, and he takes his time; he bounces baby Padraig on his knee, and if I've been missing him, I bring down some homework I know he can manage, and he helps me with it. It's just a way of being near him. The GAA pitch is only a short walk from the house, he goes down with the boys to watch the hurling and football. That's where the real bonding happens. I have no business there, so I miss out. They always come back laughing or remarking on something from the match, but they can't explain it, so it stays their private thing. He is a good father; we just seem to drift past each other.

My mother, like most Crossmore mothers, is in the house all day. She doesn't think that she gets enough thanks. Maybe she's right. Although the boys model themselves on Dad, they look so like her. The four of them have the same gently sloped noses, and soft eyes that make them look disappointed even when they're not. Even little Padraig is starting to resemble her. I don't think they realise how close to Mother they are, especially when they take such care to replicate everything Dad does, Tadgh especially. He has embodied all of Dad's mannerisms – the way he answers the phone, the way he stands, the way he jokes. Even when Dad is cold in the ground, he will still be out working the fields as long as Tadgh is around. He has started to do the evening milking on his own so that Dad can come in and watch the news.

One day, Tadgh will inherit the farm; it isn't a secret, it isn't a dream, it is a custom that Dad won't allow to fade. Whether he wants to or not, Tadgh will be a farmer until he dies. It might make us sound very grand, that there is land to be passed down, but the fields are very rocky, and so the cows never fatten as well as they could, and so they don't milk as well as they should. Even when Dad has gotten different bulls in, the cows never turn out much good. It all goes back to the land. Every Christmas Eve, Dad tells us a story that he was told as a child, about the old tenants of the farm who were evicted from the land after the Famine. He says that the daughter of that family put a curse on the land, so that it would fail anybody who took it after them. When the new tenants came in, relations of my father from generations ago, rocks had come up through the earth and rendered the fields useless. Mother leaves the room when he tells this story. She doesn't believe in it, but she is afraid of it.

'Sure you're all talk. How could any woman make rocks come up out of the earth?'

She calls in from the kitchen, trying to make Dad shut up, and when she thinks we can't see her, she quickly blesses herself.

A curse probably couldn't turn the fields to rock, but it's a very easy way of explaining the cows' poor yield. Stories like that carry weight. Even when nobody really believes them, they are taken as a sort of fact. Tadgh is getting a cursed farm that doesn't make half the money it's worth, we are not as grand as we might appear. Isn't it convenient that the career he wants most in the world will be gifted to him?

Maybe if he didn't spend so much time on the farm, Tadgh and I would be closer, but as it stands, I don't know very much about him. He isn't mean to me, but he isn't kind. I suppose it's hard to be either when we are so distant. Even sitting across the dinner table from each other, I feel like an imposition to him. He treats me more like a flatmate than a little sister. In school, he spends his lunches with the smokers behind

the hedges, and in the bathrooms, older girls will ask me,
'Is it true that your brother is with Claire Hayes?'

The name of the girl in question will change every so often, and I must pretend the reason I don't answer is because I am loyal to my brother, not because I don't know a thing about his personal life. I think if we made the time to talk, we could get along very well. Maybe when we're older, we will. For now, he is only a shadow to Dad, the same way I am trying to be a shadow to Mother.

The girls come from families exactly like mine. Maria is the last of the Kealys for the moment. Her mother is the youngest of seven daughters, and Maria is the same. Long ago, that would have made her a healer, but these days it doesn't mean a great deal. With so many daughters, there is every chance that Maria's mother will try once more for a son. Eimear has little sisters who we play with. Sometimes I like playing with them so much that I fear they are only humouring me, when it should be the other way around. Susannah's brothers are long gone from home, although they did both promise to come back for her when they are settled somewhere new. They have been gone for years, they have long since settled elsewhere, but still she clings to their promise, and she reminds us of it all the time.

'None of this will matter when Damien and Joe come and get me.'

She always says, tossing her responsibilities away. It's just a way of keeping her family together in her head, it's harmless enough.

After me, there were six years of quiet at home, and then came Ciarán, who still sees the farm as a playground, and me as interesting. Martin is on the junior hurling team, and he comes over to coach Ciarán in our garden for hours on end. It makes Dad warm to Martin, it gives me something to do. I wonder if Ciarán and I will always get along, or if he will outgrow me and only be nice to me when he needs something. The day is quickly coming when I won't be good for anything but drink and money, which is all Tadgh has been good for since last year. When that happens, I will have to be accommodating, because I am the older one.

I never expected a sibling after Ciarán, but last year Mother surprised us – and herself – with another pregnancy. Ideally, she would have stopped having children after me, because she only wanted a boy and a girl. In that life, there would have been room in the house for us all, and there would have been money to go around. Mother thought for sure that she was done with babies, with her youngest boy fresh from his Communion and her oldest headed for his Leaving Cert, but then she felt her belly hardening with Padraig. Dad told me I would never be stuck for attention, being the only girl among three boys.

I almost feel closer to Padraig than I do to Ciarán, probably because I have been tasked with changing his nappies and feeding him, and because he does not yet have the language skills to tell me to get lost. It appears that motherhood is the nearest thing to an inherited career that I can hope for.

Before us, and before Dad, Mother worked in the bank in Ballycove, and she made alright money, from what she has told me, but she gave it up to get married. She worked her last shift on the Friday, and she got married on the Saturday. When she tells us about her working days, she gets all wistful, like they are a dream she has just woken from and is struggling to remember. I suppose that is the case. She doesn't often talk about it; when she does, it is brief, as though she is breaking a rule by reliving it. It's not that she doesn't like to remember it, I think it just upsets her because that part of her life is over.

'They used to all wink at me, all the men who came in. It was annoying.'

She says, and I wonder if she means it. It's hard to imagine Mother being winked at, wearing high heels every day and blushing. At home, her days are more than full, but being busy isn't the same thing as being satisfied. She could be slowly cooking and cleaning herself towards her grave. Or she might enjoy it. Whether she regrets leaving her job or is very happy as a housewife, I will never know. Mother is not the sort of person to be honest when she could be ideal.

It's presumptuous, yes, but now that I'm getting older, I can't help but wonder about her experience as a mother, and as a woman, and how different her life might have been without children or with different children or at least without a daughter. Who would she be with one less child standing between her and freedom? Would she be an entirely different person? These days it seems like running to the clothesline to save the laundry from the rain is her biggest thrill. Maybe I'm wrong, she is probably fine. I can't imagine she thinks about her life the way that I think about it. Not often, at least. Something must happen when you get older that makes you see the joy in these small things. Though there are days when I catch her at the window, her apron sunk into her waist, twirling her short hair around her finger and looking out at the garden, and her thoughts seem very far away.

Right now she is present, in the kitchen, as we always are. She is bleaching the cloths, and Padraig is trapped in his wooden highchair. The window is open wide, and a dense rain is falling. Again, Mother is reminding me about how Granny and Dad said we should throw the highchair away because there would be no more babies, but Mother knew there was sense in keeping it. Of course, she thought one of Dad's sisters would need it before her, but still she was right not to throw it out. Everyone knows that she always ends up right, I don't know why we fight it. There is a harmony in the smell of bleach and warm rain. Padraig has a baby-sized flat cap in his hands, which he is putting on and taking off because I keep applauding him. As he squeals and kicks his legs, I see Mother watching us from the corner of her eye.

'Don't get him worked up, Lucy.'

The fun of babies is gone for her; poor Padraig is not cute or spoiled, he is just a little creature who gets overexcited and needs constant maintenance. The cap was a gift from my father's third sister. Mother thought she might be the one to take the highchair off us. Since she still has no children of her own, they made her godmother to Padraig. He is an enormous novelty for her.

'Pure waste of money!'

Mother always tries to be annoyed by the hat and its impracticality, but still she has a framed photograph of Padraig wearing it in her bedroom. She is not as harsh as she seems, she is just too busy to be sweet.

'Take it off! Put it on! Take it off! Put it on!'

I quicken my commands, and he quickens his responses, laughing.

'Aren't you smart? Aren't you so smart? What are we going to do with your big brain?'

He is giggling and I put the hat on his head, then on mine, his, mine, his, mine.

'What will you be, Padraig? A doctor? A farmer? Will you be a priest, Padraig?'

He is laughing, and it makes me laugh.

'Lucy!'

Mother warns. We're not supposed to laugh about priests. I lay the cap on my head.

'Well, I'll be an actress, I'd say, or a vet.'

'You might find a bit of time to find a fella.'

Mother keeps shoving herself into a conversation that should be one-sided.

'Mammy!'

I don't know why I am so embarrassed. It's not like Padraig can understand us. Still it all makes me shudder. Since I first crept into her room looking for sanitary towels, Mother has been hounding me about posture and diet and manners, readying me to impress boys and their mothers. Is she really so afraid that I will end up a spinster? Nothing stops her from reminding me that I will soon be a woman, and that there is a certain sort of woman that she wants me to be. That woman is the same as her, really, but with more money and a bigger house.

All along I've been ignoring Mother when she says these things, but last week Maria's sister Alison announced that she has been accepted to Mary Immaculate College. There's only three or four years between Alison and me, and already she is on her way to becoming a teacher. We used to play together in Maria's garden, but suddenly, we are not playing age anymore. The next three or four years won't be long passing, especially in these years when we are caught between children and adults.

Not just Alison, it seems that everybody around me is suddenly grown, and they're all coming up with grown ideas and plans. The Kealy girls that aren't teachers are nurses. It's just another pattern. Recently, Maria has started saying that when we finish school, she will train as a teacher as well, because the holidays are far better than a nurse's. Isn't she so clever to consider things like holidays? I don't even know what area I might like to go into, and Maria is already considering Summers and mid-term breaks. Maybe if I had all those sisters to model myself on, I would be a little more mature too. Tadgh isn't much for a guide, and with Mother breathing down my neck, I can't help but feel rudderless in a storm.

Right now it seems as though I only have two options: either I can be who Mother expects me to be, or I can be whoever I want to be. Each seems as treacherous as the other. I will find myself, soon, I just need to stop acting my age and grow up. Mother only wants the best for me. We are old and new versions of each other. I see pieces of her in me, and pieces of myself in her, and still it's like we speak two different languages; I in my funny rural blabber, and she in whatever tongue grown women speak. When I leave Crossmore, maybe I'll get it.

I always talk about leaving Crossmore like it's something I am definitely going to do. As if I would know how. I don't know where I would be going or who I would be going to or what for. Perhaps it's a risk not worth taking. Perhaps domesticity is a good thing to work towards; it's more than I'm working towards right now. Maybe I'll marry a farmer's son, who would give me a few children and a home to keep. I might enjoy it. I might drown myself in the baby bath. Who knows? Oh, I am faint from not knowing.

Perhaps next month, or after the Summer, I will have the drive to secure a future for myself. Perhaps I will forget the effect that homemaking has had on Mother, with her bright eyes now dull as old dish rags, her spark extinguished by my father and the house and all of us tireless children. All my life she has been my only role model, my greatest aspiration, but since I started to see her as a person beyond a parent, I have seen her as a grave misfortune, and now I cannot go back to the way I saw her before. Without all the mysticism of being my mother, she is just a woman, exactly like me, only with less time ahead of her, and – I'm beginning to think – all the same uncertainty. Maybe I'm just immature, maybe I could be happy too. Really, I don't even need to be happy, I just need to be the same as everybody else. It's an awful lot to think about.

Although at times their perfection amplifies it, the girls mainly keep me from thinking like this. Even when we exist as diametric opposites, I never feel lonely when I'm with them. Apart, we are weeds, but together, we are wildflowers, we make a beautiful garden. We make each other. I wouldn't make sense without them. I might not even exist. I know how to be like them. It's easy to imitate the way that they glide from children to women. All I need to do is dedicate myself to being passive and cute, and to this easy glide. As long as I don't allow Mother's words to filter into my head or give myself any room for introspection, my days will float by, vapid and simple. I can gossip and slack off and leave my choices to the democracy of the girls. When I am offered a cigarette, I'll smoke it. When there is a stupid joke, I will laugh. When Maria asks,

'Who do ye fancy?'

I will answer as if it is the most serious question in the world, because in a world as small as mine, it will be.

Maria, Godly Maria, who has always been miles ahead of the rest of us. Being the baby of all those sisters, she has long been exposed to the hot miasma of female hormones, which accelerated her puberty – or so she says. I wonder if there is any hatred in that house, among all those sisters. She turned sixteen last month. She feels like she is basically an adult now, and she is doing all she can to get us to catch up to her. One morning, not long ago, she woke up with her career chosen, her future children's names decided, and what she claims is an adult interest in men. I think she just repeats what she has heard her sisters say, so that she appears to have matured before the rest of us. Whatever the reason, it is no longer enough to blush at the mention of the boys; now we must make assumptions about their lips, their teeth, and their tongues. It all seems very graphic and unnecessary for girls of our age. Those rude, unwashed boys, why would I want to imagine such intimate pieces of them?

'You first, Susannah, who do you like?'

And when she turns to me, I regret asking, because she looks at me as if I have asked the wrong question, and when she answers, I know I have. She rolls her warm green eyes.

'Isn't it obvious?'

She says to me, smoky voiced, and I don't know why she is so hard on me or why she looks at me like I'm stupid, but I know I must be stupid, because she doesn't make mistakes. Susannah has her own language of looking, and this bitter look is one that she saves only for me. She wouldn't look at anyone else like this, it pushes my heartbeat up to my throat. It could be nicer, but at least it's mine. It isn't obvious who she likes, nothing about her is obvious. Susannah is a beam of the sun; we can't look directly at her.

It isn't fair that she gets away without answering. Everybody was satisfied without her even offering a name. I must learn how to do the same. I've always been the one to squirm in my seat and swear blind I don't like anybody. That was fine until somebody learned the meaning of the word frigid. I said it a few times before I realised what it means and that it describes me perfectly. A cold and unfeeling thing. A piece of sod, broken off from the heap. Perhaps Mother is right to be concerned.

To avoid being found out, I've started to casually mention boys' names and make up things about them that I like. Derek Twomney's unwashed hair, and Ryan O'Toole's tiny white football shorts, these small details that could potentially drive a person mad. I pretend so well I almost believe myself. Attraction is a very easy thing to lie about in conversation. It's only saying a boy's name and then a part of his body. It's just words. There's nothing to it. I will like somebody soon, when I find the right person. A sensitive boy, with long hair and nice bone structure and a soft voice, I'm sure. Until then, I can just keep playing the game.

Of course, there is always Martin. Sometimes I look at him like I want him, just to see if it will spark a feeling in me. It would be so wonderfully convenient if I did start to fall for him. The girls are driven demented with jealousy over our friendship, because they all crave a deep entanglement with a village boy of their own. There are less than forty telephone poles between his bedroom and mine, we counted one evening. His roof can be seen from our landing. Little details like that haunt the girls. Our friendship is now as it was when we were small children, very easy and innocent, and the girls' blood blackens to see us so natural together. They would like nothing more than to have an honest and open window into the life of a teenage boy. I don't see Martin as an opportunity the way that they do. I hope he knows that.

He and I walk to and from school together or, as the girls see it, he walks me to and from school, and we spend our long and rainy Saturdays watching television in my front room. He has a swing set in his garden for the sunny days. It was supposed to be taken down years ago, but his father sees that I like to swing on it still, and they like to keep me around.

When Martin turned twelve, his parents started allowing him to go into the village on his own, which meant that I, at eleven years and five months, was allowed to go with him. My parents would let me do anything if Martin was doing it. They trust him to look after me. They think so much of him, they think a lot of his whole family. The only flaw that Mother has found in the Burkes is that the boys grow their hair long, and the parents don't stop them. Besides the step in Martin's hair, Mother has full faith in him. He can hold a conversation, he doesn't smoke, and he is a skilled hurler. In Crossmore, that is the making of a fine man. It seems the boys have to do less to be considered impressive, in my house at least. It is insulting that my parents trust Martin more than they trust me, but I have not mentioned this to them. If I need a chaperone, I will take a chaperone, as long as I am allowed out.

Martin seems to like the responsibility. He likes it when Dad nods at him and Mother calls out what time he is to bring me home. It makes him feel like an adult, like a clever and strong man who I need. And I do need him. He is the wonderful anchor that stops me from drifting away into my worrisome thoughts. I love him, everybody loves him. My parents, my brothers, the girls, everybody. Soon, I expect, I will start to see him in a new way, the way Mother has wanted me to see him, the way that I think he sees me. I am looking forward to it.

Recently Rita Hegarty has started to see Martin this way, and the girls assume that this has made her the greatest bane of my life. She is thinner than me, and darker haired. She is the captain of the junior camogie team, and she excels in maths and sciences. She lives with her father. They go on hikes, and he smokes so she always has cigarettes.

'An absolute nightmare!'

Eimear often calls her. People think that Rita and I are in serious competition for Martin's attention. We are not. I don't have to compete, I always have his attention. I think Rita is far too interesting to like any boy from Crossmore. I also think she is far too interesting for me to dislike. Nobody believes me when I say that. It's like everyone else knows something that I don't. Perhaps I have unknowingly left a mark on Martin that makes him mine, I don't know. Rita is a perfectly nice girl, and if Martin wants to get together with her, then he should. For now, at least, while I am still unfeeling.

Although she knows all of the things that make her interesting and intimidating, it appears that Rita is still afraid of me. I see her out of the corner of my eye, a brunette-and-white line always darting out of view, fearing what I might do if I catch her. Wherever I got this witchy reputation, I don't know. Am I vindictive? Am I nasty? Does she not know that I am a lonely island? It might not be me that she is afraid of, but my group. Although we are such nice girls.

If she likes him, there is no issue, and in the reverse, if he likes her, there shouldn't be an issue either. It isn't as if she would be replacing me, because I am not Martin's girlfriend, I am not as important as a girlfriend would be. There's room for both of us. I keep telling myself this. In a year or two, when Martin grows into himself, girls will be lining up for him, I am sure of it. Rita should take him while she can. This is something I find difficult to communicate without sounding like I am in love. I wonder if I will ever fall in love.

4

DURING THE LONG AND TEDIOUS stretch of Lent, I realise that I am not the only one to notice startling things in Susannah. It happens on Wednesday, after school, when she, Eimear, Maria, and I decide to break Lent. It is Maria's idea. She says that if we all do it together, it won't be as bad.

We slip into the corner shop, where Liam Collins is working behind the counter. Liam is a year younger than us and generally unremarkable. We know him but we don't notice him. His uncle owns the shop, so Liam works there off the books after school. When we file in, he doesn't seem to care that a group of older girls have appeared before him; all he sees is that we are sugar starved and without adult supervision. There is no manager, there isn't even another customer to police this. It's just us, and Liam, and countless plastic tubs of sweets. Another boy would have been taken with at least one of us. Normally we can feel their eyes move across the group, but Liam is less interested in us and more worried about what we might do to his stock. A late bloomer, maybe; but watch, we are about to see his blooming.

'How are ye, girls?'

He tries to lower his voice to establish some authority, but he goes too low to be believed. We are huddled around the shelf with the boxes of penny sweets, our backs to him. Nobody ever pays for these sweets, and they rarely get caught.

'Not bad, Liam, yourself?'

Maria answers him, filling her pocket with cola bottles without stopping.

'Era, grand now. Fine day.'

Liam is doing what he can to appear grown-up, like we haven't unnerved him. Susannah gives him the attention that he is looking for, meandering over to the counter and leaning on the stack of newspapers in front of him, and her voice melts as she says,

'Warm day, isn't it? Very close like, very heavy. Warmer than you'd expect for this time of year, isn't it?'

Each dull word is weighted, slowly dropping off her tongue, and I can't help but watch as she leans further into him, like she is telling him a secret, and I wish that she would tell it to me.

The girls take the opportunity she has given them to fill their coat pockets with sweets, a cue that I miss entirely. Instead, I am watching as her heel rises out of her worn-out shoe, his throat bounces, and his eyes widen, as Susannah welcomes him into the world of her beauty. Now he is seeing in colour, now he knows light, and all she is doing is describing the weather. I cannot look away, I am too warm, and my throat tightens. Liam can't answer, his mouth is drying before her, and it makes her laugh. She laughs right in his face, and he doesn't seem to mind. The girls use his daze to run out of the shop; if I don't follow them now, I might not ever move again. It could be Liam and me, stood frozen from her, forever. And still I wait for Susannah at the door, holding it open with my foot, because I don't want to leave her alone with him. I don't want to spend a minute without her. My very best friend, my most frightening interest, I hope I am not as laughable as Liam. She takes a lollipop from the plastic box at the till, puts it into her coat pocket, and winks at him. She breezes past me without paying, and he lets her.

On the stone wall near Eimear's house, they all empty their pockets, taking from each other's piles. There is nothing in my coat.

'How did you do that?'

Eimear asks Susannah, her cheek newly swollen by a jawbreaker.

'Do what?'

'"It's so close, it's so heavy!"'

Eimear laughs, trying to make a joke of Susannah's seduction.

'Dunno.'

Susannah laughs with her lolly in her mouth, like she really doesn't care or understand what power she has.

Seeing that I didn't take any sweets, she sucks her spit off the lollipop and, unaware of how her saliva has flooded my thoughts since July, she offers it to me.

'Wanna share?'

Petrified, I do as I am asked and taste the lollipop. The mess of her chewed-up burger has come back to my mind; it is met by her liquid voice, the close weather, the heel of her sock exposed as she leaned over the counter, and the sting of sweetness from the lollipop at my back teeth. It's her spit in my mouth. It's her racing through my mind. I don't mind it. It makes me sick. I like it.

Spring continues to unfold, while me and Liam, and half of Crossmore, do what we can to stop ourselves from noticing her. These are futile efforts. Does she know the effect she has on people? Does she know that she is this adored?

Just when I think nothing could ever distract me from her, I am offered the most unwelcome distraction. Odd rumours have started to circulate about our lady immaculate, Niamh McNamara. Old rumours, that shouldn't have surfaced. I have heard that, while she was trying to choose between being Séan or John's Debs date, she decided she had to get to know them both a little better. Did you hear this one? She got to know one of them a little too well, and in Autumn she had to make a trip to England to sort it out. I don't know if I believe it. Apparently, she told one of her friends just before Christmas, and the news has slowly leaked all over Crossmore, permanently denting her reputation.

Bernadette heard that she had her pregnancy blessed the day that she found out about it, because she knew it would have to be terminated. Niamh McNamara, imagine. Secret and stunning Niamh, somewhere in England, her perfect ankles in stirrups. What a terrible distraction.

Rumours like this are one of the sorry ways that we entertain ourselves in Crossmore. Wild, nasty rumours, which are scarcely confirmed and forever remembered. Whether it is true or not, this will follow Niamh around the village, always. If we can't even find out what colour bra she wears, I doubt we will ever know the truth about this. I wonder if John and Séan have heard about it. I wonder if Niamh has heard. Sorcha quietly told Maria that Niamh was late for assembly every morning that September, until she went away for the weekend with her aunt.

'A shopping trip to London, she said, but she didn't come back with any new clothes.'

I don't know if I believe Sorcha, I don't think it would matter if I did. She will spread the word, and everyone will hear it. I dread to think what sort of things Sorcha knows about me, and the ways she could mar my name. I wonder if Maria will turn out as violent a gossip as her sister.

It is shocking. I am happy to be shocked, so that my mind doesn't wander back to where it was. But then, just as she has us all hooked, Maria tells us that we shouldn't engage with the rumours anymore. She says it was months ago, and it is nobody's business but Niamh's. Although she is right, I have to wonder where these morals have come from. We follow whatever rules she puts in place. Why ever she decided to change her mind about gossiping, I'm glad she did. I cannot imagine the panic of having such a deep secret spilled in Crossmore. This is not a forgiving place. The fear of it takes me over. It takes us all over. We all have secrets, everybody is hiding something.

For a brief spell, Niamh's problem leaves us afraid of intimacy, which is lucky for me, as it helps to disguise my faint, flickering interest in boys. Any day now, I will want to do the thing that got Niamh in such trouble. If it can happen to her, it can happen to anybody. Even those among us who are without their first kiss, those with unfinished puberties to focus on – they are equally interested in and afraid of sex.

Although the girls and I promised each other we wouldn't have sex with anybody until we were eighteen, our fragile virginities have already started to crack and fade. We pretend not to know who has lost theirs, and who is still clinging on. Eimear maintains that she hasn't done it yet, but everybody knows that she and Thomas Gleeson spent New Year's Eve in bed while his parents were out at the village party in the parish hall, where I was doing the YMCA with Bernadette and Joan. When I found out where Eimear had been, I felt so embarrassed for enjoying that childish dance. Maria has given some cloudy details about how far she lets Cian Whooley go when he takes her out driving. She has such wonderful power, if she tells Cian to wait, he will wait. I would like all of us girls to have that power. I would like all of the boys to have that sort of respect. Some of them will rush things. We all know that Sarah Wheeler was rushed by Mike Hurley last Summer, behind the grotto. When I look at Sarah now, all I see is mud on her shins and a chalky stain on her chin.

When I was young, I really did think that I would wait until I was married for all that, but my small world keeps expanding, and my opinions keep changing. More and more, I think that sex may not be the sacred union that I once imagined it to be. Rather, it seems to be a secular thing: condensation on a car window, squeaking skin on rain-soaked bales, a wonderful disgrace. That's what I have learned from the talk of my friends and from the talk of the older girls. Although it sounded shocking at first, those types of affairs now seem much more likely than the holy romances that we are told to wait for.

For the sake of my reputation, it's probably good that I am uninterested in these things. It's a blessing, it must be. It means my greatest fear is not teenage pregnancy, nor is my greatest shame a sordid affair with a boy in the year above, nor is my greatest regret a funny taste in my throat. My fear, shame, and regret are elsewhere; I know them all combined in one sickness when I stare at Susannah, deep and long, and without permission.

She must have noticed that I have been staring and getting muddled up in my thoughts, because she has started to pay me special attention, that is nastier than usual.

Her little bursts of bullying are coming more often. They are acute and swift, and although it seems they mean nothing to her, these moments of her attention shake me right down to my cold and dark core. She hides my schoolbooks. She chews the paint off my pencils and leaves her teeth marks in them. She stands on the backs of my shoes in school Mass. And then, when I turn around to say something about it, all the sunlight of March comes in through the stained-glass windows and dyes her strange colours. I am too stunned to be angry. Sometimes she is very mean, sometimes she leaves me very embarrassed, but always, I endure it.

When she doesn't like me, she makes it clear. I like that. Why can't everybody be that way? I would like to be that way. I would like to tell Patricia that I have run out of sympathy for her, and I don't want her around anymore. I would like to tell Tadgh that he is a stranger to me, and I don't think that is fair. I would like to tell Martin that I don't feel for him the way that people assume I do, and that I only encourage love that I don't reciprocate because the attention is good for me. Instead, I tolerate the constant rolling of Patricia's eyes, I let Tadgh ignore me, and I welcome Martin's intensifying attention. The slow and sluggish creep of it, coming ever closer as we walk quiet evening boreens, under a dim sunset, the hood of his jumper covering my eyes. The comfort of him. The threat of him. Yes, if I were direct like Susannah, I would tell him the truth. That I don't want to be with him, but I cannot be without him. It is selfish, but I don't want him spending his thoughts on anybody else. Maybe that's love. I don't know. It's best not to think about it. It's not like he is going to make a move on me, I think he would be too embarrassed to let me see him trying.

Besides the subtle weight of his longing, our friendship really is perfect. Of course, there are all sorts of rumours about us, and maybe Martin would have people believe them, but there are rumours about everybody. A part of me would like them to be true. It would be very convenient if I would fall for Martin, it just hasn't happened. If not for these rumours, people might deduce that Martin hasn't even had his first kiss. There are plenty of girls who would like to be with Martin, like Rita – she has not been shy about her feelings. So why does he not take the opportunity? My stomach curls up to think that he might be waiting for me.

Tonight, the boys are like barking dogs around him, hyping him up. They said that he is going to make a move that he has been dying to make. The excitement of a Friday night has them heated, they are like loaded guns, and they are trying to get Martin up to their level. From where I'm sitting with the girls, I pretend that I can't hear them. I ought to go home now, before something happens.

We have congregated in the playground, my girls, his boys, and some other people's girls and boys. We are dark shapes in the twilight. The Winter cold has stretched out to March, and I wonder if it will try to follow us all the way to the Summer. I hate gathering here, it makes me feel too young and too old at once. When I was little, I would have been so intimidated by big girls in the playground. And yet, here I am, one wasp in a swarm around the swing set. The younger young people head home before it gets dark; I'm sure we aren't bothering anyone.

There isn't much of a distance between them and us. We are near enough that I can hear the revving voices of the boys, just not near enough to make out the words said. Martin is pale eyed and tense as he looks over to us. I wish he would look right at me, so I could smile at him and laugh, and he might relax. Instead, he looks past me, to the other girls – my goodness, he looks like he could drop dead. Just out of his eyeline, Aisling Bennett is gently pushing me on the swing. Her lazy, long arms pull the chains towards her, and then she lets them go. Rita is leaning up against the bars, staring at Martin while he tries not to stare at me. She will have to watch as he approaches us and gives me all his attention and then gets turned down; it's good that she has something to lean on. Couldn't she pick up all the pieces of him then, wouldn't that be fine?

Poor Rita, she is hardly breathing so that she doesn't draw attention to herself. It's like she's trying to blend into the night. The girls hate her because they think that she is my competition. Rita is not my competition, she cannot blend in, she is far too pretty for either. How awful she must feel, I would hate to be on the wrong side of the girls. It's not that we are a mean group. In fact, I have always thought that we were exceptionally nice – but then, when girls as nice as Rita are afraid of us, it makes me wonder. I could say that it's our loyalty to each other that makes us behave viciously, but sometimes I think we are just vicious. I'm glad to be in the group and not outside it.

Aisling is telling us all about these new shoes that she wants, and we are all sort of listening. Nobody needs to mention Martin. It's in the air, we already feel it. Isn't it funny that some of the girls have already slept with boys and some of us are still this afraid of kissing? Any minute now, Martin will approach, it is unstoppable. He will come in like a cold wind and chill me to the bone. I will have to reject him, or accept him – I don't know which is worse. Can we not just remain islands?

The trees are black against the sky, and, high up, the birds are loud, aggressive in their evening song. The noise of them is all that I have to distract me from the chattering of Rita's teeth and the chanting of Martin's boys.

'I love your belt, Lucy.'

Rita says in a shy voice, and I feel so sorry for her. This is just an ordinary brown belt; it might as well be a length of rope for how unremarkable it is. Listen to her, trying to keep peace between us, when there is nothing that could disrupt it. Poor, confused Rita, making a victim of herself.

'Thanks. It's old.'

When I try to be self-effacing it comes out like sarcasm, as if I'm trying to make a fool out of her for complimenting me. She sinks further into the bars, making herself a little bit smaller. Joan laughs, and it sounds sour. She thinks she is helping. There is a tension building around the swing set. Yes, I know I said we are an exceptionally nice group. Maybe it would be more accurate to say that we are exceptionally nice to each other. It isn't that I need Rita to think we are all lovely or even to like me, I would just like her to know that I don't hate her. It's more for my reputation than for her state of mind. The tension is peaked by a boy's voice, cracking behind us.

'Here, Martin wants to talk to you.'

These words come to us like the news of a disaster. Why must the boys behave this way? We are too old for this. Could Martin not do this to me later, when we are walking home? There is no need for this messenger, and all the publicity. Perhaps alone with him, I would feel something new. Perhaps if we were closer, on a dark, thin road, where it's just us and the night air, I might see him in a new way, the way that I have been wanting to see somebody. Perhaps there, alone, I would find an easier way to let him down. Why does he make it so difficult?

Heaving a breath up from low inside me, I twist in the swing to see which of the boys Martin has sent over, and I realise with a shock that the invitation is not for me at all. Rita has peeled herself off the bars, and, without looking back at me, she follows Jack over to the benches, where the boys are dispersing and leaving room for her to sit down. Aisling holds tight on the chains of the swing, and it stops me from turning away.

'No way.' She says without thinking.

Then, with her arms thrown like branches in the wind, Maria starts to tell a wild new story about Niamh McNamara: that she was seen planting a tree in her garden, trying to hold some sort of memorial. All ridiculous, tasteless lies, obviously, but Maria goes on and on with the rumour, and she talks about how brave and how heavenly Niamh is. Did she not make us all agree that we wouldn't speak about Niamh's trouble anymore? Is Martin not supposed to be in love with me? My Maria, breaking her own rules to distract me, can't she see I am already distracted?

I'm just a little shocked, that's all. It's just a little bit humiliating. Not because Martin wants somebody else, but because I am not as important as I assumed I was. Although the girls are pretending to listen to Maria, I can tell that they are looking right over her shoulder, to watch Rita laughing softly, and Martin leaning ever closer to her. Then their eyes twitch back to me, as if they are waiting for me to explode. Do they expect me to get up and beat Rita into the ground? I didn't realise that people thought I was so feral.

Do we really have that bad a reputation? Soon there won't be a breath between them. They will make one new creature. I cannot help but laugh.

'If she's so afraid of me, why did she get up and do that with literally no hesitation?'

I say, and I am surprised by the force in my voice. I might as well spit on the ground. Why would I suggest that anybody should be afraid of me?

'The dirty bitch.'

Joan says, not caring that Aisling will hear, and that Rita will be told. No, I don't think that we are nice girls at all. How disappointing this evening has been. Doesn't Martin deserve a little love? Anything that I say about it now is going to sound like an insult, and yet staying quiet will sound like I am grappling for a scrap of dignity. Aisling is slow to speak in case the girls turn on her. I know by the feel of them that they are just waiting for her to say something, so that they can attack her. Rita is a slut now, she will never be anything more, the girls will make sure of it. Just as I think I should stand up for her, I am stopped; as if Martin doesn't love me, as if he doesn't care about me, as if I really am just a piece of frigid sod, he kisses her.

'Let's go.'

Joan says, and Maria puts a hand on my shoulder.

'But I'm supposed to walk home with him.'

'I'll walk you. I'd say he's here for the night.'

With that, I am escorted from the playground, and Aisling is left on her own, gripping the swing chains and watching Rita kiss Martin with a braid of envy and fascination forming inside her.

All the way to my gate, the girls list the endless flaws of Rita. She isn't as bad as they say she is. I am glad that they don't list the flaws of Martin, because I know them, and I would regret ripping him to pieces. It isn't that I want him, it's that he wants somebody else. Since when am I not enough for him? If I'm not enough for Martin, I may never be enough for anyone. There's no dignified way to say that to the girls. When we get to my house, they want to talk at the back step all night. At eleven, Mother knocks on the kitchen window and beckons me inside, and I'm so glad to see them leave.

I spend a long weekend in my bedroom, trying to get comfortable with my defeat and sudden inadequacy. If I can come up with a way to appear unbothered by this, I can face everyone again. Then maybe I will begin to understand why I am so badly bothered. By Sunday evening, the humiliation has subsided, sort of.

Martin has every right to take affection where he can get it. He would have been waiting an awfully long time to get some from me. It's all terribly confusing. After Sunday dinner, he appears at the back door. He stands on the step, waiting for me like always. His mother smooths down his hair for Mass. She makes him and his brothers wear shirts. If his mother only knew how he embarrassed me on Friday. I don't like it when he looks this clean. This morning, after the service, when all the adults were chatting in the churchyard, he walked right past me, out the gates and towards the car. I knew better than to follow him. Martin isn't one for apologies, and neither am I. We have never been emotional people, we don't like talking things through. It means that the cold spell we are in now could have gone on forever; he has surprised me by coming here this evening. He must have gotten over his pride. Perhaps Rita has had a good influence on him already.

Ugh, Rita. I don't want to think about Rita. Not now, when Martin is here on my back step, where he belongs. Solemn and full of dread, his fist knocking heavy on the glass, and I can hear Mother asking him why he didn't walk me home on Friday night. How mortifying. I'd love to listen to him trying to answer that question, but there is no point in looking for little pieces of revenge. I go to the door and save him, because I am exceptionally nice. I must be. Here he is, his tender and downy face waiting to be slapped. I am sure that he brightens when he sees me.

We sit on the stone wall at the end of the garden, because he doesn't like to talk where my family can hear us. Since we came into the liminal space of adolescence, he doesn't want to do anything in reach of the adults. For a long time, I thought he was silly to think that the adults would care about our small dramas.

He takes a deep breath, readying himself to speak. A small part of me wants him to apologise for Friday night, but most of me knows that he has nothing to apologise for. All he did was kiss a girl who likes him. That's allowed. It doesn't mean he will disappear from me, it just means that he won't be my back-up plan anymore.

'Did you hear about Niamh McNamara? In Sixth Year?'

Why is he asking me about Niamh McNamara? Why now, when we have other things to talk about? I have strange feelings, and so does he, and this time I don't think we should pretend they are not there. The boys are always so late to hear about these things. It isn't as if we are living in different villages. It isn't fair that we agreed to stop talking about Niamh, and yet everybody continues to talk about her. Whenever there is a silence to fill, it's lovely Niamh who must fill it. What she had to do has not cheapened her in the way that I thought it would. In fact, when the scandal of it wore away, I realised that Niamh has been through a piece of womanhood the rest of us cannot imagine. Where before we talked about her in awe, and briefly in shock, we now talk about her in prayer. Her endurance has canonised her in our small world. I don't mention any of this to Martin, because he doesn't understand these things. I hope that neither of us will ever understand it. He continues to say her name like she is just something he stepped in and smeared into the carpet. As though she has done him some injustice just by living.

'It's only a rumour, don't spread it. Niamh is grand.'

I tell him, stealing his momentum. He expected me to lap up the news, as though I would want to hear his opinion on something so personal. Martin, who until Friday night had never even known the inside of a girl's mouth. Where have his informed and crucial opinions been gestating? Maybe last year I would have wanted to hear them, but I am growing now, and I'm understanding things differently. There are so many important things that Martin just doesn't understand. He and I are growing in different directions, I think. I let him change the subject.

'Did you have fun on Friday?'

'I think you did.'

I only mean it as a joke, but he has taken it to heart. Perhaps he thought that we would not address his kiss at all. It has made him very defensive.

'Right, look, the lads made me do it.'

He looks at me very sincerely, as though it is very important that he is understood.

'I wouldn't have gotten with her if, you know.'

He stops talking before he makes a real point. What he means to say is, he wouldn't have kissed Rita if I had asked him not to. Why doesn't he just say that? If I am so dear to him, and it's so important that I know this, why doesn't he just tell me? Why has one kiss complicated things so much? Suddenly, I'm glad not to be interested in anybody. I must stop this all now, before he thinks that he has a reason not to pursue Rita. Before I convince myself that he should always stay available in case I change my mind about him. There is no more room for grey areas, I must spell this out for him, for us both. His infatuation and my selfishness must be destroyed before they are allowed to grow any larger. I must take his beating heart, cut myself out of it, and bury it right here in the garden.

'I was so delighted for you! Rita is such a star, and it's so class you found someone who likes you as much as you like her. Ye are so cute, honestly.'

Oh, look at him, look at his eyes drop, and the new hunch of his shoulders. There goes his heart, falling into the little grave I have dug for it, right next to the stone wall. He feels the disappointment deep in his gut, and however well he thinks he is hiding it, I can see him understanding that I am not an option.

'Come on, she's such a ride. Are you gonna see her again?'

For the first time in years, it's like he has actually heard me when I speak, and he laughs, and says,

'You sound like one of the lads.'

Such a warm and welcome insult. I feel the most wonderful relief as I devolve from a glimmering image of unknowable beauty to the uninteresting tomboy he once knew. At last, we are going back to ourselves.

5

APRIL 1991

IN THE LAST YEAR, THINGS have changed. These days Martin cannot pull himself away from Rita for long enough to even look at me. Only once, on my seventeenth birthday, does he take himself from her to give me a peck on the cheek and wish me a nice day. As he leans in towards me, I swear I can hear a low sound of longing, gurgling deep inside him. Sometimes I just hear what I want to hear.

It's hard not to convince myself that he still wants me when everybody tells me that he still wants me. Isn't it sad that we are still at this? Mother, the girls, all of Maria's sisters, they tell me to be patient, because soon Martin will realise that he never cared about Rita and that he should be with me instead. It makes me feel bad for her. Even when she has him in the palm of her hand, nobody believes that she has him at all. I wonder if he realises all the things that people say about us; I wonder if he hates me for it. All year he has had an arm around her and ceaselessly talked about her and been happy with her, and yet the weight of me is on his back. His mother won't let him forget that I am only down the road, with my lovely farm, with my two parents and all my nice, traditional ways. Similarly, my mother won't let me forget that teenage romances don't last and that all that camogie will give Rita awfully muscular legs and that men may wander but they always come back. The expectation for us to be together doesn't weigh as severely as it once did, but it is there, undeniably, and will only get worse when they break up. If they break up. The girls keep whispering about how fat Rita looks in her school jumper. I pretend to care. Poor Rita. Poor Martin! They're only trying to have a nice time.

They only want me with him because they want me to fit expectations. There are plenty of other ways for me to do that. I can be a social, busy person, who knows all the girls and likes all the boys. So I go out every evening, I let the boys walk me home, I know every vile detail about the girls, perhaps even more than they know about themselves. It's easy to understand other people and their feelings, and why they all think they are protagonists with important stories to tell. When Patricia bosses us around I know it's only because she has no control at home, and I know that the reason Bernadette is so concerned with her appearance is that she wants a boyfriend more than the rest of us but thinks she is the least likely to get one. When I am this deep in them, it's easy to forget about myself. My own feelings are a hedge of briars that I can't bring myself to touch. There are so many unhappy people, I just don't want to find out that I am one of them. They walk among us, they touch you, and you become them. Introspection is like cyanide. Life is fine this way, ignorance is easy, I do what is easy. Doesn't that make the most sense? I think that is more sensible than worrying about Martin and how he has forgotten me for Rita or worrying about how mean the girls and I really are. It's surely safer to be ignorant than to let myself go on thinking about the many greens of Susannah's irises.

Ms O'Neill, our Home Economics teacher, is one of the unhappy people, and she wants to infect us all. Today Susannah has not brought any ingredients to class. Catríona didn't get home until after eleven, and by then all the shops were closed. It was a human mistake: she just didn't get a chance to buy anything. We are supposed to be making meringue, but instead Ms O'Neill has Susannah standing at her desk and is shouting at her in front of the class.

In September, Ms O'Neill's boyfriend of eight years left her for another woman. We all heard about it. The sky was coloured like pink lemonade, and with a fresh gash in her heart, she walked around the town in a daze, trying to digest what had happened to her. Susannah was there, in a halter top outside the chipper. As an older boy put a lighter to her cigarette, she locked eyes with Ms O'Neill. Because they weren't on school property, Susannah didn't put the cigarette out, rather, she sucked on it as she held her teacher's gaze. The glowing top lit a fire deep inside Ms O'Neill. Since then, Susannah has been her favourite student to pick on. She thinks Susannah is disrespectful and too young to look the way that she did that evening. Coming unprepared to class is just another reason for Ms O'Neill to justify hating a teenager. When Susannah told us about that evening, she said she felt really sorry for her teacher, and she didn't even laugh. It's April now, Ms O'Neill should be getting over that old boyfriend. Something about the Summer coming in makes the students lazy and unafraid; the frustration makes her heartbreak harder to heal from. She cannot understand why Susannah didn't go to the shop this morning.

'I didn't have any money.'

Susannah says softly. We all feel it. A small gleam comes to Ms O'Neill's eye, because she likes making the girl from the biggest house in Crossmore admit that she didn't have as much as a fiver lying around. Since Phil left, and took his income with him, Susannah and her mother have been asset rich, but nothing more. She doesn't even get pocket money unless she begs for it.

In truth, it doesn't matter that Susannah won't get to make meringue today, because this will be the third time we have made it. None of us has ever been able to complete one without it cracking, and Ms O'Neill insists we will make it once a month until somebody gets it right. She says it's something about the way we beat the eggs. I don't know why it matters so much to her. I could bet my life right now that we will be attempting it again next month. We are seventeen, we don't care about meringue. Ms O'Neill won't stop shouting at Susannah; it's not even interesting, it's just uncomfortable. Another teacher admonishing another student would be entertaining, but Susannah is mortified, we don't want to watch this. Ms O'Neill might never stop ranting, if Eimear didn't interrupt her.

'Sorry, Miss, I've no eggs.'

She says, as she slides her carton of eggs over to Joan's side of the table.

Ms O'Neill likes Eimear, but not enough to abandon the tone of aggression she has set. Huffing, she rolls her eyes like a teenager, but before she can give Eimear a watered-down version of what she gave Susannah, Maria says,

'I've a load of eggs. I've enough of everything, sure, Susannah can help me.'

Ms O'Neill hates this, because she loves Maria, because of her brightness and her bright sisters before her.

'Well, that's very nice of you, Maria, but it isn't really the point. This class is supposed to be about responsibility.'

'Not being cheeky, Miss, but would it not be irresponsible for me to waste all these extra ingredients?'

What angels I have surrounded myself with. How well-assembled our group is. I knew that we were nice girls. For a second, Ms O'Neill is quiet, she is exhausted by this. In the end, she lets Maria share with Susannah, because she can't be bothered arguing anymore. Susannah does not let on that she is upset. She pretends it's all very funny that she got in trouble and that Maria has gotten away with being cheeky, rather than admitting that she wants to cry and that Maria was just allowed to be charitable. I didn't do a thing. I just sat and watched as she was torn to pieces. And still, somehow, I am the one that she chooses to whisper to,

'Ring me after school.'

How am I supposed to get past this delusion when she comes directly to me? My heart lurches, as if it wants to leave my awful body and go make a home in her. All I want is to avoid what I feel, yet it seems that all Susannah wants is to bring these feelings to the centre of my attention. How lovely it would be to ring her and listen to her. Imagine making her feel better. But I could not say the things that she deserves to hear with Mother listening on the other line. As is my greatest talent, I disappoint Susannah, saying,

'I can't stay on the phone long, Mam will kill me.'

She knew I would say this. It's the attempt at talking that she needs, the thought of actually being listened to terrifies her. That's why she always comes to me, because I never want to listen. The worst of it is, Mother wouldn't really care. There's just something about being on the phone to Susannah that is intimidating to me. Our backs are straight, our heads are down at our bowls, I don't need to look at her to know that she is scowling at me. It's nice to have her staring at me for a change, even if she is cross. Although I can't talk to her on the phone, I am still here for her. I want her to know that I would always be here to disappoint her, if she would only give me the chance.

'Write me a letter then.'

All that venom in her voice. She never talks to me like this. For the rest of the lesson, she ignores me. I mustn't give in, I really can't talk to her on the phone, it's too dangerous. Her sadness would be coming down the line, and even with Padraig crying and Mother breathing into the receiver of the phone in her bedroom, I wouldn't hear anything but the warmth of Susannah's voice, saturating my cochlear fluids and deafening me to everything but her. There are ways of avoiding my infatuation; talking on the phone would only invite it. I need to ensure I take the right ways, not the ones that she tempts me with.

Susannah knows that I've been avoiding anything intimate with her. I think that's probably why she always seeks it out. There have been times – rare and far apart times – when she has talked to me and I have let myself hear what she is saying. When we are the last two awake at a sleepover, or when we have been drinking, we get brave. She talks, and I don't ignore her. It's only in the darkest dark, and in a voice that isn't her own, when she admits that she's very lonely at home and that she misses her father and that she doesn't have the things she needs. It is very difficult not to let the heat of her whispering burn up my cheeks, not to let the closeness of our hearts affect me. It means the world to me to be so near to her, and so I don't let myself be near to her, because I don't think it means the same thing to her. It is a terrible dynamic, but I don't know what to replace it with.

Maria flicks icing sugar at Susannah's face. They are sparkling, I am ignored. It's probably for the best. When she is close to happiness, I don't mind being a casualty.

Ms O'Neill is squawking about the correct way to hold a whisk.

'Forget the wooden spoon, girls, this thing is nothing like the wooden spoon!'

She spent a year in France, which is the reason the school allows for her temper. Nobody else who applied for the position of Home Ec teacher had studied Culinary Arts in Lyon. Principal Sheehy thinks that it is an attraction for parents considering our school, as if parents don't just send their children to whatever school is closest to home.

Principal Sheehy has notions about St Joseph's that have made teachers like Ms O'Neill untouchable.

When she knows enough people are watching, Eimear discreetly spits into her bowl and asks Ms O'Neill to taste her mixture, to check that it isn't too sweet. Ms O'Neill dips her little finger into the white goo, sucks it off, and in a very local accent tells Eimear,

'C'est parfait!'

'Pervert.'

Eimear says under her breath.

Mine is the only meringue that survives the oven. It has somehow come out perfectly, while everybody else's has cracked in one place or another. I hit its centre with a dessert spoon, so it cracks right down the middle. I want Ms O'Neill to lose all confidence in her ability as a teacher.

I want to ring the school pretending to be Catríona or write to Principal Sheehy on Phil's letterhead, but Susannah is too cool and too proud to let me. Ms O'Neill doesn't realise how threatening Susannah's parents could be, or how threatening I could make them out to be. Nobody seems to realise how obsession has weakened my limits.

Against my better judgement, I write Susannah the letter she asked for, and which she definitely does not want. There's a good chance that if I give it to her, it will be insulting and I will make things worse; but there is just as good a chance that she will think I'm stupid and funny, and it might make her laugh. The small effort might make up for not phoning her.

Each sentence is very carefully considered; I don't want to write anything to upset her further. It comes out very boring, but it is authentic, and even if it is embarrassing, I would like her to know me authentically and to be taken away from the house she is so lonely in, even for a minute.

Susannah,

This evening was dull skied and mild, the type of weather that makes the day seem pointless.

Martin told me that Ronan Breen cut his hand open in Woodwork. The table saw went right through his palm – he said it nearly hit a vein. I don't know how we didn't hear all the commotion. He said that Colm Cafferey fainted and Mr Smith screamed. You'd swear they never saw a drop of blood before. Isn't it typical that we would miss the most exciting thing to ever happen in St Joseph's?

We had veg and chops for dinner. Three pork chops between the seven of us, the state of it. My plate was mostly veg. We could have had one each if mam would buy cheaper meat. She can't afford her own standards.

Tonight has been quiet. Martin is doing my Irish homework for me. I tried to do my Maths homework but I can't figure it out. I'll have to copy Joan's tomorrow. I don't really need to tell you that. Padraig is crying. I think he's getting a little old to be crying so much. What age do they stop being upset all the time?

It's such a clear night. Don't you love the country sky? I hate so much being in the city at night, when you look up and the sky is orange from all the lights. Things like the sky make Crossmore so nice. I hope you had a good night.

I hope your bed is warm and you sleep well.

See you tomorrow,

Lucy x

PS Sorry about Ms O N, and sorry I didn't say anything.

When I read it back, I cringe at all the things I have said. I shouldn't have told her that we missed something exciting; I should have said more about Ronan's severed vein. I shouldn't have said that we cannot afford enough meat for all of us. That is mortifying. I should not have mentioned her bed, or its warmth. What a disgusting intrusion. Her bed is none of my business.

In the morning, she is in a sunny mood, like always, like yesterday didn't happen. It might annoy her if I remind her of her cold snap, but still I give her the letter, very casually, like it's a joke. She asked me to write it, and I always do what she asks, doesn't she know that?

Her eyes widen, like she is embarrassed, like this is my petty way of mocking her. But she is sort of smiling.

'Jesus, you didn't actually have to write me a letter.'

'Yeah, I did.'

She puts it in her skirt pocket, and all day I see her touching its folded corner. I don't mind. I don't think about it all evening, or as I go to sleep, I don't.

A new morning comes, and in school, she quietly approaches me and hands me a note of her own.

L,

Sound for the letter. I hope you weren't taking the piss when you wrote it, because I read it while I ate dinner and on the sofa and in bed, and I think I'll read it a thousand times more. It was nice to have some company. I know that sounds sad. I'll take another if you want to write it haha. You're the best.

x S

The best. Tonight and every night, I will defend my title and write her more letters that chronicle my tiresome evenings and do all that I can to keep her warm in her big empty house. And she will read them while eating, lounging, and in bed.

We're sitting in the garden, Martin's back against the bumpy oak tree, mine against the stucco side of the house. He is pulling up clumps of long grass in his fists and dumping them back down again. Last year we would spend so much time together that we hardly had anything to talk about, but now he is with Rita so much, I feel that we are always catching up. It isn't a bad thing. For the first few months that they were together, I felt myself becoming less alluring to him every day. There is no more fascination with my bra straps or a patch of armpit hair missed by my razor. If he is still interested in me, he hides it very well.

It's so nice these days, just me and him hanging out. Everything he says makes me laugh. It's different to the girls, they can't make me laugh like this. Nobody can. When I talk, he listens differently to how he used to, and it is better. Even though he is less intent on what I'm saying, he's also less intent on agreeing with me. It makes things much more interesting. For a while, he was so biased toward my opinion that talking to him was like having a conversation with myself. Now that I'm just an ordinary girl, there is less for him to be careful about.

Although the sun is pale, he is squinting to look at me. And I suddenly notice his legs. Look, they are dark with hair. They were never like that before, were they? Boys take so long to change, and then they seem to do it overnight.

Eimear likes his friend Ryan O' Toole, who doesn't go to our school. Martin knows him from hurling, Eimear likes to go to their matches and watch as Ryan shakes his hair around when he takes off his helmet. She keeps telling me not to tell Martin about it, knowing that I will tell him and that he will tell Ryan. Though Ryan is a little unruly, Eimear could do worse, which she has, and which she will likely do again. Martin has no objection to helping her out.

'You're mad for setting people up, aren't you?'

He leans his head against the tree, passing a long blade of grass between his fingers.

I shrug my shoulders. I suppose I am always setting people up. It's not a passion of mine, just a task that keeps finding me, and that I have no reason to turn down.

'You don't want to be set up yourself?'

He asks, looking down to the piece of grass, almost like he is asking it and not me.

Again, I shrug, I shake my head. I know everybody that he knows, I wouldn't need him to set me up.

'You never like anyone, do you?'

He sounds shy, like he is concerned with me always being single, as if it's dangerous for me.

'Dunno.'

It's all I can manage, because I really don't know. Nobody has ever asked me so directly before, and I'm not sure how to skirt around this. I'm sure I like people, just not in the way that he means. I don't like any of his friends, if that is what he's asking. Of all people, I think he is the one I could talk to about this honestly and openly. And yet I don't. What would I even say?

When I answer, he looks smug, and he rubs the piece of grass up to pulp in his palms. He seems satisfied with what I've said, as vague and far away as it was. It will be fun to get Ryan to notice Eimear. We like sharing these projects, because ultimately, we don't care about how they turn out.

It's so good to do things like this together. I miss him always being around. It's stupid, because I was never going to be his girlfriend, but I do miss being a priority. Sometimes I wonder whether I've missed out on him. Sometimes, when I indulge in my insecurities, it feels like Rita has surpassed me in importance. All the time Martin and I have spent together is forgotten, because Rita has come along with her warm mouth and easy body. I'm jealous, but I'm not jealous. It's complicated, I think.

6

MAY 1991

Lucy,

Daddy won't be coming home this weekend, will you come over instead? I'm waiting for one of us to get heatstroke with all this time we're spending in the garden. It's a shame you stay so pale. We could have the weekend just us. I'll get a bag off one of the fifth years.

Susannah

IT STARTED A FEW WEEKS ago in her garden, a few innocent hours of sunbathing, which has mutated into me offering her every free minute that I have. The other girls never get invited. I am as grateful as I am terrified. Since the weather started improving, Susannah has wanted to spend every afternoon lying in the garden, where she likes my company. I cannot deny her. Although I try to keep a respectful distance between us, gravity always brings me closer and closer to her, until we lie inches apart. There are frantic moments, when I feel we couldn't possibly get close enough. She tells me that this is the best time to tan, because as soon as school finishes, the weather will go bad. And she is proving herself right, every day turning up to assembly a little more golden than before. She lets me fall asleep in the sun; it never seems to annoy her if I stop talking and drift off. I once woke to her putting more suncream on my shins. It really felt like she cared about me – I don't think she would have done that for the other girls. I would like to say it feels intimate, if that isn't weird.

Today I arrive to her lying out on the front lawn wearing a flannel shirt and socks, her handbag lying on its side. Catríona is hurrying back and forth from the car to the house, preparing to go away for the weekend, her kitten heels lightly tapping up and down the garden path. Susannah says that she relishes these little chances to pretend she is the woman of the house, she does not mention how painfully lonely she gets. Normally, she will do something to ensure a little attention from Catríona on her return. It might be a drained bottle of wine left in the fridge; she once asked Joan for a pair of her teenage brother's underpants, so that she could leave them where her mother would see. Recently, there have been slices of meat around the gates of Croft Hall, as though she has been trying to lure stray animals back to the house. It's safe to assume that this time her stunt will involve a filthy new pet.

Catríona often assumes that one of Susannah's older brothers will phone or drop in to check on the house while she takes these weekend holidays. But the last time either of them had much to do with Croft Hall was on each of their eighteenth birthdays. When the O'Shea children get their inheritances, there isn't much of a reason to stay around. Susannah considers it a survival instinct that her brothers left, and she never lets on that she is upset with them for leaving her behind. Sometimes they do phone her, but not often. Joe is married now, living past Ballycove with two children of his own. Damien lives in London half the year and travels for the rest. They are busy people. Susannah doesn't allow herself to become bitter over their absences. Instead, she fills the spaces that they left with unending love and waits for them to come back and retrieve her. She is quite a bit younger than her brothers but has never considered herself an accident. She is quite a bit older than her stepbrothers but does not consider herself a burden.

'There's ten quid on the side, love!'

Catríona calls out as she heaves an overnight bag into the car. With neither of her parents home, a vacuum is created, in which Susannah will have an unclean, unproductive weekend. When Catríona gets back, their arguing will unseal the vacuum, the volume of which will shake the birds from their nests. Then, in school, Susannah will lash out at me or some deserving boy or somebody like Ms O'Neill. I will allow it, because I don't know how to help her.

This is the best time, before any of that emotional fire is spread.

'What are you wearing that for? Aren't you roasting?'

I hope this won't startle her, but she doesn't even blink. It's like she sensed me coming, like she could smell me from a mile away. Can she hear me before I speak?

'Mother's orders.'

Although Catríona often disregards it, a maternal urge exists within her. When she sees Susannah's young body half-dressed, it flares beyond ignoring. She doesn't want Susannah on display so near the road, where anybody might see her. It's sometimes strange when such rules are set and followed in this house, because Susannah and Catríona do not have a typical mother-daughter relationship. They are more like sisters trying to best each other, or old friends who don't really get along anymore. They understand each other very deeply, probably better than Mother and I understand each other, but then they clash so violently, where Mother and I are more like a quiet storm. They are a mess, but we are all messes. It's easier not to interfere.

It's hard to believe that there was ever normalcy in Croft Hall, but, once, Catríona and Phil were happily married, with all their young children living in one home. Susannah swears that her parents were madly in love, that she could never have guessed that Phil was going to leave them for a new woman and have new children. I don't remember the last time I saw the five O'Sheas together. Phil and Catríona seem to plan their lives around avoiding each other.

'Money brings trouble.'

Mother always says, although Susannah and her mother are currently broke. The old money that sustained Catríona's family had just about run out by the time she met Phil. If not for Croft Hall, their descent through the class system would be much more obvious. Every few months, she will sell off a piece of antique furniture just to keep things going. When she needs to, she sends Phil their bills – his big income is enough to sort those out. They are still legally married, he cannot pretend she doesn't exist. What little Catríona has is still an awful lot more than my family has, but their story is always told as a struggle. It makes me glad to be squeezed into one small farmhouse, sharing three pork chops between seven of us.

Susannah expects us to laugh when she calls herself Phil's practice daughter. For the sake of normalising her situation, we do. At the moment, his new woman only has sons; if she has a daughter, Susannah might not take it so lightly. He lives on the border of Cork and Tipperary, which makes his commute to Susannah dreadful, with the country roads, but his commute to work very short. He is a medical lawyer – I don't know how busy that sort of job keeps a person. I'm not sure if Catríona works, nobody is. Whatever she is doing, she keeps her hair blow-dried for it, and it takes her on a lot of weekends away. It could just be endless girls' trips. It could be an affair. It could be that she just goes to a hotel for the weekend, to get out of Crossmore. Perhaps all her skirt suits and heels are just a way to make her time-wasting feel important. Maybe she does work, maybe I'm being unfair.

Susannah talks about the whole thing like it's very normal. I suppose to her it is very normal. Maybe it only seems dramatic and interesting to me because I'm on the outside of it, or perhaps because nothing dramatic or interesting ever happens in my life. She knows that her inheritance is coming and that this drama isn't forever.

I drop last night's letter on her stomach. It's so silly that we have become pen pals when we spend all day together. There isn't much I can report in my letters, except for the things that happen in my head, where another version of her has taken residency. Maria told me recently that she wishes somebody would take the time to write her letters. She suggested we all start writing to each other. That would be very nice, but I'm not about to start writing six letters a night to people I see every day. It's only special when it's for her.

'Read it to me.'

She says, and although I'm embarrassed, I do as I am asked. I write nicer than I speak, so it feels fake reading these letters aloud, like they are not my words.

Susannah,

It's a shame you don't go to Mass. The last day, Father Twomney was talking about the Harrowing of Hell. About how Jesus went down and set Eve and Lilith and all the whores free. I don't think he realised how empowering it was. I'd say Jesus would save anyone, in fairness to him.

Lucifer

How mortifying. Still, she laughs. Catríona gets into her car and slams the door shut, announcing her departure.

'I'll give you a ring tonight, pet!'

'Talk later!'

Just as soon as the car is gone from the drive, Susannah pulls her socks off with her toes, loosens a few buttons, and tugs the shirt off over her head, revealing a bright blue bikini. I've never seen anything so cool.

'Where did you get that?'

My jaw clenches. I am suddenly starving.

'This?'

She cranes her neck to look down at her body, creating a concertina of neck and chin.

'Dunno. Tell me more about that Harrowing of Hell thing, would you?'

She lies her head back down, as if it's nothing, as if I'm not here. It's probably something she has stolen from Catríona's wardrobe, brought back from one of her abroad holidays. Mother wouldn't let me wear a bikini if all our lives depended on it. She decides when I am a woman and when I am a child. When it comes to dressing, I am definitely still a child. Until seeing Susannah in a bikini this didn't bother me. Now it seems wearing anything else would be childish and embarrassing, neither of which I am. She reaches into her handbag and takes out the bag she promised to provide. As she begins to roll a joint, I look over to the fuchsia bushes and keep my attention there, not on the imperfect way she wears the bikini. Too big in places, and too small in others, and yet she wears it so defiantly that it suits her, like it's supposed to fit wrong. Parts of her are burning in the sun; I will not look. The pride, the nonchalance, the honesty of her body. I could never invite imperfection this way. How well she wears it.

I lie next to her. I lie next to a sea of stars, breathing in the smell of the grass, of the sweating marijuana, hoping for a shower of rain to quench this awful and addictive fire. I tell her about the Harrowing of Hell, about Jesus heading into the inferno, meeting the damned women, seeing their raging beauty, and dragging them out of the flames. If I could lie on my side, if I could reach out and touch her. Touching seems quite radical right now. Disappointingly, when she passes me the joint, the tip is bone dry.

Until now, I would have said that Susannah's body was the least interesting thing about her, but I am ashamed to say that this afternoon it is immorally captivating, stretched out on the grass like a centrefold. I want to look like that. Does she practise, or is she like this naturally? With great dread, I begin to take Catríona's side and realise why Susannah was told to cover up. Anybody could drive past and see her now, with eyes even more advantageous than mine. I would drape my own soul over her body to protect her from eyes like mine. Remember that, left alone, Susannah would just be a piece of the earth. She cannot be held responsible for my reaction to her, for the scream of her sun-kissed skin against the blue bikini. Remember that, without the sweat on her sternum and the Autumn colour of her, in her most basic and fleshy form, she is only another piece of the earth, the same as me. We are all just pieces of the earth. I must take a breath.

After hours of straining to avert my eyes, she says she is thirsty, and so we go inside. Only now, while she is bent to drink from the kitchen tap, do I really see the new colours of her. An impossible sunburst, her hair turning from rust to gold, burning, browning, save for a few white lines. These new colours now my favourite colours, these tan lines now all that I revere. In the kitchen light, with my hunger, it is easy to forget that she's just Susannah; lonely Susannah O'Shea, four months younger than me. She takes a drink. I wait to hear her swallow.

'Am I burned?'

She turns around and lifts her waves of hair so I can see her back, pinkening.

'A bit.'

'Catríona will be delighted with that.'

Hunching over, she takes the ice tray out of the freezer and empties it into a tea towel, and she hands it to me.

'Will you do my back?'

It isn't really a request; she knows I will. Nothing could stop me from doing her this favour. I put my hand flat on her shoulder blade, and she jumps a little.

'Your hand is cold.'

Just to fill up the silence, I laugh. It's a way to distract myself from the burning, tight skin under my palm. Very slowly, I bring the ice up to her back. She feels the cold coming from it before it even touches her. When, finally, the tea towel meets her skin, she lets out a little gasp, a jolt of cold goes through her. I want so badly to take a raw ice cube to her back and watch it melt against the heat of her. How terrible it must be, to feel my dreadful eyes crawling across her skin. The light of the freezer brings soft yellow to her face, and she half turns over her shoulder, suddenly seeming very shy, and says the slow and warm words,

'Thanks, Lucy.'

Some parts of her I keep in my memory, others in my heart. This, I keep in my blood. And all night in bed, my blood slowly drags through my veins, bringing that moment to every piece of my body. It is beyond words. This isn't a feeling, it is a state of being. Susannah has done to me what she did to Liam Collins in the corner shop, and what she did to Ms O'Neill outside the chipper, and what she does to her mother every day. She has put herself at the centre of my attention, she has taken control of my emotions, and I feel her thrashing around within me, so intensely. I pray she will never go.

The days go on this way, melting into one another while I drop deeper into her. The only thing that keeps me here on earth is the ringing of the school bell. Today, between Irish and Maths, she asks me to come with her to the hedges so that she can have a cigarette. It wouldn't be worth getting caught for any of the other girls, but I love to be brought up to the hedges with her, even with the awkward eye contact from my brother's friends. It is entirely different to the way they look at Susannah. She belongs here, they can't stare. She belongs everywhere she goes. It feels so good to be with a cool girl. Perhaps that is why I am so fascinated by her, because she is so cool, and I want to be cool too. She has been talking about Patricia. I do what I can to seem like I care.

'The poor thing. She was telling me about her dad again yesterday. It's so rough what she goes through.'

Susannah sighs. What a wonderfully big heart she has. As a bystander, it wouldn't be difficult to have sympathy for Patricia. It is rough, what she goes through. Of course it is. But truthfully, I find it very difficult to care about her home life. Perhaps I'm the only one that feels this way, because I'm the only one she doesn't really like. It isn't fair, the way that Patricia treats me. It's almost as though I'm being targeted. Like I've done some awful thing that only she knows about, and this is her way of punishing me. Now that Susannah and I are so close, I feel for the first time I could air my grievances, although I don't think I would ever have the neck to do it. And yet, I find myself saying,

'She can be such a bitch though. I don't know she likes me at all.'

I expect to be scolded, but Susannah turns her head to me and smiles.

'Don't mind her. She's only jealous of you.'

This is the sort of advice Mother would give me when I was a child. And yet, when Susannah says it, I believe it. With so few words, she has soothed such an embarrassing insecurity of mine. I wonder if she knows what a cure she is. In the evening, I begin to write a letter that says,

I am all wounds, Susannah, and you are the loveliest pus. Flooding in to heal me. Yellow as the sun.

I stop writing then, because it seems like too much.

If I allow myself even a moment to reflect, everything feels like too much. This Summer has been just a little bit too warm, the sun has been a little too bright. My thoughts have been a little bit too uncontrollable. And my emotions a little too humid. They only grow more humid. It all just gets stickier. Soon I think I will be unable to go even one day without lying on the grass with her. There are times when I get a little bit too high, and while she turns onto her back, I begin to panic. What has happened to me that I am suddenly so absorbed by her? Is this healthy? When will I get to go back to how I was before? And do I want to? I get hot, and my mind races, my heart pounds. And then I get a look at her, and it doesn't matter. She is just so easy to look at. So good to look at. Such a treat to look at. And to listen to. And to speak to. It just doesn't matter. The panic goes.

I resolve that, for the rest of the Summer, I won't worry about what I feel. Rather, I will just offer her all my time and energy and hope that she takes it. That she lets me listen to her musings. That she writes me a thousand more letters. That she lets me settle closer to her. Ever closer.

Lucy,
Thanks for keeping me company last night. It was so nice to eat dinner with you. Cooking and cleaning aren't boring when we do it together.
Joan was asking if we want to go over on Saturday to her house. A part of me wants to tell her no, so we can just lie on the grass for the day. I'm sure it will be fun, though. I'll go if you go.
It's absolutely boring here in the evenings. I wonder if Catríona would let me bring the telly up to my room. She doesn't watch it.
Right, that's it, I'm probably boring you now. See you tomorrow.
Night night,
S

I do what I can to breathe the air, to metabolise my food, to speak and to listen, but it is not easy. Her softest exhale is like my own personal dog whistle. When she taps her nails on her desk, I feel the same rhythm in my throat and in my stomach as my food turns to vomit.

She walks out of school behind me, I feel her moving, like I'm being stalked. Maria, all my praises for Maria, and Eimear, who catch up and make a group out of us. It feels so good to be part of a group, this group. We are so safe with each other. We pass by those waiting for the school bus; rather, my body passes by them, my mind is elsewhere. Martin is waiting for me at the bottom of the road, I see the blur of him from back here. I might kiss his cheek when I see him, anything at all to take me away from the strain of being alone with even a thought of Susannah. Eimear starts talking, I want to thank her for the distraction.

There are a lot of people in school who don't have any close friends. There are girls who cycle through different groups, each cycle ending in a series of blazing arguments that leaves them on their own again. All along I have regretted this loneliness for them, but now, since feeling the intensity of company, I am beginning to feel envious. In a nearby yard, a dog is barking. I focus on its bark, rather than the clacking of her school shoes behind me, the burn of her eyes on my back. The lonely girls and bus children look at us while we pass by, they wave and we wave.

Without the girls, I don't know who I would be. They are a very big part of who I am. All my life, they have been laying a beautiful path for me, and I am so grateful for it. We lay paths for each other. They lead us back to each other, to who we should be. They see me from the outside. I like what they see in me. These rigid and clear paths. I want to be tied down to my path.

The girls and I are friendly with everybody, but we are friends with so few of them. We are so well able to pretend to care about people we don't like, and even better able to pretend not to care about people we are delirious over. We always say being fake is a waste of time, but we are fake. There's nothing wrong with it. In fact, I'm beginning to see it as a wonderful way of protecting the mind from madness and the heart from explosion.

Susannah's pace quickens. Girls, please keep me on my path.

'Did you see Thomas looking at you there?'

Eimear says, and I don't realise it at first, but she is talking to me. The dog loudens, my heart follows, and so do Susannah's shoes, and a heat comes to the back of my neck.

'Sure, she doesn't care about Thomas. It's all about Martin! Isn't that right, Lucy?'

Maria walks on the edge of the footpath, keeping us all off the road, nodding to the shape of Martin ahead of us that is becoming clearer.

'Go on, so, Martin or Thomas?'

I can't think about the banality of this question, let alone an answer. All I can think of is bright blue on sunburnt skin. There is nothing else.

'I wish that dog would shut up.'

'She's a dog, dogs bark, what do you expect?'

I feel giddy, and it's so strange, and so funny. This isn't like me at all, but I like it so much. Is it because of Martin, there ahead of me? I know he will get me a 7up in the corner shop for the walk home. He treats me like I'm special, even when Rita is around. Maybe I'm just high because I have friends or because it's Friday. Martin is water, I am smoke. She is fire. He keeps things in line. He makes me what I am. We are inevitable. I hardly think of my answer.

'Martin! Sure, I barely know Thomas.'

The record is set straight.

Everything is as it should be.

Until Susannah says,

'You don't like Martin, you like me.'

Everybody laughs, and although it feels as though it has stopped, I'm sure my heart is beating as normal.

'Girl, would you get over yourself!'

Maria pushes her. Susannah is self-involved, it's funny, it's cute. We are all laughing. I am swallowing a flame. She is so sweet. She looks at me with such an intensity that her eyes could make a diamond of me. We exist for a moment, above the laughter, the barking, the sound of her shoes. It's just us, our eyes meeting on the school path. I just look. I can do nothing else. I would look forever.

Susannah is right. I like her.

Isn't she clever? Doesn't she know me well? Of course I like her. I like her so much sometimes that I wish the other girls wouldn't talk to her or touch her, and that it was only me and her. Is that too much?

At home, with my bedroom door closed tightly, I give a real chance to what she said. Nobody can hear me thinking in here.

I don't like Martin, she was right, I knew that, I've always known. At least somebody has been listening when I say he is just a friend. The way I feel about Susannah isn't the way I feel about anybody else. Not Martin, not Maria, not Rita. It's miles away. She makes me feel molten. Why didn't I know this until now – am I really so repressed? Why did she have to tell me like that? What a thing to be told about yourself.

It makes me panic. People say 'lesbian' sometimes, they say 'dyke' more. People are always hurling that word around. I've said it plenty of times. Sinéad Kelly has a lesbian cousin who used to live in Crossmore but has since moved to Galway. The village isn't supposed to know about her, but we all do, we all call her a dyke. Does liking Susannah make me the same as that? I don't want to be a thing that the village isn't supposed to know about. How can I fix this? Do I want this fixed? I wouldn't want to live not knowing the goodness of Susannah. She is fresh air, and warmth, and mornings in July. What is there to fix? There is evil in my yearning, I know, I just can't see where yet.

And does it matter? There is no way that she has the same feeling that she found in me. We aren't a match, not like that. Susannah is golden sunlight, and I am a struggling sapling at best, crippled by heliotropism; she does not need me the way that I need her.

But then, how would she recognise this odd sort of attraction if she did not know it herself? Maybe she doesn't like me, but she might like another, different girl.

She sits next to me every lunch break. She writes her name in the margins of my copybooks. She has me in her garden every day and never invites any of the girls. Maybe. But I have always seen what I want to see. Why would she do this? Why would she look at me that way?

All I am doing today is putting a name to a feeling. I like her, that's all. That much feels fine. It makes sense. I can leave it here a while. She already knows about it, she doesn't seem to mind, she doesn't seem to want it advanced. So I'll just wait, and if she makes another revelation about me, I will listen, and if not, I can just sit quietly with my feelings until I understand them. Okay. Okay.

Dearest Susannah,

Today you let me know that I like you. If I could only tell you all the ways that is true. Isn't it sad, that you have such a hold on me, and yet you are not mine? What I feel goes beyond words.

I stop writing. It would be altogether too much for me to confirm her suspicions. This confusion is torture, the unknowing is a hand on my throat, tightening. Lethal, glorious, inviting Hell. I want this Hell to last.

And it does, all Summer long. I watch helplessly, hopelessly, dying as the hue of her goes from sunrise to sunset, and I fall deeper with each new shade. We lie out for hours and hours every day, speaking lightly, laughing, cloud-watching. I read in one of Sorcha's magazines that aloe vera helps turn sunburn into tan, and so I dig through the couch and car ashtray until I have enough change to buy Susannah some. She gets me to put it on the back of her calves, where her peeling skin is like lace, and I watch very closely to see her shiver when it touches her. The skin begins to come away in my hand. Another layer of her, laid bare before me. This Summer is breaking my heart into pieces, to reveal a new and better heart that only beats for her.

There's always weed in her handbag, there's always a bottle of wine in the fridge. With that and the heat, my heavy head always finds space right next to hers. The days go on forever, forever is only the length of the faintest new heartbeat with her; it is always a surprise when the end comes. It's the same signal every day, when the heat has worn away her perfume and she wants a shower. The honest smell of her sweating skin, the truest evidence of our time together. It suits her very well, but then, anything would. When she catches the smell on us, she ends the day, always saying,

'Same tomorrow?'

And I always agree to it, and I always feel the surgical wire I have sewn between us ripping through my flesh when I try to leave. Could she not just heal onto me? Could we not prevent the sting of leaving? She always walks me down to the end of the drive, her bare feet on the gravel. She wouldn't do that if she didn't care, would she? My head reels wondering what she does when I leave. I suppose she showers using expensive soap, the bathroom filling with steam. I suppose she sings as she washes, the crooked tone of her voice filling my mind.

In bed at night, I smell weak, sweet silage on my sheets. I have been leaving my window open all day. I don't ever want this smell to go, it is the Summer. The Summer means everything to me. I feel the coolness of the sheets against me as the heat of the day leaves my body. I won't shower until the morning, I must keep her with me. Susannah was wrong when she said that I like her. I love her.

7

AUGUST 1991

ON THE LAST FRIDAY OF Summer, Susannah and I are taken from the garden, because Eimear is turning eighteen. She is the first of us to do so. It is the only good reason we have to haul ourselves off the grass. Eimear's parents aren't making a big fuss over the day, it's just cake and cards in the kitchen. Her mother, Deirdre, passes out party hats. I love these childish things. Her grandfather, neckless and shaped like a bullfinch, is at the table, and when he sees me, he takes me in for a hug, his huge, stiff hands covering mine. Again, he tells me how like my own grandfather I am, and what good friends they were. He passes out ice cream and wafers. He tells me more about my grandfather than anyone. Since I was little, I have adored him.

Later on, there will be a big party outside the village. Even now, as we chat in the kitchen, the boys are in the field building a bonfire. For the moment, it's very nice to all be squeezed in this one small room, my sun-tender skin chafing against my clothes, my wild and perverse heart unknown. Eimear's three little sisters are racing around, pulling at our clothes and looking for our attention. Where did the time go since we were the tiny children, looking for attention from Maria's sisters and idolising the big girls? What of Niamh McNamara, what of all the dire rumours and uniformed dreams that followed her around the school? It feels like they only just graduated, and still their shining lights are so distant.

'Would ye leave Lucy alone, girls, don't be annoying her!'

Deirdre's voice makes the girls scatter. Should I be afraid? What does Deirdre know? Everything puts me on edge these days.

'They're grand! Come back here, girls.'

Even when it is inconsequential, it is nice to be brave and assertive, it is nice to bend down to their height and ask them about school, and to whisper silly things about the nuns to them. I am not afraid of the nuns anymore. I have been in Eden all Summer long, I know divinity better than they ever will.

'They're mad about you, Lucy!'

Deirdre laughs, and lets the girls crowd me once more. What a nice mother she is. What a feeling I have now, like I fit in so well. I could stay here in the kitchen forever, celebrating Eimear's day. I get a sick feeling knowing that, eventually, I'll be alone in my bedroom again, with just my buzzing thoughts. Deirdre gathers us all in tight for a photograph as Eimear blows out her candles and makes her wish. In the photo, everybody is smiling and laughing, Eimear's granddad with his hands on her shoulders, her youngest sister on my hip, the girls fanned out around us. What a loud and happy house.

'Deirdre, will you take one of me and Lucy?'

Susannah asks as she pulls me in her direction, in front of Deirdre and her camera.

'Go on, girls, smile!'

And Susannah takes my hand and holds it very boldly in both her hands; our freckled shoulders touch, I hear her smiling, I am blinded by the flash. Deirdre does not realise the love she has photographed. I am already nervous for the day she gets it developed and sees the thirst I can scarcely conceal. What a special picture.

'Ye're lovely girls!'

It's only a second before Deirdre has moved onto the next photo to be taken. Clearly, she doesn't realise how significant it was. My goodness, my life, I am so in love. Eimear got a denim dress for her birthday. A denim dress, with a belt and collar. It looks so amazing. We spend a great deal of the party making her twirl around in it.

'Did ye never see a dress before, girls?'

Her father is laughing, but he does not understand how wonderful this dress is. She is made to take it off before we go out. We have all told our parents that we are going to Susannah's for the night, and that Catríona will be home.

When it is time to leave, I almost don't want to go. We step out into the evening, and the Summer air is still warm around us. Maria walks before me and lights a cigarette. The sky ahead of us is peach, bruising where it is nearest to Heaven, and behind us, black. Each of Maria's spiral curls stands out against the sky, the smoke from her mouth is icy blue.

'Got a tenner off Grandad.'

Eimear is very smug when she pulls the note taut before us. Good for her. Good for us all, because whatever she buys with it will soon make its way around the group.

'Come here, Eimear, we didn't forget about you.'

Joan stops and takes from her bag a long bottle of vodka in old Christmas paper.

'What have you wrapped it in?'

'Mammy saves the wrapping paper, shut up.'

'Maria's sister sussed it!'

Eimear is smiling, and she holds the bottle up to the streetlight, which is marbled through the glass. We all look.

'I hope ye thought to bring a mixer.'

The bottle is passed around, and we wince at the taste. I never liked vodka, but it's Eimear's favourite drink and it's Eimear's night. It tastes hot and cold at once.

When we reach the boreen before the field, we stand into the ditch and drop our bags. Now we are far away enough from Deirdre, we can get ready for the party. We take off our tights, tighten our bra straps, Bernadette passes around a little mirror. I try not to stare at Susannah when she smears on her eyeliner, and she asks Maria to check if her eyes are even. We all smell of the same perfume that I took from Mother's dresser. Joan puts gloss on my lips and ties a knot in my top. They all look at me, and I know by their eyes that I must look pretty. It makes me feel pretty, although I don't look in Bernadette's mirror for very long. We are a little old for this now. Eimear is eighteen, we shouldn't be getting ready in ditches anymore.

'Who's coming so?'

'Everyone! All our lads, Aoife's gang are coming, and the lads from the boy school.'

'I told Rachel and all her friends too.'

'Feck, I should have got more dressed up.'

'No, it's casual.'

This is a different sort of party to what was in Eimear's kitchen. Not bad, just different. Not a party I could be honest with Mother about. As we approach the field, we see the night has already started. The grass has all been bailed and stacked, the stubble that is left beneath us is dried out and yellow. A bonfire is lit with a big circle of cars backed around it, and people are hanging out of the boots and sitting on blankets. Susannah bumps into me as we walk, she is just playing. I feel I can do the same back. One drink could provide all the bravery I need to declare to everybody how deeply this Summer has changed me, and how gracelessly I have fallen for her. I must be very careful. There will be all sorts of stupid things happening tonight, my bleeding heart does not need to get involved.

We take a spot by the fire, and one by one, small groups come to speak to us and tell Eimear happy birthday. There are also those who don't know Eimear and who have just come for the party. It doesn't matter, they probably won't come near us. Eimear is so happy with the firelight bouncing off her cheeks, it's as if she's not used to being the centre of attention. The fire suits her so well, her and her yellow hair.

It's so lovely to be here. There isn't a person here who I wouldn't want to spend the whole night with. I love everyone here; that's not like me, is it? Something about tonight has made me so happy. Maybe it's the turning season and the still night air, maybe it's the drink. It's having Susannah beside me, starry and giggling. I am laughing at something Joan said, almost hysterically, when Patricia says,

'Calm down, Lucy, it wasn't that funny.'

It slows my laughing. Why is she like this?

'Patricia, don't be so dry. You're always giving out to poor Lucy.'

Susannah says. It doesn't create the atmosphere I expected it to. In fact, the girls hardly even react. Perhaps they think it's justified. Susannah then goes on talking, taking the group's attention with her. Isn't she good? I can't believe she stood up for me. How wonderfully thoughtful. While Patricia doesn't apologise, she leaves me alone for a while. I am too happy to notice. I must remember to thank Susannah later, when we are sober.

Here comes Martin, my lovely Martin, with bulky, long-haired Diarmuid and skinny, long-haired Ryan, who is carrying a box of bottles.

'For the birthday girl.'

Ryan hands Eimear two bottles. He's so smiley, with dark hair and warm skin. I can't be bothered looking for something in him I am attracted to. Eimear tries to pass one of the bottles to Patricia, who has been quiet and hasn't had anything to drink yet. She doesn't see Patricia dropping the bottle on the ground or Bernadette picking it up and opening it. Her bright pink lips stain its rim, and suddenly, she is all talk.

'You're good for something, Ryan! Come here, it's a good crowd! Pure relaxed like!'

She faces the boys, not us.

'Yeah, everyone is behaving so far.'

'What are you drinking, Lucy?'

Martin is already a little drunk, and he doesn't wait for me to answer before he opens a bottle and puts it in my hand. This is not like him, is it?

'God, he's a real gent! Aren't you lucky, Lucy?'

It's like Bernadette saves up all her observations for when the boys are around. Without them, she is so buttoned-up. In moments like these, I have no interest in listening to her. Still, my good mood prevails, and I find patience for her.

'You're some woman for the jokes, Bernadette.'

It's all just a laugh. Nobody minds that we are snapping at each other, nobody takes it seriously. Martin rolls his eyes, but it's only a performance of annoyance. Really, he is very happy for people to tease me like this and to notice how well he treats me. Why wouldn't he be?

He only handed me a drink, that's all. It shouldn't be such a big deal, but I feel everyone quietly watching us. Rita is around somewhere, and Rita is in love with him, and still he keeps a piece of himself for me – he even flaunts it – so that everybody will think, poor old Martin, all the girls want him. I ought to shut up and let it go, but now, more than ever, I'm aware of male attention.

'How's your mam, Susannah?'

Diarmuid snickers. How surprising. I wouldn't have expected it of a nice boy like him. I can feel the heat of embarrassment off her. I must say something. She only just stood up to Patricia for me. Look, she is about to say something herself. She can handle herself. I want to say something.

'Don't be a prick, Diarmuid.'

Martin says, and Diarmuid clears his throat, now as embarrassed as Susannah. I hate myself for not saying anything. I hate that mentioning Susannah's mother is a mean thing to do. I hate Martin for taking my chance at looking after her. How infuriating.

'Aren't we lucky it didn't rain?'

It's a very pedestrian and adult way to break up the conversation, but it's all I can think to say to move things along. While nobody starts talking about the weather, my comment does break our large group into several smaller conversations.

'Sorry about them.'

Martin says quietly, as he leans into me. He likes to get close, to remind me that there is trust between us. He likes to make his behaviour seem like other people's behaviour. Even with the smoke of the fire and half a bottle of Mother's perfume in the air, I can smell him. The smell of his house, his mother's laundry, a little drink. That's my whole life in a scent. There's nothing for him to be sorry for, it's just Bernadette's mouth that's the problem. Normally, I would just push him away and we would laugh, but I don't think I can be bothered with that anymore. Where has my good mood gone? Tonight is meant to be wonderful, I'm supposed to be having a wonderful time. I love everyone here, don't I? I must grit my teeth and keep it that way.

'Where's Rita?'

I saw them together when we got here, but now she is nowhere. If she would come and join us, I might be able to relax.

Maybe I'm a narcissist, but I feel a spotlight on Martin and me. Drink makes me paranoid, maybe. I'm just so nervous that he will get brave. So many things will happen tonight that will be infinitely more interesting than the gap between me and Martin. Patricia is about to try and start an argument with us for drinking; Ryan is going to start a fight when his drink is stolen before bringing Eimear into the backseat of his car; Declan has brought his new girlfriend, and there will be a rumour that her handbag is full of pills; the Guards will visit – and yet, I feel everyone is waiting for Martin to slip an arm around me. Surely he knows better. Surely I know better than to worry about that. It isn't like he's never put an arm around me before. It wouldn't be altogether bizarre if he did. Perhaps I'm just jealous that he stood up for Susannah. Yes, that must be it.

I must be more in love with myself than he is to assume all this attention is on me.

He shrugs his shoulders, he doesn't know where Rita is. I'm not sure he cares. But there is Susannah, smiling in her conversation, and suddenly, I don't care either.

The night melts past, and I get back to bliss when I stop thinking about Martin. There are guitars, I dance, I think I even sing, and I drink more than I ever have, which probably isn't that much. Around two, it starts to get cold, and the crowd begins to thin. Rita is among those leaving. She goes with Aisling and her friends, who are collectively fuming that Martin didn't offer to walk them home. He is too drunk to be upset by it. It isn't nice to see him like this, not his usual considerate self. On another night, I would have taken his jacket when he offered, but it wouldn't be worth the talk. I can't afford mixed messages tonight. I can't be friends with my friends, just in case people get the wrong idea. Our boundaries, our language, our movements, they must all be monitored, I must bend over backwards to stop from hurting or arousing his feelings. Despite my hopes, I was not being narcissistic, because as soon as Rita is gone, all the girls want to talk about is me and Martin, what a pair we are, and what a shame it is that she gets in the way. As ugly as this talk is, at least it means that I am doing an excellent job of concealing my feelings for Susannah. Perhaps I ought to lean into it.

A few of us have moved onto a blanket when it starts again.

'Oh, Martin, don't look now!'

Lauren Hayes has appeared at a car boot with two older girls and a bottle of wine. Lauren is in Sixth Year now, rail thin and just five feet tall. Her grandmother is from Shanghai, and even though her parents are only from down the road, she is considered wildly exotic in Crossmore. A perfectly palatable mix of foreign and local. Tonight, her hair is so glossy it almost looks wet, and when she looks at Martin, she tosses it over her shoulder and smiles, before slowly turning her back on him. The older girls have an unbreakable confidence, even when they are only older by a few months. A tension passes through our circle, a moment of silence offered for Rita, and then they turn in my direction and offer one for me. They expect me to explode with jealousy – maybe I will, maybe I should put on a show. I would love nothing more than for Lauren to seduce Martin, and for everybody to see it, I'm sure they would love that. Then she could be the other woman, and I could get up and leave without causing a scene.

'Jesus, she doesn't look too bad now.'

'She's like a rake.'

'You wouldn't say no, though.'

'She's dreaming if she thinks she'll manage the whole bottle of wine.'

'They're late arriving.'

The boys are praising her, and the girls are attacking her, all to get a rise out of Martin and me. Maria nudges my side, and she winks her beautiful eye as if to tell me, it's alright, you are better than Lauren, you have nothing to worry about.

'I don't care about her.'

Martin says to me. His words run together, and he looks so sheepish, as if he has done something wrong, as if this is exactly what I wanted to be told.

'They all think I'm after her, but I swear I'm not.'

He goes on and gets closer to me. Oh, why has everything tonight been so embarrassing? Everybody can see him getting closer to me; surely they can see me blushing. Why does this bother me so much? Do I actually like Martin? Is that why this is so upsetting?

Everyone pretends not to be looking, like it is a very tender moment between us. Perhaps to Martin, it is. Perhaps I should let it be a tender moment. But it's all too close. And so totally, wonderfully, I ruin it. I have to.

'Nobody cares if you fancy Lauren. Would you ever piss off and give me a bit of room?'

It seems harsh, but I am allowed to speak to him like this. Best friends are allowed to do this. He won't care. He only moves away because I have asked him to, not because he is upset. I know it.

The circle gets quiet, they're all looking. I take a breath and choose not to feel embarrassed or guilty. The sting of it will be forgotten by tomorrow. We're all drunk, it's allowed, I'm sure.

'Nice one, Lucy.'

He laughs like it's all fine, but he gets up and walks away; after a sweet moment of hard, unmoving awkwardness, his friends follow him. My lovely horde of girls rush to my side like I've done nothing wrong. Why does nobody believe me when I say I don't care? Is there any way to really communicate that and have it sound real?

'It's Eimear's night, let's just have a bit of craic.'

And we do, they all very kindly brush past my outburst. I go and talk to Declan's new girlfriend, to see what she has brought, and if any of it will take me out of my head for the night, away from all my muddled and panting thoughts. Eimear's vodka is long gone.

I could cry when I see Susannah across the field. She is so beautiful it hurts me. Standing with Bernadette and some boys, they are all giggling and touching hands to shoulders, they are in the dark. She looks very happy. The rest of the night is just a smear on my eyes – I would like to remember it, but I'm not sure it would do me any good.

It's time for a few more of us to leave, I think the morning is coming. We make sure to go without telling Martin, because he would only want to walk with me. I can't deal with that right now. He would speak too honestly, I would feel too protected by him. Even if I told him no, he would walk with me, and he would say it is only because my parents would be cross if he didn't. I don't want to have to say sorry to him yet.

Bernadette and Maria are in cars with boys, Eimear is talking to Ryan, and Patricia went home to her own sour bed hours ago. Joan says she is ready to go, and my skin buzzes when Susannah says she will leave with us. The others will come back to Susannah's at some stage, later.

The last of the dark is slowly burnt up by the dawn as we walk away from the field. It is so good to see the orange glow of a sunrise coming to us. The night and all it's nonsense can be dismissed soon.

I can still hear the loud crack of Ryan's fist meeting that other boy's cheekbone. Everybody heard it. Everybody saw the thick clot of blood he spat out onto the grass. Perhaps it isn't a good sign that Eimear was so enthralled by that. In fact, she was more than enthralled: when it was obvious that Ryan was going to win the fight, I saw Eimear unhooking her bra and creeping away to his car, where he was told to meet her. We agreed not to tease her for that, because the birthday girl can do what she wants. She didn't cry or vomit or start a fight, what she did do is very excusable. Joan is stiff speaking, maybe she is a little bit jealous, I don't ask. I do what I can to stop conversations about the boys from blossoming, because I can't listen to another word about Martin. Lovely, nasty Joan saves me from this.

'Here, Patricia was driving me mad tonight.'

We gossip about a lot of people, but we never gossip about each other. Almost never. When we do, it is usually about Patricia. It's so refreshing when the girls own up to their feelings. I don't know why we aren't this honest all the time. Normally, Susannah would be the one to stop us, but she is too drunk to really hear what we're saying. Nights like these are the only times I am glad of Phil and Catríona's absences. If I had to go home to Mother in this state, I might never be seen again. Now that Joan has started, I don't want to give her a chance to stop.

'She was like a dog.'

'Why does she even bother going out?'

'She only goes out to judge everyone else.'

The sky is renewing, the new sun is a ripening peach on the horizon. I take Joan's wrist to see her watch. Just after five. Finally, Susannah joins in,

'She needs help, I was afraid to even speak in front of her because I knew she'd just jump down my throat.'

Another good reason to justify my hatred of Patricia.

'She's her mother's daughter anyway.'

I am afraid that we might all be our mothers' daughters.

It feels like hours might have passed by the time we get to Susannah's house, though it isn't even half past five. On the porch, she takes the last of her wine from her bag, and she offers us the bottle, but Joan is already making her way to the sofa, calling out,

'Goodnight, ladies!'

And suddenly, it is just her and me looking out over her garden, like we have been all Summer. Like we should always be. The quiet of the sunrise, the cool air of the dawn. Being alone with her now, I feel I am the nearest I have ever been to God. It is her, she breathed my soul into me. It is Crossmore, our small rural Heaven. It makes me nervous, how could it not? I take a deep drink of the wine and wince as I swallow it. It's so dry and sharp, it wakes me up a little bit. Our fingers overlap while I hand her back the bottle, and I feel the rough edge of her bitten nails. For a minute, I pretend that she knows how I feel, and it's nice. She makes me think about cooking her dinner and reading to her and cleaning up for her. The domestic things I once pitied Mother for are things I now crave. These subtle and romantic thoughts don't surprise me anymore, this is just the way my mind goes when she is with me.

'Martin is some prick, isn't he?'

She is laughing, but she doesn't mean anything by it. She is swaying trying to keep herself upright. In the rising sun, a new green comes to her eyes, a new shine over her heavy eyelids, and when she looks at me, it puts me under deep, warm water.

'I think he just has a crush on me. He'll get over it.'

I try to look away, but she locks her eyes on mine, and she is so quick and so earnest when she says,

'No, he won't.'

I bite my cheeks. Does she know what she is saying? I must keep my mouth closed to stop myself from yawning, I don't want her to think I'm tired, I don't want to go inside. I just want her to say that again and again and again, even if hers is the last lovely mouth that should be uttering his name. The light is yellowing on her jaw, showing me the acne where her makeup has faded. Soon, the dawn will be gone. We must go to bed now, or I will stand here all day, watching as the sun changes on her blessed face. There is no need to talk, the birdsong fills the silence. She knows how I feel about Martin, she understands me.

Her bedroom smells of trapped heat and lavender. The curtains are closed, and bulky, they reach all the way down to the floor, and her white pillows are trimmed with lace. We lie down, sharing one side of the bed. Tonight, her hair smells of cigarettes. She is looking to get warm, and without asking, tucks herself into my side, her face just under mine. My body reacts so subtly, but definitely.

'What was your favourite part of the night?'

She asks me through a yawn, and in the dim light, I can make out the shine of her back teeth.

'Eimear's house.'

'Same...'

She wants to keep talking, there is more left for us to say. Maybe I'm getting too brave, but I wish she would finish her sentence. My patience for things unsaid has grown very thin, I don't see the romance in it anymore. There are things I have wanted her to say; maybe she would have said them tonight. Maybe she feels safe with me. In this thin place between sleeping and waking, there is room for honesty.

Rather than speaking, she moves further into me. This says much more than I could manage with words. Where her body is pressed into mine, our skin glows. These parts of me are beautiful.

I should move away now, before she gets too comfortable, before she falls asleep against me. The more I think about this, the staler the room gets. I turn away from her and feel her breath on my neck for a long and upset second before she moves to the other side of the bed, a mile away. The pink heat of her bedroom, the burn from inside me. I am melting with love. I am close to disgrace. Long after tonight, this heat will stay inside me. These aches, these urges, one only amplifies the other. Listen to her, as she sighs to sleep. I could not go on without her.

The small hours swirl by, and I wake up with dry eyes and a sour tongue. I see her, far from me, her head on pillows I cannot even reach, but the slant of her body and the length of her leg has left her ankle on top of mine; I feel the lovely bump of her bone. Sitting up, Eimear is revealed to me, wrapped up and sleeping in a pile of blankets on the carpet near the bed.

Knowing what torments me, the duvet has hidden Susannah from my sight. All it has left for me is the bare slope of her shoulder, dusty with freckles and tinted blonde by the morning light breaking through her thick curtains. It is so early, too early for her to be defiled by my looking. I must leave now before she rolls over and gives me a reason to stay, before I fall in love with the remains of last night's eyeliner under her eyes. Her makeup is on the pillowcase, the sweat of her neck is on the sheets, and I wish that a piece of me would be left behind the same way. Is that dirty? Is that fair of me?

Without another breath – what Heaven that breath might be – I slip out of her bed and take my bag from the floor as quietly as I can. For just a fraction of a second, for a lifetime, I look back through the crack in the door and see her stirring.

Downstairs, Joan is still asleep on the sofa, her long feet over one armrest, her hands stretched out over the other. When she wakes up, her back will be destroyed. At some stage last night, Bernadette and Maria came back and joined her in the living room. They are sharing the other sofa, though Maria's snoring has kept Bernadette awake. She looks up.

'You going?'

By her face, she hasn't slept for five minutes. I pull my tights back on and, using her mirror, I do what I can to clean off my makeup with a little spit on my finger. This does nothing for the way I smell, but right now I wouldn't dare step into Susannah's shower. I nod to Bernadette and say,

'I'm dead.'

She laughs, once, and mumbles in agreement. I shouldn't smoke right before going home, but I take a cigarette from her anyway. On the back of the box, there is ugly, undeveloped handwriting that reads *BRIAN 02338140*. Good for her. I hope this will settle her insecurities a little bit. She is such a wonderful girl, it's a shame she is so fragile.

The morning is soft, and Susannah's perfectly manicured garden is easy to look at. It's the only thing that Phil looks after in Croft Hall. He wants Susannah to have everything, what he gives her is nice grass and hedges. I know I'm too young to get hangovers, but still I feel disgusting. Mother will want to do all the back-to-school jobs today. Susannah's bedroom windows are closed, as are the curtains, but I know she is still up there, sleeping, her shoulder still bare and coloured by a shadow. Why don't I just go back to bed?

That thought makes me pull the big door closed, separating myself from her and all the girls. Me and all my feelings are alone in the morning dew.

The night comes back to me in pieces as I walk. Declan's girlfriend just had hash, which was a disappointment. Still, she smoked with me, and she wasn't even cagey about sharing with a stranger. Rita went home early because Martin was ignoring her. Ah, Martin.

I could be annoyed at myself, I could be humiliated, but right now I'm not. The mess we made last night is one we have been making for a while now. He's making me make it. Everybody will have forgotten my outburst by Monday, it will be like it never happened. The more I think of it, the clearer it is that I'm the one who made a scene, not him. Do I even have the right to be angry? Poor Rita.

I really do think that, in another life, Martin and I would be together. In every life but this one, we would probably be together. Absolutely, we would be, we are so alike. Even in this life, we should be together. He wants his girl next door. I want the girl in the big, echoing house on the other end of the village. She wants a normal life. We will all be disappointed in the end. The swans stare at me when I pass them by.

I hope that I am a better admirer than Martin. I hope I am kinder and more considerate, or at least more subtle than he is. I hope my feelings haven't made her as confused as his have made me. It's strange. It's all very strange. He is supposed to be my best friend. Perhaps all this time, he has only acted like my best friend because he fancies me. Why else would he carry my bag to and from school and waste his Summer nights tutoring me in Irish? Why don't I want him the way that he wants me? I could have a chance at a beautiful life with Martin. Instead, all I have is an unrequited obsession with a girl who is probably straight.

It's hard to feel such heavy things like this while pretending that I don't feel anything at all. That Martin is just my friend. That Susannah is just my friend. That neither of them have me torn apart.

If I ignore Martin's feelings, they might go away. If I ignore my own feelings, they might go away. Although I realise that I could never ignore my feelings when I catch myself carefully keeping my hair dry in the shower, so I can keep the smell of her bed on me a little longer. I have only been washed and dressed for a minute when Ciarán shouts up the stairs to me,

'Lucy! Martin is here!'

Will this night not end?

I suppose it's best that he is here now, so I can face him and get it over with. I don't bring him into the house. Normally, and especially after a night out, he would come in and make us both tea and we would watch telly. He would have told me everything from the boys' night, and I would have told him everything from the girls' night, and it would be a lazy and funny afternoon. Instead, we are sitting on the step at the back door. Morning light suits him. He has grown into himself. At the moment, he is easily the best looking of his brothers.

'How's the head?'

This is so like him: when he is sober, he acts like he did nothing stupid the night before. He will be the next one of us to turn eighteen, although suddenly, he looks older than that. All along I have felt like the grown-up one, but just look at him. Listen to him. He is grown, I am only a child. I just nod, because he is so nice, and I am too tired to keep up with him. Perhaps he has forgotten about last night.

'Did you see Ryan?'

He means the fight, I assume, and not after the fight, when Ryan was with Eimear. I should have the information about what happened in the car, but the last I saw her, she was asleep on Susannah's bedroom floor. I just nod again and pull my hair away from my face. A starling is singing nearby, and I want to concentrate on that noise. The atmosphere between us is so strange. We never fall out. I want things to go back to normal. Even if his feelings make me uncomfortable, and even if he is wrong for wanting me while he is with Rita, I just want to put all this behind us. It's too awkward. Maybe it's best that we don't talk about it at all. I am still not one for apologies, but now that he is a man, Martin seems to be creeping towards one.

'He was in such a state after it. I don't think the drink suits him.'

'I don't know if it suits any of us.'

I am too harsh for this soft morning, I know. He thinks I am talking about myself.

It's normal for a while. He goes on to ask me about Eimear, and what she and Ryan got up to, and all of the girls. He tells me that Declan's girlfriend is actually really nice and that he doesn't think she would have brought drugs to a party. If nothing else, I am gathering gossip to tell the girls later. It's all fine, until finally he says,

'God, I was so drunk.'

'Yep.'

'I don't even remember half the night.'

'Don't you?'

I do what I can to sound uninterested. As though there is nothing to remember. I don't want him to remember it. I don't want him to think I could be annoyed with him.

There is a short silence, and he reaches down to flick dried mud off his shoe, and I hear the words trying to leave his sticky mouth.

'Did we have a fight or something?'

This is a poorly disguised lie. Martin remembers our small poisonous exchange. He remembers it well enough that he could recite it like a scene from a play. What I said surprised him so terribly that he will remember it verbatim for years and years, although he won't ever understand what he did to provoke it. I have to laugh. Will he even mention his old wound, Rita? Is he waiting for me to explain myself?

'No, we didn't have a fight. I think I told you to piss off, but we didn't have a fight.'

'Oh, right.'

He is not satisfied.

'So what happened?'

Why is he digging here? Am I supposed to be honest?

'I don't really remember.'

He's annoyed, it's funny. I'm annoyed too, it's obvious, and neither of us is brave enough to be truthful about it. Aren't we stupid?

'I'm sure it didn't matter.'

It is a dissatisfying and frustrating end to the conversation. That's it, we don't say much more. When he gets up to go home, I am so glad to see the back of him getting smaller and smaller until I can't see him at all. If only we had more Summer left, that way I could stay out of sight

SUNBURN

until our mutual disgust burns up.

I spend the rest of the day in the garden with Padraig, playing with as much energy as I can to convince Mother I wasn't out last night. I show him how to suck the nectar out of a fuchsia. I never have tasted the sweetness before, but I pretend for him that I can. Padraig laughs at everything I do, he is such a cure.

8

WHEN THE AFTERNOON IS ENDING and I am bitten up with the fear, the telephone rings in the hallway, long and loud. It cuts through all the awful weight around me, and I know before I answer it that it is the high scream of Susannah calling my name. I know her ring apart from others, I rush to answer it.

'Hi.'

'Oh, Lucy?'

Is there any sound like her breath in the receiver? My private symphony, call me Lucifer, just once. She is probably lying on her front, on her big double bed, or perhaps her long body is draped across one of her sofas. She is probably wearing one of her father's shirts instead of one of the many satin nighties I have seen in her wardrobe. There is music drifting out of her record player, coming down the line to me. Perhaps I shouldn't listen so closely, it could be private. The music she likes is all old-fashioned, records and cassettes her brothers and parents have forgotten that they once liked. Folky, sad seventies sort of music, high-pitched and full of longing. She doesn't care when we tease her for this. Mother would be disgusted to hear music on the other end of a phone call. No manners, she would say. But this is not her call, she cannot hear a word. Mother is so far away; all I hear is Susannah's breathing and this faint song.

She talks, I listen, I don't have the strength to stop her. Discussing the plainest things is exhilarating. Today's weather, a grocery list, a dandelion out the window, I am breathless.

'You left my house really early this morning, were you okay?'

She noticed me missing, can you believe it? Imagine if she was disappointed to wake up without me.

'Yeah, just I had to get home.'

'You should have woke me. I wanted to say bye.'

You were too dreamy to wake, I stared at you too long, it was foul, I wanted to say goodbye too.

'Sorry.'

Maybe she is sitting on the kitchen island. How decadent she is. She's probably up there painting her toenails, eating out of the fruit bowl, the fructose slowly rotting her teeth. Mother calls my name, we both hear, and Susannah knows she needs to hurry up.

'Listen, what are you at tomorrow?'

'Dunno.'

'Wanna go on a walk or something? We're probably fooling ourselves sunbathing now.'

'Alright, call over after dinner.'

There won't be dinner at Susannah's house, I wish I never said that. Even if she comes home, Catríona won't make Sunday dinner. The fruit bowl will be running low by then. I thought I would have to wait until school to see her, but she is granting me one last look at her in the Summer.

'Alright... see ya.'

She hangs up before I can say the same. The dial tone throbs in my ear, its heavy, low sound. I hold the phone to my heart, and its beating falls in line with the beeping of her goodbye. Mother calls out again. She only wants to know who is on the phone. Everything here is so dreary, but now I have a tomorrow of Susannah to look forward to. I go to bed early so that it will come sooner, and I wonder if there is any of me left on her sheets.

At four o'clock on Sunday, she arrives in jeans and a cardigan, and a glaring diamond ring. This is very typical of Susannah: she is opulent in ways she doesn't realise. She often wears her mother's engagement ring as a casual accessory; to her, a diamond isn't particularly interesting. While there isn't food in the fridge, there are a few diamonds lying around her house. This is a real diamond, not small, worn on her own ring finger or a chain around her neck, once even on a hair tie at the end of a braid. Once, while making bread, I asked Mother,

'Mam, why do you never wear your engagement ring?'

And she said,

'I never had one.'

Without sighing, she kept on kneading the dough. That was when I first realised about money. For years, I thought everyone in Crossmore had the same amount of money. Then I came to know that there were rich and poor people, I just had never known where we fell. After considering Susannah, I can categorically say that we are not rich. Then again, Mother doesn't work, so we can't struggle too much. I'm still not sure. I suppose if we were very poor, I would know about it.

Although people say Susannah is made of money, you really wouldn't know it without seeing the house. In her school uniform, with her unbrushed hair, she is no different to any of the rest of us. At home, she has a plethora of expensive clothes, perfumes and jewellery from her father, but she mostly just wears old bits and pieces that her brothers left behind. Only for her address, nobody would know she had a penny to her name. I wonder what she will do when she is eighteen and she gets her hands on the money. It is probably more than enough to get her out of Crossmore. I dread the day that she goes, and leaves me behind. No matter, she is here right now. She is stunning, and standing at my door. How well she timed her arrival. She knows me well.

Our walk is long, we take many back roads, we go on for hours.

After our summer together, after I let myself crumble, talking to her has become so easy. Somehow she makes everything so smooth, so alluring.

'I'm dreading school.'

'I can't wait.'

And,

'You love those flowers.'

'Yeah, my favourite.'

And,

'Which Brian gave Bernadette his phone number?'

'Oh no, actually he gave it to me.'

She tries to brush past this, like she doesn't want me to ask questions, like she doesn't realise she has winded me.

'Who is he?'

'Brian McCarthy. From the boy school.'

His name drools out of her mouth like it doesn't mean anything. Perhaps it doesn't. Perhaps I don't.

'Do you like him or something?'

'So what if I do?'

What an awful blow. Though she looks very serious, she keeps a laugh in her voice, like there is a joke I have missed, like this is funny. It reminds me that it's none of my business if she likes him. The small view of her that I've been given is a gift, not a right. It's more than most people get. I should be more grateful.

'I just need him to stir up trouble at home.'

Here we go.

'Next time Mam is home, Brian will be there too. We're just gonna make a scene, that's all.'

My deepest sorrow, she is so alone. This poor fledgling, at home with half a mother and less than half a father.

'But you still haven't even got in trouble for what you did this weekend.'

'Exactly! She came home yesterday, and the house smelled of drink, the girls were thrown around the place, there was even vomit in one of the downstairs bathrooms, and she didn't say a word!'

It must be so exhausting to live in a house like theirs, where they are both raising each other.

'So basically, drinking isn't enough anymore, I have to start sleeping around.'

She says this so casually. Is she so attention-starved? It's only a joke, of course it's only a joke, but still I am appalled. She keeps going.

'You know, not actually sleeping around, I just need to make her think I'm doing it.'

Every move she makes in that house is a cry for help, but what can I do to help? I don't have anything to offer, I have no experience or advice worth listening to.

'Obviously, I don't actually want to do that with the boys, it's just pretending.'

I will hang onto this sentence forever.

'Lads are a hassle. I don't want to end up like you and Martin last night.'

This curse. She stops walking, standing before me, in front of a bright hedge with drooping foxgloves, letting me know she is about to lay it on me.

'Will you drop it? I'm so sick of hearing about me and Martin.'

'You're not the only one.' She blesses me with a warm sigh. 'I know you don't like him like that.'

'I know. I keep saying I don't like him.'

'Yeah, it's getting old.'

What would she have me do?

She is looking at me with bad eyes, her hair is fire against the foxgloves, and the last of the summer sunlight is sacrificing itself to fall on her. The wind slows till it is less than a breath. How calm the air can be; look at how she smoulders.

'So am I supposed to be sorry that he likes me? I don't think I can stop him, Susannah.'

I could shout at her, I could fall to her feet. Nothing is about Martin. Not one thing. There isn't a millimetre of space for him in my heart, she has filled up all four ventricles.

'You don't have to be sorry about it, you should just be honest about how you feel.'

'I am being honest, it's just nobody ever listens to me!'

A fever comes over me. I am not understood, not by the one who matters the most, not even by myself. I've never known her to drag me around like this. Does she need me to scream it out? Does she know what truth she is about to uncover?

'You're not being honest.'

She is so calm, so cool. I could slap her, she is always right. Kill this painful talking, these sweating feelings, this heat. Does she want me to say it? Does she really? Does she know what she's asking for?

'So what if I'm not being honest?'

The way she is looking at me now could slow my organs to a stop. Where has this look come from? This is a new way of looking. It is weighted, expectant. It says: don't wreck this.

My throat dries. There is no room for confusion with this look, this passage of electricity. This talking without words. Her look of longing, begging, demanding. I want her to always look at me this way.

'So just be honest with me. Take what you want.'

Look how she shrugs her shoulders, like we are nothing. Like we could touch. Like she would allow every part of us to collide, if I would only move. How is it that she is always so calm and confident and yet she expects me to be able to speak and touch and be honest? She is too cool for my frenzied heart. I will come to her, she knows, she waits. The chance is waiting to be taken, or to disappear forever. Every occurrence of my life only passed to lead me here, to this, and here it is, she is so close to me, this is no time to be afraid. God bless me if I am wrong.

Suddenly, the worry goes. How could I be afraid? How could I be nervous with her? This is a moment of great peace, when, for the first time, I am not afraid of my feelings. I want her, I just want her, there isn't anything sordid about it – actually, it's the most beautiful feeling I've ever known.

It is simple. It is natural. I move, I kiss her.

This instant is eternal. My hand on her cheek, her lips against mine, her perfect and glorious mouth. The nervous breath stammers out her nose and onto my cheek, one she has been holding in all her life. Her hands find my back. We are eternal. Oh, at last, her mouth.

A cow cries. A pair of song thrushes sing. This is not the explosion I expected it might be. Rather, it is a quiet and soft making of sense. It is the late August sky, the dew forming on the snowdrops, a far-off car rumbling. Her hands have found me. I have been let into her mouth. We are so far away from everything. Mothers, money, men, all miles away. Our small world explodes and is made new. We are the only two people in it. Long may this last.

Moving away from my mouth, her eyes look so deeply into mine, deeper than my cells, deeper than my soul. With this look, she takes a piece of me, and she will have it forever. I don't mind. For the first time in my life, I am not afraid to be seen for what I am. We don't say a thing. I feel so delicate, like if we stand still long enough, we could blow away with the pollen. I kiss her again, because I know I am welcome, because I know I want to, and because I have never felt anything like it. Her warm, velvet mouth, the perfect blackness of my closing eyes. The cow cries out again. What beautiful music she makes.

She holds my hand and walks me through the fields. It's like she is showing me Crossmore for the first time. We can see the ocean from here, where it meets the sky. Blue on blue.

Susannah,
Save this letter: it marks the moment that my life finally started. I have never felt closer to Heaven than I felt today on the road with you. I can only hope that it was real, and that you will not change your mind.

Now I am away from you, I have never felt further from home, further from myself. Susannah, since the day I met you, I have wanted to let you know that you are a spill of gleaming gold on my otherwise dull and pointless world.

Yours always,
Lucy

9

SEPTEMBER 1991

IN THE MORNING, SUSANNAH COMES ten minutes late to assembly. Principal Sheehy glares at her for arriving late to the first day of Sixth Year, but he ought to know by now that it will take weeks for her to break out of her Summer sleep schedule. When she races to her place in the line, she doesn't look at me, although she does wave to Bernadette. We are given a long lecture about Sixth Year, and about how we must forget about daydreaming and focus on our schoolwork or we will be in a deficit for the rest of our lives. It's all very dramatic on this side of the exams. She stands there, yawning and whispering with Kevin O'Shea and Dermot O'Sullivan. Why won't she look at me?

There isn't a chance to speak to her alone before the bell rings and we are whisked off to class. A little doubt has come in around me. There's every chance she doesn't want a chance to talk to me. I wish I wouldn't let myself think like this, but I do.

Our Sixth Year commences with Geography – what a tiresome beginning. I only took Geography because the other option was Woodwork, and I would be even less suited to that. She and I are assigned seats on opposite sides of the room. Without another option, and without the patience to wait to speak to her, I scribble her name on last night's letter and have it passed along the room to her. It's already gone from my hands before I consider that somebody might open it, but they don't. It lands on her book, and she stares at it. Twenty minutes into the lesson, she asks to go to the bathroom. I watch as the letter goes with her.

I couldn't feel any different to how I felt yesterday. When she reads the letter, she will know for certain that I am in love with her, and that our kiss was not just a silly, girly thing, and not just one animal pawing another – it was a dream realised. Maybe I was too honest, maybe I put a little too much love into the letter, and a little too much of myself into the kiss. Maybe if she thought it was just a funny, slutty practice kiss then she would let me do it again. If I could only run to the toilets before I vomit my nerves onto my desk, but Susannah could be in any one of them, with my letter, which reveals my whole heart. Writing it was so natural, but that was last night, when I was high on her spit, and anything would have seemed like a good idea. Now, in the Geography classroom, in my school uniform, hearing about the process of denudation, everything is so staunch, and my romantic ideas seem brainless.

She comes back into the room, careless as a breeze, and sits down, and still she doesn't look at me once. If she wasn't so far away, it would be easier to confirm what I believe I'm seeing, but I think, and I hope, I am right, that she has unfolded my letter in her copybook. I think she is reading it again. And again. I think I see her neck redden, and for better or worse, I know I have embarrassed her.

When the bell rings, she leaves the room without a word, without a glance in my direction. Why does she do this? She goes straight to her Higher German class, and I go to Ordinary Irish. All through this lesson, Bernadette is trying to catch my attention, and I do what I can to giggle and whisper along with her, but my mind is so far away.

It is not until French, our third class of the day, that she drops a note on my desk and disappears to the back of the classroom to sit with the boys. I wonder, just for a second, if she is showing them my letter, and my hideous affection, and laughing at me. One hundred and eighty minutes of agony, unknowing, waiting, and here is my answer: a red-and-blue lined sheet, torn out of her German copybook, folded up with my fate written inside. I wait until the class is deep underway and steal her idea of reading the letter in the bathroom.

There are two First Years at the mirror, who hurry up and leave when I enter. Normally, I would relish this little piece of power, but I hardly even look at them or my reflection or at how many doors are shut. I go straight to a stall, lock the door, and sit on the lid of the toilet. I take a very fast, deep breath, and read the letter. Let's just get it over with.

L,

You're very dramatic. I wish I could write something as dramatic as you, but it isn't easy when Fraulein Becker could call on me at any second. You keep putting me in these nervous and intense situations – that is not a bad thing.

I have not changed my mind. You seem to think I have all the power here, like I was going to decide not to want you anymore. I'm powerless.

If you want me, I'm yours.

S x

She is power. She is mine.

I rejoin the class. I understand now why she could not look at me, because I cannot look at her. At small break, I wait at her locker, because if I don't talk to her now, I might never talk to her again.

But I don't need to be afraid, because she's coming towards me now. Look how bright she is, look how the corridor around her brightens. The volume of the locker-lined hall fades, I don't hear a thing but the clacking of her low-heeled Mary Janes. And it gets louder, she is nearing. The sun floods the high windows and fills her coppery lips. She hasn't had a new school shirt since we were fourteen. Phil could afford to buy her a new uniform every year, he just can't afford the time it would take to bring her shopping. Her knee highs don't reach her knees anymore, and even though I spent the whole Summer looking at her in a bikini, there is something wildly enticing about this exposed inch of her shin. Look at her hair bouncing; she sees me, and her eyes are smiling.

'Lucy!'

She puts her arms around me without hesitating, and because we are girls and we are blessed with an anticipated level of intimacy, I can do the same. Nobody notices as her hands fall on my back again, nobody cares how tightly I squeeze her. If even one of us was a boy, we couldn't do this. It only lasts a second, because she must get on with her lovely day. When she pulls herself away from me, the noise comes back to the room. She smiles, she is sheepish as she tucks her hair behind her ear. That's it, there is no more wondering. Another girl like me exists, and she is the most perfect girl in the world. The awful deed is done, our perfect love comes to life. I am hers, and she is mine.

Those first few heartbeats of her leave me ecstatic. At last, I am defined. All my lonely days were not wasted, they led me to this most perfect union, this weaving of our two souls. The parts of me that were once afraid can no longer be found. Perhaps they will come back to terrify me again, but for now, I can't feel them. For now, I allow myself to be wanted by her.

From that first moment in the school hallway, time starts to move differently. I no longer count the hours or the days, it's only the time that she is with me, and the time I have to wait until she is with me again. The seasons change, and she changes with them. Susannah adapts so well. I have started to adapt too. As the leaves oxidise, her hair darkens, and new, cold air is breathed into my lungs. Crossmore rusts into Autumn, Dad weans the calves off their mothers, and Susannah grows pale as the sky. She convinces me to cut my hair again, so it curls up around my ears the way that it used to. She likes to pull it straight and let it bounce back into shape. I like doing whatever she likes.

This day last year, I could never have imagined calling Susannah my girlfriend. I could never have imagined having a girlfriend, or being in a relationship at all. How quickly things have changed. It seems Susannah has often imagined having a girlfriend, as none of this seems particularly strange to her. It makes sense, I suppose. She has never officially been linked to any of the boys. She has never done much to suggest she cares about them. Now that I know Susannah in this way, I can't imagine her ever being with one of them. She is too mature, too clever. I feel so lucky to know her this way.

The Winter shows me more stars than I have ever seen. I know them now, and they know me, because of her. I think she might light the stars. In this dark half of the year, the isolation of Crossmore intensifies. For the first time, it is liberating. I always thought a place like Crossmore would kill a person like me, but I realise now that places like Crossmore are made for people like me. There is space for me, for us, out on the edges, among the ruins and the hedges and the stone walls. These things are immovable. They belong to the world and cannot be altered. I hope that Susannah and I are like these things. I carve our initials into trees and scratch them onto rocks, hoping that a piece of us will remain in the landscape. While I do this, she has no fear in scrawling our initials into school desks. What nerve she has. It takes all I have not to bat at her hands and stop her.

Yes, for all our glory, denying her has become second nature. Did you expect anything less from me? Neither of us wants to be a cousin that the village isn't supposed to know about. Although if Mother ever found out about us, that might be the best that I could hope for. Even if I told her that I finally feel like a proper person, that I can breathe, that I no longer need to imagine what it is to feel peace, it would be my end. If she didn't try to cure me herself, she and Granny would send me off to the nuns. My father and brothers would be told I got very ill in the night and died, and I would spend the rest of my life locked in a convent, staring out at the bare trees of Winter, shivering in anticipation for the sight of Susannah's shadow below.

She says that Phil wouldn't mind us being together.

'His woman has a load of gay friends in the city. They're all lads, but I've met some of them and they're sound.'

She calls from the sofa while I wash the ware in her kitchen. I hate to think of her standing up for something as monotonous as washing up. I like doing little chores for her. Perhaps doing little jobs like this makes up for my behaviour. Even with all the love that I have for her, I'm not ready to be out. Not yet. I'm just somebody in love with Susannah. That's enough.

I wring out the sponge. There is a little silence, which I hum to fill. I'm not sure what else to do. She is waiting for me to say the right thing. She will be waiting a long time for that. As I am drying my hands, I feel her behind me. She puts her arms around my waist and drops her head on my shoulder.

'It's a shame that you can't even come out to me.'

She says into my ear. Her thumbs rub against my sides. There is no need for me to come out. She and I are just two people who understand each other. What would I even come out as? I wouldn't dare disappoint her with a statement as pathetic and vague as that. It's much easier to kiss her and say something to make her laugh. She doesn't push it. She lets me make her laugh.

'Will we dress up for Halloween?'

She asks me. Isn't she lovely to so willingly change the subject? She brings me back over to the sofa. I wonder if Catríona buys any sweets for the trick-or-treaters. We are too old to dress up, and yet I tell her,

'Whatever you want, honey.'

Perhaps all the time I spent daydreaming about her, she spent on self-reflection, because she is so alright with who she is. When did she do all that thinking? I like to remind her that if her father was okay with us, then her mother would not be, and it's her mother that she needs to live with. Susannah is sure that as soon as she finishes school, she will be kicked out of Croft Hall. There is no point in accelerating that for the sake of a little honesty.

It isn't often that she mentions it, but I know she would like to come out. I know that the only reason she hasn't is to look after me. Sometimes she pushes it, just to see how it feels. Like in the Art room, when Cathy Mooney is loudly asking everyone who is a virgin and who isn't, Susannah says,

'Don't be vulgar, Cathy, we don't have sex with boys.'

And Cathy says,

'So you're a virgin, Susannah?'

And she says,

'I never said that.'

All the girls laugh at Cathy. Susannah loves to light these little blazes. And although the whole exchange makes my skin crawl, I am compelled to kiss her. When she talks like this, and touches me in her quiet ways, it is almost too much to take. When I am falling apart with love for her, it brings us so close to being caught. Sometimes I wonder if I am only a funny crush to her. I hope I don't ever have to find out.

Later, she passes me a note that says,

Lucy,

Isn't Cathy such a dick? Imagine if I had told her the truth. I'd love to see her face. It's hard to feel like this, to be always guilty and upset. It's hard to watch you feeling that way all the time. I think you feel it a lot heavier than I do. Sometimes I think I make it worse for you. I promise if you get through it, I'll make it worth it. I'll marry you if you get past all the shame of being with me.

Susannah x

It's awful that our perfect existence is punctuated by her dejection. Little things like this have been happening more recently. Her nerve is mounting. She tells me I am insecure. She tells me that the girls wouldn't care, that we are all one thing anyway, so nothing would change. That isn't true. I don't know if she is pretending or ignorant. The very best outcome would be the girls reminding Susannah that I don't have any money to spend on her, and reminding me that she has a wandering eye. I love the girls more than I love myself, but they would not love me if they knew. I know this, and deep down, Susannah must also know this. Why would we give anyone the chance to stop loving us? Why would I let them confirm my worst fear: that we are not a normal couple at all, but one strange sin spread across two people?

It's too heavy to think about. Instead, I light her cigarettes, and when they go from my lips to hers, it's close to a kiss. When changing back into our school uniforms after PE, she puts on my jumper, and I put on hers, so her perfume is there whenever I want it. It will be there until Mother washes my school clothes on Friday evening, then it will smell like me when we swap back after PE on Wednesday. She can put an arm around me while walking, just briefly; she can blow kisses my way if she does the same to the other girls. They love this newfound feminine affection – they think it's very sophisticated. As long as she is good to them, and a little mean to me, nobody notices. It's all so subtle that nobody thinks twice when Susannah comes over and spends all day in my bed, playing with my hair. It's just female adolescence, nothing we do is taken seriously.

Halloween comes around. Although Aisling has invited us to her house party, Susannah and I have decided not to go. It's all very suspicious that Rita would allow me to be at Aisling's party, given that she supposedly hates me. I used to love Halloween, but since we've grown up, it isn't the same. I don't really like getting off with people at parties, and I don't really like dressing in a sexy way. There doesn't seem to be much else to Halloween these days. I would go to the party, probably, if I didn't have another option. But then Susannah asked me to stay in with her. I think she is only doing it to make me feel better. The girls can't believe we aren't going. It's all they have talked about today. I wonder if they suspect anything.

'You're so dry.'

Joan says, while rolling up her skirt in the school bathroom.

'Would ye not just come?'

'It's gonna be unreal.'

They are all going to dress as cats. I don't want to dress as a cat. I would feel ridiculous. The girls take so easily to things like that: dressing up, being alluring and girlish. Susannah takes easily to it. It makes me feel very peripheral that I don't. Even Patricia will be there in a black skirt and cat ears, looking and feeling as though she belongs.

'I can't be bothered with it.'

Susannah says, pulling the back of Joan's skirt down to even it out. Why am I not saying anything? Why does this make me feel so uncomfortable?

'They don't have to go if they don't want to.'

Maria says, which stifles the girls. Isn't she so lovely? I wonder if they will miss us. I wonder if Rita will convince Martin to wear a couples costume. What trouble will we miss out on?

It is so cold as I walk through the evening, down Susannah's road. All the leaves have fallen off the trees already. There is a little bit of lilac sky left on the horizon. There are scarce yellow lights from the houses on the hills. I breathe in the cold air. I could walk this road forever. A part of me feels like I should be going to the party. I feel like I'm going to regret not being there. Like I should be drinking tonight or trying a new drug or meeting people. It's a weird feeling of guilt for something I haven't even done. That all falls away when Susannah opens the door to me. The glow of the fireplace fills the doorframe and outlines her in orange. That lucky light. She is wearing a black nightdress and a witch's hat. I can hear music coming from inside. She pulls me into the house.

Now and again, there is a knock on the door, and Susannah will race to answer it. She very earnestly compliments the children on their costumes while handing out sweets. I could watch her doing this all night. She is so excited every time someone new comes to the door. How wholesome this is. I am so glad that I am not drinking or on drugs or meeting people. She fills us a bucket with water and apples. Isn't she sweet, wanting to play these childhood games?

I cheer as she plunges her face into the water. She has not remembered to tie her hair back. The bubbles of her breath are bursting before me. With her hands behind her back, she tries to catch an apple in her mouth. I feel so warm, watching her. When her face surfaces she is laughing. Her eyelashes are wet, and she blinks her eyes open. With her chin in the water, she tries again to pierce an apple with her teeth. The water from her hairline is dripping onto the floor.

'Go on, honey!'

She pushes an apple towards her mouth and bites into it, then throws her arms into the air. We cheer. The music seems louder now. Her mouth is wet, she is chewing on the apple. I pull her close to me. When I kiss her, I feel the water on my face and taste the warm apple spit in my mouth. She laughs.

'I used to stare at your mouth so much.'

I tell her. She puts her arms around my neck.

'You should have said. I'm always staring at you.'

I don't know if I have ever felt so secure with another person, with myself. Being with her is so fulfilling. It is so affirming. I should be here with her, I know that. I am not just an admirer who she is humouring. We are equal parts. It is such a good feeling. I didn't realise this feeling existed. I didn't realise how badly I needed to feel it. All along I thought Susannah was like a god. Now I kind of feel like a god too. It's funny that another person could make me feel this good. We stay up, talking. I could listen to her talk forever. In the morning, we sleep in late. Later Mother will be upset that I didn't go to Mass for All Saints' Day. I will go tomorrow. Perhaps Susannah will come with me. Perhaps she will spend every day of the midterm with me. Wouldn't that be dreamy?

There is a little drama when Catríona gets home. Susannah left the kitchen light on all night. It isn't enough to argue about, but enough to set a tone in the house. We sit through it. Later on, Susannah gives me a letter that says,

Lucy,

Thank you for earlier, when Catríona was banging around in the kitchen and you squeezed my knee. I don't know if you realised you did it. But it was so nice. It just felt so good to know you were there. And I

thought, if Lucy is here with me right now, that's enough goodness to last when she is gone. A few minutes of you would really be enough to keep me going for years. Thanks for always making me feel like you're there.
Susannah xo

I felt that squeeze the same as her. It was a moment of real love. It would be enough to keep me going for years too. Maybe forever. Even when she puts pressure on me, even when I am filled with guilt, I get so many of these precious moments. And then she thanks me for them. She is the sweetest sweetness. It's amazing that we have all these private touches of Heaven and nobody sees a thing. I sometimes forget that we are meant to be keeping ourselves a secret. It's hard to do sometimes, when we feel so natural.

The closest to being caught we've been is when Mother once saw Susannah's name was stitched into the label of the school jumper in the laundry instead of mine.

'I never knew such a pair of friends. I don't know where you end and she begins!'

Mother laughs as we hang the uniforms up to dry. Somehow Susannah's jumper always feels a little softer, even when it is washed in Mother's generic detergent, even when she hasn't worn it in days. Her name is stitched in the collar; how could it not be superior? I breathe it in and get stoned.

Even with all my gnawing fear, I can't help but look at her with glossed eyes. Somehow they all miss it. Somehow they miss the glisten of blonde fuzz on her top lip when she drinks from the tap. They have missed her in morning assembly, yawning and exposing a stretch of her navel. Those poor pities, how have they missed these things? Sometimes when I'm with her, it all becomes so much that I don't care what people would think of us. Susannah is so powerful, she is too much to be denied, she is the sort of woman that could pull rocks up from the earth.

I have so much to be ashamed of, small things that I've said and done that come to me at night and keep me awake. I don't want her to be one of these things. It's just sometimes that I don't care about what people would think. Maybe when we are older, sometimes will be all the time. For now, let it be our perfect and precious thing. The privacy makes loving easy.

And the privacy makes loving sad and frustrating. I have to save all my affection for the solitude of our bedrooms or the cold, dark outdoors. Even old frigid couples who have fallen out of love are more obviously together than we are. There are times when sneaking around makes me feel pathetic. She deserves better than someone pathetic. But then I get a look at her, and it's like a honeymoon away from my thoughts. Even on school mornings when I am frozen to the bone and exhausted, being near her is always sunbathing in the garden. It makes it easy to put my conscience away. I must remind myself that she is not trapped, she could go if she wanted to. It seems that for now, the scraps of intimacy that keep us alive are enough to sustain her too.

The other girls have started to swap jumpers, they don't get it. We let them play along, we don't care. It's funny. All along I felt so far away from everybody else, but now I think I was just far away from myself.

Now that I am with her, I can't imagine being without her. I can't imagine being who I was before. I don't want to. These days my life is perfect. I like sharing my lunch with her. I like her massaging my hands while we watch television. I like listening to her uneven singing while she potters around the kitchen. School is better. My life at home is better. She came along and made it all better. I want to tell her that I love her.

My Susannah,

Thank you for the nicest autumn of my life. I want you to know that I appreciate the helpless position I have put you in, and although I keep it quiet, I am so devoted to you. Thank you for always being patient. I didn't realise that I was ever unhappy until you made me this happy. I promise that I am proud of you. One day everybody will know how proud of you I am. Until then, Susannah, I hope that you will continue to grace me with your perfection.

Yours always,
Lucy

This is the closest I can manage to an admission of love. It's too early yet. I don't want to say it too soon in case she thinks I don't really feel it. I have never felt anything so strongly.

It is a wonder Susannah has grown up so lovely when she was made from a woman like Catríona. I don't know if anybody is more miserable than her. I have heard her shouting more than I have heard her talk. Parents usually wait until they are alone with their children to shout, but Catríona seems to enjoy having an audience. She isn't an evil person, she's just stuck in a life she isn't happy with. She wanted to be married with a big family, with plenty of money and plenty to do. Instead, her husband left her for another woman, two of her three children have disappeared from her, and she has nothing to do but wait for weekends away from home. You would think that she would cling tightly to Susannah and make the most of her while she is young. It must be easier to be bitter. With this soap opera way of living, it's surprising that Susannah hasn't been made bitter. It has taken a toll on her, undeniably, but in ways that are softer, more painful. She has been made needy and dependent and sometimes very angry, but not bitter.

They are downstairs fighting right now, while I am lying on Susannah's bed, pretending not to be here. If I hadn't told her to go and make us something to eat, they wouldn't have crossed paths at all. If she was up here doing her homework with me, Catríona would only be the sound of faint footsteps; even if she started wailing, we could ignore it. But Susannah is downstairs, flaring her mother's temper, because I put her there. Most of the time, she doesn't think anything of their fighting. Maybe she is too accustomed to it. Maybe it isn't as bad as it seems. There is a very good chance that I haven't heard Catríona's fullest anger. Susannah might not have either.

This is the most explosive argument I have heard in a long time. Of course, I miss a lot of it. Susannah told me that only yesterday morning, they fought to the point of tears over the last yoghurt in the fridge.

'Just because you don't see it doesn't mean it isn't happening.' Susannah said to me.

Perhaps that is what started this argument, perhaps she is trying to prove to me that she and her mother are not fine. Since we got together, Susannah has stopped pulling so many stunts to get Catríona's attention. I have not saved her, but I have certainly distracted her.

They seem to get louder with every argument. I dread the day that Susannah gets angry at me – I don't know if I could manage this wrath. As lightly as I can, I creep across the floorboards to lean my ear against the door and listen to their shouting. It cannot be too private an issue if Susannah has allowed it to get this loud while I'm in the house. Slowly, I pull the door open, afraid of a creak that doesn't come.

'Do you want me to tell your father about this?'

'I'd love you to tell him! Shame you can't talk to him without making it about yourself!'

Susannah is laughing, like it's only a game, and it makes Catríona worse. The tone that Susannah takes with her mother, the things that she says, it's unbelievable. I would be crucified for even having thoughts with that much attitude. And somehow Susannah gets away with laughing in Catríona's face while she shouts. The lengths she goes to for a little attention. The wild and outlandish things she does. Things like me.

Surely I'm more than just a trick to get on Catríona's nerves. But then, surely I would be the ultimate way to break her mother's heart. Perhaps she is letting it build up.

I press the bedroom door shut, very hard, and I hope that they hear it, and I hope it knocks Susannah off whatever trip she's on. I get back on the bed, as I was. Susannah wouldn't use me, not like that. I mean more than the likes of Brian McCarthy, don't I? She would use somebody else – I've seen her do it – but not me, I don't think. What a statement we would make. What better way to offend Catríona than for Susannah to parade around the house with the sheen of me on her chin?

Here she is at the door; she creeps across the floor to me. Is she embarrassed all of a sudden? What I wouldn't give to roll my eyes at her now, to pull my hand away as she tries to hold it. The luxury of being annoyed at her is something I cannot afford. Normalcy, it seems, is something I cannot afford. I dare not risk bursting the little bubble that we exist in. If we fight, this might all end. She gets as close as she can to me, and I let her, I even put my arm around her, because I can't help myself. Is this safe? Is this exactly what she wants?

'You're the only calm thing in my life.'

She says into my neck. Oh. There isn't a note in her voice. She isn't trying to lure me in or sweeten me, not right now. She means it; she is too sad to bother with anything but the truth.

Catríona and I stand on opposite sides of Susannah. Wherever I see beauty, she sees rot, and where I see misery, she sees a lesson learned.

Susannah the Daughter is so different to Susannah the Lover. And still I know that we know the same girl, one who could show her mother an erosive sweetness just as she could show me a torturous evil.

I must take her mind off her mother. I must say something to keep her from herself.

'Are you still onto Brian McCarthy?'

I could have said anything; why did I say that? Why did I shake her up when she was settling down? I can't tell if she is insulted or confused. She is trying to place his name, and when she lands on it, she sighs, annoyed.

'Brian McCarthy? Don't be stupid, I don't need him anymore.'

She smiles at me, even with her red eyes, it is the brightest smile she's ever shown me. Each tooth a shard of glass. She is trying to be endearing, and she is trying to reassure me, but all she has done is spike my paranoia. My love, you are a poison.

We are a dream together. Why am I trying to confuse things? Why do I allow my greatest pleasure to be my greatest panic? Just the mention of her name is enough to fill me with butterflies, with bile. Yes, I have kept us a secret so I don't have to face the reality of what our relationship means. I just wonder now, without reality, and without accountability, is there any relationship at all?

All we have to do is enjoy ourselves. All I want is to enjoy it. She takes my homework and starts filling in the blanks I have left. I let her do it. I let her do whatever she wants. Perhaps I shouldn't.

Spending all this time with her has left me with no time for Martin. He doesn't have any time for me either, since he is always with Rita. It's a little bit sad. I wonder if he has noticed a change in me, that I am newly happy. Of all people, he must have noticed. Of all people, Martin is the one I want to tell that Susannah O'Shea is not just a girl from our class, but that she is a seraph who found Crossmore, and that I don't have time for him because I am too busy kneeling at the altar of her navel.

He looks so disappointed every time she joins us as we walk home from school, as if he has secrets that he has been waiting to share, that he must keep inside when she is around. As if he will be expected to carry her schoolbag just because he carries mine.

'Any craic with the boys, Martin?'

She asks him, and is always met with a sigh. Not my sort of Susannah Sigh, but a different, dejected one, the sort you would expect from a teenage boy. His moods don't seem to deter her, because she could talk to anybody, even when they won't talk back. Her steps stay bouncy, even when he ignores her and says,

'See ya, Lucy.'

He takes the turn to his driveway without even looking at her. It's so embarrassing. Why does he have to behave like this? I will have to have a word with him when I get the chance. Susannah takes my schoolbag from him.

'It's so annoying that he carries your bag.'

She says, lifting it onto her shoulder.

'No, it isn't. He's only being nice.'

I pretend not to see when she rolls her eyes.

At my house, we drop our coats in the kitchen and race up to my room. Mother and Granny never look up to see which of the girls is with me. At Susannah's house, there is seldom anybody there to say hello to, and when there is, the house is big enough to hide in. There is hardly room to think in my house, and there is always somebody home. My younger brothers share a room, but since Granny can't walk up the stairs anymore, I have a room of my own. A small chapel for Susannah and me.

This is warm. She will look at me for just a second, just long enough to drag the air out of my throat. As her hands take my jaw, her lips take my cheeks. Each touch of her is nicer than the last, each time is different and new. I could touch her forever.

'Be honest, how long did you fancy me before we got together?'

It's the sort of daring question I could never ask, but she asks me. I am sitting on the edge of the bed, she is on the floor, pushing her old school socks down to her ankles, revealing a pink ring around the top of her calf from where the elastic was too tight.

'A while.'

The early December sun is lowering at my window, on us both. She looks up at me.

'I liked you first.'

Everything is easy. Everything makes sense here. She takes off her jumper, and drops it on my dresser, knocking over my statuette of the Virgin Mary. In the dresser, there are two sets of rosary beads, a Brigid's cross, and an iron pendant on a chain. And then there is her, more worthy of worship, with a knee on either side of my hips. When she is here, it is so easy to forget what I have been made to believe. She tells me she is mine, and the guilt goes away for a while. Padraig is playing army outside: I can hear him throwing pebble bullets against the stone wall. She and I are as the stone wall. Balanced, dirty, unmoving.

Before, I would let boys do a little with me, but not much. I expected that these attractions were an acquired taste. The way that Maria talked about triceps and body hair sounded so grown-up, I wanted so badly to feel her fascination. Now I feel it, and it's shocking to think there was a time when I didn't. With Susannah, I don't need to bother acting coy or well-behaved. Sometimes when we make love, we melt out of shape and become one thing. A thing that wants nothing but to touch and be touched, to be real and make noise. We can be heavy against each other, without any need to impress one another. This is so far away from what I ever felt with boys. There is no pressure. I can just exist as a conduit of pleasure and love. I want to always be this way.

When I compare this to what Sorcha has told me about boys, it seems strange that anybody would bother with them. There is an unwritten rule with boys, Sorcha explained to me, that you can't go all the way with them. She said that they use you, and they don't come back. I was told to give them little tastes, but never the whole thing.

'Not until you're at least engaged. Sure, he'll never come back otherwise.'

She warned me, like this was a fact, and not just her experience. It sounds like so much work for no reward. Susannah gives me what I want, and more than what I want, and I can't imagine not coming back. I'd come back on my hands and knees. She bites the fat on my hip, leaving the signature of her teeth on me, and when its red bruise fades away, she does it again. There won't ever be a time when I have had enough. I will always come back.

10

JANUARY 1992

MARTIN BEGINS THE NEW YEAR with heartbreak, as he finishes with Rita. The girls say it is because he never got over me properly. They only say that because they think I haven't gotten over him either. Besides a little ruffle in my ego, there was never anything to get over. They all say that she will be out to get me, but I doubt that's true – although I did find a rotten banana in the bottom of my schoolbag, and Eimear swears she saw Rita drop it in there. It could just as easily have been Padraig.

'She won't get over him until she gets under someone else.'

Eimear says, and though it sounds vulgar, it's probably true. Whenever I see Rita now, I stretch out my mouth, giving her the biggest smiles I can. Why not? I have no reason not to smile. Today I even stopped her in the bathroom to tell her how long her hair has gotten and that I hope she is okay. I don't know why I expected it to fix anything. It didn't. By the way she looked at me and scoffed, it was clear she thought that I'd only got out of Martin's lap just long enough to come and mock her. Well, that's just rudeness. Rita is not stupid, surely she knows that I don't actually care how upset she is and that I'm only trying to be nice. She could have just taken the compliment and stopped things from becoming awkward. It costs nothing to be nice, that's what Granny says. There's probably nothing I could ever say to Rita to convince her that I didn't have a part in her breakup, so I think I will give up on it. If she needs to hate me to get over Martin, that's totally fine; I'll still smile at her. I want the girls and me to be as nice as we think we are.

It's lovely that Martin will have more free time again. Although working out how I will share myself between him and Susannah makes me nervous.

The darkest days die out, and we evolve. Wildflowers begin to grow. Nobody notices, nobody cares. Our mock exams edge ever closer. I don't notice, I don't care. How could I, when I could listen to the way that Susannah says my name? She makes a dull sound into a song. In the early peach-coloured evenings of January, the sky almost looks like one of Summer, and I feel the perfect happiness of her garden coming back to me, even though it's only three degrees. I see Ciarán out in our garden, filling the watering can from the hose. There are distant, crying seagulls, and closer, there are crows and blue tits and thrushes. A passing car frenzies a nearby dog to a state of roaring. Then there is a sudden silence, when everything seems to stop, the lungs of the back road filling and readying to begin again with a new rush of wind. I smell the water from the hose in the warming air, and I want to live in that smell. The sky is preparing to stretch, the seasons are about to change again. Yes, our shivering and love-haunted Winter is truly over. Spring is pointing a pale and eager sun on us, and I doubt I am ready for the light.

This evening, like most evenings, my parents watch the television. Just a quick hour before Dad falls asleep. *The Angelus*, the news, then, if they can manage it, they passively absorb whatever comes on next. From the kitchen, I can hear the television mumbling, and David Norris beginning to speak, before Mother sighs and turns the volume down until he is done. I am very glad; I would rather not know what he is saying than have a debate started over it.

'There was something about the football in the *TV Guide*.'

Dad starts, trying to clear the air. It's only awkward because they let it be awkward. My parents don't like to see people looking for equality, or for any change at all. They like the world as it was, not as it is becoming. If they could choose, Crossmore would revert to the way it was when they were my age. Instead, the country is changing, much slower than the rest of the world, but it is changing, and it is dragging Crossmore along with it. These pushes for equality have been uncomfortably received in my house. Tomorrow, in the chipper, I will briefly tell Susannah about this, and she will tuck a curl of hair behind my ear and sigh. We will share a long look, and it will be broken by Eimear laughing at us, and saying,

'Ye dykes.'

It would be as easy for Eimear to just say something nice. It would be even easier to say nothing. It will be a full fortnight before I will let Susannah touch me in front of her again.

Before all that, I must listen as Dad fumbles for the *TV Guide* and convinces Mother to watch his GAA programme.

In the Winter, Susannah didn't mind that we were a secret. Perhaps because it made us seem a little less serious. Now she seems ready to be serious. She says that she is tired of the best thing in her life being an embarrassing secret; I've never been the best thing, I've always been embarrassing, doesn't she know that? Her patience is wearing out, I can feel it. Since we came back to school after the Christmas holidays, she has had wild eyes, she hints at exposing us. It's that damned Spring sun: it has heated her blood and given her a terrifying urge to be free. If not for me, she would have come out by now. Think of all the mad and wonderful things she could do without me.

We are sitting on the long sofa in her living room, sharing a can of Coke, her hand in mine. Chaos always begins with peace. The television is on in front of us, though we are not really watching it. We are thinking faraway thoughts. I am staring at the screen, she is staring at my face in profile. Does she like the ugly parts of me? My weak chin can't be hidden from this angle. My hair is growing out, it is an awkward, unflattering length. Does she worship me the way I worship her?

Her leg is bouncing, she is biting the rim of the can. Perhaps I ought to do something to calm her down.

Before I can, the front door opens and slams closed, and Catríona comes into the room carrying the post. Suddenly, the air around us changes, and grows stale. No longer is the living room a private haven for Susannah and me. Now it's just a room in a house that I am a guest in. I tense up a little, I sit up straighter and get ready to lighten my voice. Without even realising it, I have dropped Susannah's hand.

'Oh. Okay. Hi, girls.'

Catríona says, and sounds surprised that we are here, like she has forgotten that Susannah lives with her. Not breaking eye contact with her mother, Susannah takes my hand again, quickly, and firmly puts her arm around me – so firmly that I cannot move away. I love that she wants to be known, and I hate it. Catríona drops a very heavy breath.

'Are you out tonight?'

Susannah asks, and puts our joined hands in her lap, where anyone could see them.

'No, love, I'd say not.'

Catríona speaks softly, like she cannot read Susannah's tone.

'Oh, that's a shame.'

Susannah smirks, and as her eyes tighten on her mother, her grip tightens on my sweating hand. If I don't escape this conversation, I will faint. Susannah is going to make an argument out of me, I feel it coming, I feel her temper rising. I shouldn't even be here. Catríona doesn't say anything about us, she keeps leafing through the post.

'A shame? Why?'

She feels that she has no reason to trust her daughter, and she's probably right to feel that way.

'Me and Lucy just wanted to be alone, that's all.'

Her sincerity cuts so close to the bone. Is she standing up for us, or is she weaponising me? Yes, my love is using me. I am just another way of getting her mother's attention; I am only as important as Brian McCarthy's phone number scrawled on the back of a cigarette box. We are dangerously close to being exposed. One small jolt in Susannah's temper would be enough for her to tell Catríona everything. We didn't discuss this, this isn't fair. And then Catríona spots our hands. She knows. It's so clear. In that one uncomfortable and confused glance, she figured us out. It's too much for her, I can see it in her face; she won't dare speak its name. After all the love I have received, I can't say it either. For our own reasons, none of us can call this what it is. And yet, in our strangled silence, Susannah is making us all look at it.

The air gets thicker, nobody breathes or swallows. Susannah's eyes narrow on her mother, her hand tightens further around mine.

'Don't start with me. Not tonight, Susannah.'

'Lucy is sleeping over, so maybe make yourself scarce if it's gonna be a problem.'

The post twitches in Catríona's hand. If I weren't here, she would drop it on the floor and pull Susannah's hair. Instead, she smiles as the letters shake, and warns,

'You're on thin ice, girl.'

And she leaves us. The quiet stays until we hear her bedroom door slamming, and Susannah rolls her eyes, as though she is the mother dealing with an unruly teenager. Then she smiles at me, like she is satisfied, like she has done something to be proud of. The carnage does not bother her, she is delighted with the attention. What a sour atmosphere they have created. My heart is hammering. I need a cigarette, or to scream. I need to get out of this house. If I spoke to Mother like that, I would never be heard from again. Now her hands are sweating around mine, still holding on tightly. A very small part of me is proud of her, but more of me is terrified, and appalled, and enraged. In the reverberations of her mother's slamming door, she whispers,

'That was class.'

I could slap her. I think I want to. She is smiling. She keeps going.

'That was the closest I've ever got to coming out to her. I think I basically did? Like she must know something is going on between us.'

Why does she keep talking? In my head, I'm halfway out the door, pulling my shoes on, running away from her mansion – but when I look down, my hand is still in hers, on her torn jeans, in her lap.

'Don't do that again.'

It's the first time I have spoken to her with real strength in my voice. I get up, she follows.

'What's the problem?'

It takes all I have not to scream. I must not raise my voice above talking, so that Catríona doesn't hear us and suspect that our wretched loving isn't going to last.

'What was that? You made such a scene.'

'So I was standing up for us. So what? That's a good thing.'

Her smile won't go.

'No, you weren't, Susannah, you were just using me to piss her off.'

Her smile goes, just for a second, and she tries to revive it. She looks genuinely confused. I regret saying this before I've even started.

'We all see you lashing out for her attention. Don't pretend that's not what just happened.'

Maybe she didn't realise how cutting I can be. I didn't really realise either.

'You're joking?'

'I wish I was joking, Susannah. You totally used me, just admit it.'

'Am I not allowed to hold your hand in my own house? This is the only place you'll let me touch you. What was I supposed to do?'

'Just admit it.'

And to my surprise, to my horror, she does.

'Okay, maybe I used you! A little, tiny bit, but I want her to take us seriously, and to take you seriously!'

'Susannah, I don't want us to be taken seriously. As far as anyone else is concerned, there is no us.'

Now she is not smiling at all. Nothing in the world can shake Susannah from her good mood, and yet look at what I've done.

'When are you gonna grow up, Lucy?'

I've never seen her so disappointed. But who does she think I am? I am not the brave and beautiful vision of Lucy that lives in her head. That girl doesn't exist, she never has. Susannah keeps talking, as if there is any need. I don't want to hear any more truths.

'There's more to life than what people in Crossmore think of you. Why are you so stuck here?'

Let me take it too far, let me cause irreparable damage. Darling, let me hurt you.

'Because I have a family here, and a mother who actually gives a shit about what I do.'

Now it's out there. She asked, I answered. Now she knows what I think, and she knows that I have seen how sad her life is. That she doesn't have a good family, not like mine. It's the only thing that upsets her, and I have used it against her. For all her wealth and all her beauty and experience, I'm the one with a mother who is home every night. It makes me the winner, somehow.

'I might not have a perfect mam, but at least I don't have to lie about who I am in my own house. Your mam will only ever love you as long as she thinks you're riding Martin Burke.'

His name in her mouth. I could cry. I could pull her hair out. Sweet and gentle Susannah, who knows so well how to love. With all that heartache, she knows so well how to hurt.

'Go home, Lucy.'

Is she enjoying this turbulence the way she enjoys it with her mother? Does it mean the same thing? I think she has been waiting for a chance to fight with me this way. Why should I be good to her now? All I want is to go home and be as far away from her as I can get. It's what she's asked me to do, it's what she expects me to do. She is so used to getting left on her own. Did her mother not just storm out of the room? Her mother, her father, her adoring brothers, they all love to leave her. And when she acts like this, I think it's what she deserves. Susannah is no child; she can look after herself just fine. If I left now, she would lick her wounds and get on with her evening alone. I'd disappoint her, but that's all I ever do. If I leave, it won't break her. Oh, but it might break me. The upset will fade, I'm sure. Whether for her sake or mine, I won't go anywhere. Will she be disappointed again?

'I'm sleeping over.'

Maybe she'll throw me out. That wouldn't be the worst thing. At least I could say that I tried. She might not need me as much as I think she does. I doubt anybody needs me as much as I think they do. By asserting myself this way, I have taken a risk that I don't want to take. Suddenly, I'm the one who could get left alone. How nice for her, to have all the power again. She comes closer, and just when I think she is going to spit in my face, she tells me, into my hair,

'Go upstairs, then.'

And like always, I do as she tells me. We take it out on each other, and when the sweat dries, we are fine again.

And later, lying on her bed, she congratulates me on making our first fight interesting. Fighting and getting over it makes me feel like we are a normal couple. My head is on her chest, and she is wrapping my hair around her finger. Every once in a while, she pulls it.

In the end, Catríona did go out, and she shouted 'I love you' up the stairs before she went. Susannah tells me that things won't be hard forever. Maybe life would be easier if my own mother was as distant as Catríona. There would be less chance of disappointing her if she didn't care. Then we could be ourselves. It would be fine.

'Did you hear Cian Dempsey is banned from the Debs?'

I ask, and she hasn't heard,

'He put a sliotar through Mr Elliott's windscreen by accident.'

She laughs and laughs.

'That's Anna's night fecked, so. No one else will take her.'

She gets quiet, she is going to say something that she doesn't want to say. So don't say it, love – things are too good right now.

'Kevin Fitz asked me would I go with him.'

She admits, as though I will be cross with her.

'Obviously I said no.'

The poor thing. She should have said yes. She will have to say yes to the next boy that asks her, because it's not as if I can take her. After that fight, she can't expect that I might take her. It's so nice to imagine I could, but I could never. What lonely, ugly love we are making.

'What would we wear? If we went?'

'Together?'

'Yeah, just if we did.'

'Green. You look unreal in green.'

'Maybe things will be easier by then.'

This is peaceful. It's hopeful, even if it's a lie. We didn't fall apart. We are looking ahead to when things get easier.

This is the easiest our life together will ever be. Everything is about to get so much harder.

11

FEBRUARY 1992

IT BEGINS WITH HER KNOCK on the door, a stunning sound that lets me know my day is about to begin. When I open the door, the hallway is flooded with February light and her. Look at her now, in the doorway, a painting in an old wooden frame. Is that not spectacular? Even though I've had her hundreds of times, when I see her looking like this, I doubt that she has ever been mine.

She's in her father's down jacket, one from many years ago that he thinks is missing, and she is in golden eyeshadow, a very expensive one that her glittering mother doesn't realise is missing yet. Mother would never ever let me out with gold eyeshadow on. She and Catríona are so different from each other, it's hard to believe they are from the same village, or the same era. Look there, so subtle and so striking, a smear of sunshine across her eyelids. There is a little fallout on her cheeks, and it sparkles there, bringing life to the bags under her eyes.

She comes in; the hint of Phil's cologne still lingers on the jacket. And she smiles. Do you hear my heart double-beat? The jacket is left on a hook at the door. The Spring has come. The last of our gentle moments are upon us.

I could not get up the stairs quickly enough. My room is waiting for us, for our honesty. The bedroom door is flush with its frame, and since it became the thing that keeps Susannah and me from the rest of the world, it has been the most venerated object in the house.

With Susannah in my bedroom, the sun perks up, and I want to ask her about her morning, but seeing her in the fresh light, I don't have the breath to speak. There are so many wonderful thoughts in her head, I would dedicate my life to listening to them. She knows all the secrets of the universe. If only she would pour a little of her knowledge on me. I want to be told the things that she knows. Oh, the way she moves through the light, the gleam in her eye. Crossing my little floor, she stands right in front of the window, talking about last night's dream, and for a moment, she is a dark shape in the glowing daylight, and I am drawn into the darkness. A black sun, taking the light from the world, and I am glad.

'Anyway, how are you, darling?'

Darling, darling, darling – my darling, you have knocked me off my feet. Just as soon as I am adjusting to the loveliness of her, she moves out of the way of the window, over to my unmade bed. The sheet has lifted from the top corner, and if Susannah moves too much, it will slip down, exposing the ancient mattress, the stains from my childhood, and the stains from last month. If she sees them, I won't care. Susannah has made love to the body that left the stains; she would lie on them happily, she wouldn't care. There was a time when I was so careful to project an image of perfection in front of her, but these days I don't have to. I like the person that I actually am now, because Susannah likes her. I think soon I will like myself all the way through, and I won't mind what people think of me.

Lying down on her side, looking up at me, she says,

'What's wrong with you, girl?'

Her voice, her blessed voice, and the small tune of her accent, exactly the same as mine, only better. It is home in a sound. Susannah is the place where I belong. This is Heaven, this is all I want. Reaching her hand out for mine, I see a change come across her eyes. She looks at me now like I am a thing that she wants, a thing worth having. I have been a wanted thing before, many times – it doesn't mean anything if you don't want the person back. Before her, I was only ever preyed upon. Now I feel I am worshipped. I feel chewed up and savoured. Even with her teeth sunk this deep in me, she is not claiming me, she is only showing me that she wants to be a wanted thing too.

Soon she will be wearing nothing but golden eyeshadow. Her hair doesn't smell of her shampoo, or of cigarettes, as I expect it to. It smells of old sweat, from days of not washing it, from walking everywhere, from this, and I love it because she wouldn't let anybody else smell it on her. She looks at me deeply, to the darkest part of me, a place so deep that my own soul would not even venture there, and she whispers,

'Oh, Lucifer.'

And with those words, I am prepared to receive the Lord.

I don't question the things that we do anymore. When they come to us so naturally, it doesn't seem right to ask questions. Why challenge our nature or happiness? For all the time I spent ignoring it, being with her in this way is my strongest instinct. I know this better than I know I must breathe; I know her body like it is my own. What she feels is what I feel, I know what I am doing here. My bedroom is a place where I belong. It just makes sense when she's here. We make sense together. We are like honeycomb, sweet and fitting. If she cut me open in this moment, I would be sweet down to the bone. Like everything else, Susannah does this so well. I am glad for her to practise on me, and perfect her perfect touch. Her teeth meet my hip bone, and this is our last gentle moment, right now. Let it linger. Let the goodness last.

I feel a draft in the air, my beautiful door swings open. We are not alone. We have fallen from the sky, we are angels landing on earth. Here is Mother, suddenly in my bedroom with a heap of laundry up to her eyes. I am mortified, I have been made mortal.

For a second, she freezes. If she hasn't seen us, she has smelled our evil in the air. Without turning to the bed, she dumps the clothes on the floor and goes, slamming the door shut behind her. I hear her racing down the stairs. Heaven is fractured; Susannah and I are among you now, all you awful sinners.

Susannah, a deeper red than she ever was last Summer, has taken her weight off me and is scrambling to dress herself, and I hear her saying that I must speak to my mother so that she can sneak out the front door. For the first time ever, I have seen the colour of shame on her. It is distracting. I can hardly hear her. I cannot even bring myself to move, and so she pulls my dress over my head for me. My body is still floating on her sea, my soul is a swollen wave, my mind is dried up and dead. Will it all be over now? Is this what it takes, will she be gone now? My dream was realised, and so the nightmare must be realised also. Is it really time to wake up and face a life on my own?

She is standing before me, holding my cardigan out for me to take, and tells me again that I must go downstairs and distract my mother. Before I have the chance to know better, I do as I'm told. How well deserved. I have always known that this would happen. I have always known that we would be found out and punished. This was always going to happen, the same way that I was always going to fall in love with her, and the same way that I was never going to put a stop to us. This is very well deserved. I put the cardigan on and go out into the hall like Susannah never took it off me, and I ready myself to go and tell Mother that everything is ordinary, that I am not in love.

I take the stairs quietly, turning to see Susannah in the doorway of my bedroom, bouncing on her toes, light in her trainers. The sun still glows behind her, and I have to walk away. Maybe Mother will be too shocked to be angry. Maybe she won't know what she saw, or who. I call out to her, with no response.

I call again at the bottom of the stairs and again in the kitchen.

'Mam, are you there? Just talk to me, will you?'

'Are you alright, pet?'

Granny calls from her bedroom.

I forgot that she was even here. Behind me, I hear the front door softly shutting, and from the front room window, I see Susannah running down the garden path, pulling her father's jacket on as she goes. The car is gone. All the love that put my queasy conscience at ease has left. I have nothing to reassure me that my treachery was worth it. At the coat hooks, I let my hand lie where her jacket was. My eyes are heavy with tears that are waiting to spill.

'Yeah, Granny, I'm okay. Thanks.'

I call to her, trying to keep my voice from cracking. How I would love to go down to her bedroom now, and chat to her like nothing is wrong. Instead, I stay still in the hall for a while, regaining my breath. There is nothing for me to do now but hide and wait.

What I wouldn't give to be outside in the garden now, where the sun is. But I cannot bear the thought that, any minute, the car might come back. Mother could see me, here in my dress and cardigan; she would have to look at my swollen lips and listen as I speak with a tongue that has committed unfathomable horror. She would have to listen while I pretend to be sorry, and she would have to hear me call her 'Mammy', as if nothing has changed and we are the same people that we were this morning.

The rest of the day passes, and I spiral, and the empty house is unbelievably tense. There isn't any space for me in this house now, and still I take up space. I stay up in my room, growing hungry, even when I hear them return. Not until late at night, when I'm sure they are all asleep, do I go downstairs for something to eat. All day, Mother has been so careful in avoiding me, but a part of her wants so badly to catch me. A part of me is the same: I want to be caught and sat down and talked to, to be shouted at, to be acknowledged. A much bigger part of me wants to be ignored forever. I am starving, I must go down, and hope they have all gone to bed.

There she is, sitting in the empty front room, the television glowing, the curtains open. Mother doesn't want to see me tonight – given the choice, she might never see me again – but I am a creak on the stairs that she cannot ignore. She gets up and comes to me.

Here in the hall, night dark, with a steadying hand on the banister, she looks at me long. This is it now, the first and only time that Mother will look at me for who I am. She sees me; I am hideous, and she lets a cold and heavy sigh out through her nose. And I swear I see her searching for the words she wants. But she doesn't find them. She leaves me, she goes back to the sofa, where the television is playing on mute. I go back to bed hungry, and I hate the person that I am. Under my pillow is an old scrap of paper, where Susannah has scribbled,

I love you x

The thrill of it makes me cry, because I'm not allowed to love her back.

I wake to a wet bedsheet. Blood, earlier than I expected. A new stain. Before I let myself fully remember yesterday, I creep down to the shower. Under the cold water, I wash myself off myself. Then, looking in the mirror as my wet legs pimple in the cold, I see a new spot on my chin. When the blood on the sheet was still inside my body, Mother loved me, I was safe, and Susannah was my beautiful secret. If I had not been caught yesterday, Mother would let me stay home from school today, she would send me back to bed with a hot water bottle and bring me cups of tea all morning. My best friend.

My sheet is already gone when I get back to my room. My stomach churns – hunger, hormones, humiliation, how could she do that? It's her bed sheet, really. Nothing in the house is truly mine. I go downstairs and see her outside, little Padraig sitting on the front step, the bloodied sheet on the clothesline, and her, garden hose in hand, rinsing me off it. These little revenges will go on forever, I fear. Granny is talking at the table and does not stop to acknowledge me. Tadgh comes to the table and looks at me as though I have disgraced the family. Ciarán does not look at me at all. Dad is gone to work, I bless myself. Tugging at my school skirt, I make myself known in the doorway and, squinting in the morning light, I say to her,

'I could have washed that.'

She turns to face me. Looking at me in my school uniform, she labours to swallow, as though it is a great pain to see me as I have always been. She turns right back to the sheet, continues with the hose, although she can't get the sheet back to white. If we didn't live on a quiet back road I would walk in front of a car to save myself the humiliation of all this. I suspect that if we didn't live on a quiet back road, Mother would never pull such a trick. This is a punishment for me, not her. She wants me to be afraid of getting caught, not to actually get caught. She puts her hand on her hip and pinches the end of the hose so the water sprays in two hard streams, to no avail. The blood has soaked the sheet, and it is not coming out.

'What a waste.'

She sighs. As she is unpegging the sheet from the line, Martin appears at the gate. I have never been so glad to see him. I take my bag and run down to him.

'You won't offer me a cup of tea or a bit?'

He asks, without realising what scene he has arrived at. I take him by the arm and pull him down the road. He doesn't ask why I am in such a hurry, he just takes my schoolbag and talks about his morning. I let him talk and hope he won't stop all the way to school. This morning, he is a lovely distraction.

When we arrive at school, I find the girls at Joan's locker. They are talking about their yesterdays, which were pleasant and plain, and I must behave as though mine was the same. They don't mention the spot on my chin, though Patricia stares at it. When Susannah arrives, she surprises me by handing me last night's letter. She says it's notes to help me in French. I didn't expect to ever get a letter again. She has one leg shaved, the other left alone. She said she couldn't be bothered finishing.

'I didn't write one.'

She doesn't look disappointed.

'I didn't get a chance, sorry.'

A weight falls on me, a sadness. It comes to us all. I wonder if it will ever leave.

Lucy,

I love you a lot more than I know how to say. Sorry I've only told you in letters. I hope you weren't killed after we got caught. I'll get my inheritance from Grandmother after the Leaving. If you can make it to the summer, I can take us somewhere for a new start. I promise I'll make sure that everything stays okay. I'll look after you.

Love, love, love,

Susannah

12

MARCH 1992

THE HOUSE IS ALL WRONG now. It feels as though I am living upside down, breathing animosity in place of oxygen, as though I have slipped into the Otherworld, and I am now an invisible thing living in an invisible place, parallel to my human family. To Mother, I am no longer Lucy. I am a fragmented memory, brought back when she trips over my schoolbag in the hall, when she hears the closing of my bedroom door and sees my empty seat at the dinner table. This memory is easily ignored. She has given up on my curfew, on my laundry, on my meals. I am thinning and unclean, and she is unbothered. At last, we have reached the long-anticipated limit to Mother's love. What I wouldn't give to be punished.

As I never bring lunch to school anymore, the girls have begun to suspect that I am starving myself. Bernadette quietly warns me that this is a dangerous habit and offers me the solitary clementine in her lunchbox. I give her a sad smile and split the segments between myself, herself, and Susannah.

This is the reaction I always expected from Mother, should she find out about Susannah and me, although it feels more extreme now that it is actually happening. Perhaps if I had been better prepared for this, it wouldn't upset me as much. Perhaps if I had a little more self-worth, I would understand that Mother's love is too conditional to want. The time I ought to have spent reflecting on this, readying myself for this, was spent staring at all the shapes Susannah takes. It seems that Susannah has done this reflecting already, and that is why she is able to embrace herself so readily, without question. Or perhaps we are just wired differently.

If only I had never spotted the tortuous loveliness of her. If only I wasn't afraid to look inside myself, that way I might know better who I am. As it stands, I don't know whether I might want a boy or another girl, or whether my heart has been spoiled beyond any other love by Susannah. How can I defend myself to Mother when I don't understand what I am defending? How is it that when you grow up and get stuck in love, that love is forgotten about? My love now seems to be an aggressive, political thing. It is the ceaseless search for an identity and then committing to that identity. It is a fight to exist in my own home. Is that not exhausting? Is it worth it? It feels like the good parts of loving have been thrown on the backseat and forgotten about.

If I were another girl, in another house, this would not be a problem. I might simply be somebody who found good in somebody else. If I were Susannah, with enough inheritance coming to get me out of Crossmore and a family so exhausted of heartbreak that they are apathetic to everything, this would not be a problem. If I were another person, this wouldn't be a hateful thing or a poor choice used against me. A part of me wonders if I should stop bathing or wet myself at school or make my father cry, so that I have a real reason to feel ashamed. All I've done is fall for Susannah. It is not shameful or radical or wild. Anybody would fall for Susannah. I never meant to upset anybody.

The evenings are growing light, the air thickens with silage. It's a sign of the Summer coming back. This year, although I breathe it deeply, I cannot find any of the sweetness I once found in that smell. It smells worse than what it is, actually. For the first time, I see the stone wall at the bottom of the garden is crumbling. Oh, all the pieces of the countryside that I held so dearly in Winter are falling away from me. Maybe it is unsightly, maybe somebody should do us a kindness and knock it down.

Mother is washing the back step, Granny is sitting at the table, they are enjoying each other's silence as Mother works. This is the last task on her list. Now the whole house has been cleaned, the four corners of every room have been blessed.

'Spring cleaning! Would ye believe it's that time again?'

She has been saying this around the house, as though she must justify what she is doing. As though I am going to reveal to everyone that she is trying to purge my perversion from the house. Every strand of my hair, every flake of my skin, a cruel reminder of the daughter that she has decided to let go. If I think about it too long, I feel myself about to drop to the floor. Look how ardently she scrubs the back step, like it will change something! Like my secret will be made secret once more. Oh, to be made secret once more, to return to that lush and heavy silence that I lived in when I had everything. Such heavens are unsustainable. I could not evade real life forever, I know. It has found me, it has come to me as a low, clouded sky, threatening to rain all over Mother as she cleans that step. The looming sky tells me that I will never be as ordinary as Mother needs, and I will never be as extraordinary as Susannah deserves. Let the rain come, let me be cleansed. Let me disappear into the fields and rise up and start again. Why can I not start again?

If I could, I would be fearless. I would be friends with my failures and nurse them until they became victories. Perhaps when I am older, I will live that way and be an honest, proud version of myself – but right now I need to eat, I need to finish school. I am seventeen, I need a mother. It isn't enough to hope that I can stay out of her eyeline until

I can leave home. I need my mammy. I won't apologise for that. If she would let me, I would cling to her side, I would be a little fruit fly in her kitchen again. Mother, look at me, I am not ready to let you go.

Forgive me, I am going to do whatever it takes to get her back, to buy myself the time I need to figure myself out, and the security I need to survive. Forgive me, forgive me, forgive me, I am going to do whatever heinous thing I need to save myself.

'Do you want a hand?'

I ask, and she does not stop scrubbing the step, she does not even hear me. Granny doesn't acknowledge me. Ciarán pushes past me, hurley in hand. Am I invisible? Mother smiles and moves out of the way to let him pass. This is humiliating.

'Mam? Do you want a hand?'

And still she says nothing. Even the girls and I have matured beyond this behaviour. What do I need to say? If she wants me to renounce Susannah, I cannot. To say her name would bring us both to tears, I cannot. Please, what do I say? A lovely break in the tension is allowed as Martin comes into the garden with his own hurley. How I adore him. Wherever he is, I am expected to be; his presence means that I can be here now. Waving at us both, he calls out,

'How are ye now?'

'Ah here's Martin.'

Granny says, smiling.

And Mother waves down to him, beaming. For a moment, the weight of me is gone from her.

'Grand, love!'

She turns back to the step and sees my shoes in the corner of her eye – the weight of me comes back to her. Martin and Ciarán begin playing under my clouded sky. They look so carefree, this evening suits them. Since finishing with Rita, Martin is around a lot more, always playing hurling and searching for first cars with Tadgh. He chats nicely to Granny in the kitchen, he talks about farming with Dad.

My Martin, under the churning sky, perfect Martin in my garden. He makes me feel like my blood is flowing in the wrong direction, he makes me aware that I am wrong. If only I loved him the way that I am supposed to. Susannah once told me that Mother will only love me if she thinks he and I are together. Perhaps if I were to fall for him, outwardly, nobody would suspect a thing about Susannah and me, or all the confusion inside me. If Mother thinks I am headed in the right direction, she might warm up to me again. Is that cruel? Should I try it?

'Martin is after breaking up with his one. Did you hear about that?'

Briefly, she brightens, and I feel myself start to brighten. Her interest is caught, but the hunch in her shoulders does not straighten, she does not acknowledge me. It doesn't matter, she is not as hard to read as she thinks. I know already how to win her back. Watch, I will make her brighten again.

'I was glad, anyway. She was always getting in the way.'

Without taking her attention off the step, Mother raises her eyebrows, almost like a reflex. Granny laughs. There is potential in what I am saying. When Martin looks in our direction, I wave. A small, girlish sort of wave that Maria would be proud of. Suddenly, there is a rhythm in the air – is that his heartbeat? Is that Mother's heartbeat? Something is bringing us all back to life. All I need to do is pretend I want him. He will be happy. Mother will come back to me. Susannah will remain my delicious secret. Did I not say that love is aggressive?

On a deep breath, she goes back to work, but I have done enough to interest her. I will deny Susannah, I will adore Martin, Mother's love will come back to me. Yes, this is pathetic, this is wildly insulting, but I already told you that I will do whatever it takes to win her back. Let me do this, do not question me while I unearth Martin's heart from the grave I once dug. There is no other man that I could hold in the palm of my hand this way. Nobody else would melt as gladly or willingly as I need him to melt. All it will take is to be caught kissing him, to be seen in his arms. Just one kiss could turn everything around. I could be back in Mother's good graces by the weekend.

When Dad comes up from the farm, the family all sit around the table for dinner, and sure enough, Tadgh calls me into the kitchen. For the first time in weeks, Mother has food for me: two slices of roast beef, which are mainly fat.

'The awful things Lucy does to her body! All this dieting. She doesn't get any of what she needs.'

I am too hungry to listen to the subtext of what she is saying. I am too grateful, and too proud of my plan to care. The boys assume that she is being passive aggressive about my figure – we are not emotionally literate enough for them to say I have lost too much weight. Chewing the jelly of the fat, I thank Mother, and she ignores me. It doesn't matter, because tomorrow, I am asking Martin out. Tomorrow, I will get my life back.

I am too determined to be nervous or guilty. I wait for our shared Religion class to make my move. Religion is the most boisterous class of the day, nobody thinks anything of it when I reach across the table and take his copy book to write,

Come over tonight x

It isn't a question. I will get him alone and give him the piece of me he has always wanted, and Mother will see me give it to him.

It's only one kiss. I am yet to inform Susannah about all this. Waiting for her permission isn't going to get me anywhere. She wouldn't agree to it, and I don't really want her to. Equally, I don't want her to try to show me sense. We have two very different ideas of sense right now. We have two very different mothers. While Catríona never asks about me, she knows exactly what I am to Susannah, there are no secrets about it. Perhaps that makes Susannah a better girlfriend than me, and a better daughter. Honesty is expensive, morals are circumstantial; if I had another mother, I could be as proud and upstanding as Susannah. It's only one kiss.

At lunchtime, I let her know that a more palatable version of me is going to emerge so that we can stay together. I expect her to be furious, but worse than that, she hardly reacts at all. It's as though she has been waiting for this to happen.

'I told Martin to collect me tonight. Him and Mam are the only people who will even know it happens.'

Any other lad in school, any other man from the village, and she might not mind as much, but this is Martin Burke. This is what everybody has been waiting for. No matter how meaningless it is to me, it will mean something. Yes, I ought to be more considerate of her feelings, and his feelings, but I am too concerned with myself. Nobody else is going to help me get Mother back, are they?

'Why him? You could have picked literally any other lad.'

And I regret the callousness of my answer before I even offer it.

'Because I trust him, and he trusts me, so I can control him more.'

This is a side of me she has not seen before. It is one that I barely recognise in myself but that has always been here, waiting. Before this, I was not a manipulative person. From now on, manipulation will form the forefront of my personality. It all seems so regressive to her, but I have always been a coward, we have always been a secret. How can this be regression when I have never progressed? As far as Crossmore knows, I have always been stuck on Martin, and he has always been stuck on me. We have always been gliding towards each other; finally, we are about to collide. I try to convince her that he is only a layer of fog to hide under. Martin Burke is only another Winter, that's all.

She skips Geography and instead spends the class crying in the toilets. She suffers the indignity of emerging with mascara on her cheeks to an audience of Second Years, who offer to go and find Eimear and Joan for her. She tells them that the principal caught her smoking and is going to ring her father, and they think she is so cool for getting in trouble and so pretty when she cries. That is what Bernadette passes on to me, because Susannah isn't talking to me anymore. When I'm packing my schoolbag in the afternoon, a letter falls out of my locker with my name scrawled across the front in red ink. It might as well be my blood. I dread to read it.

At home, I don't run straight to my bedroom. Instead, I sit in the kitchen, letting the guilt fester inside me, waiting for Martin to arrive. Mother sits in the front room with the newspaper, looking at it but not reading. She is so skilled at ignoring me, even when she senses me like a change in the temperature. If she would only stay this placid, if she would only pretend to read the newspaper forever, we might coexist quite nicely.

Suddenly, she speaks.

'Susannah O'Shea will do anything to catch her mother's attention, you know that, Lucy.'

So easily, so abruptly, she confirms my greatest insecurity to be true. All the fears I have never admitted to having, she knows – what lovely ammunition for her. My name sounds unfamiliar in her voice. It's like she is pleading with me to realise I have been put under some devilish enchantment and to walk away from it. In truth, Susannah has nothing but good love for me. I am the one who will do any evil thing for their mother's attention. I've never seen her look this way: sadder than when she stares out the kitchen window, more panicked than when

Dad tells us about the cursed land. Until now, I suppose, I've never seen her truly afraid. This is the last time she will ever show me authentic emotion; after this, every interaction will be kept to a surface level. I will lie, and she will be shallow. It's just a case of getting used to it. Not giving her the reaction she wants, I say,

'Martin is coming over in a bit. We're going on a date. I'll be home before eleven.'

Without answering, she lets her eyes fall back to the newspaper, and this time I see that she is actually reading. I wonder if she believes me. With my back to her, I bite my lip until it bleeds, to stop me from crying, to distract myself from thinking of how easily she can love and stop loving. I suck the blood from my lip and don't wince. There is no room left for sensitivity. To get through this, I need to be harder, I need to pack up who I am and pretend that she doesn't exist. It's only one kiss, why does it feel like so much more? I am being the very person that Mother wants me to be, and she won't even look up from the newspaper. At dinner time, I am fed again. A smaller amount than little Padraig, but I am fed all the same.

Martin arrives in his aftershave and Crossmore GAA half-zip. I wonder if he spent a long time getting ready. My clouded sky is clearing, and lit up by his bright, wide eyes, blue as cold water. He would be so easy to fall for. Looking at him, I search myself for some feeling, for the spark that should be there, but there is nothing. Surely that means that I must love Susannah at my very core, it must mean that she and I are right together. Maybe later on this evening I'll feel something for him. I think I would like to feel something for him.

We walk out to the low-cut fields, we sit and watch the sun going down over the pale gold grass. It already feels like Summer. If I were only sitting across from him, not right next to him, this might feel natural. But he is so near. I can feel him buzzing, I hear his pulse race, he is so transparently in love. Was I this obvious with Susannah? Could she always feel it when I tensed up around her? It's shocking how little he does to hide his feelings. It's unfair that he has the right to want me so openly. It's ridiculous that I invited him to come and feel his feelings tonight, while I do everything I can to repress mine. He might as well enjoy this, he's waited long enough.

The birds are far off and quiet. The wind is soft. It blows my hair over my cheek. With honeyed eyes, he watches me, and he feels divinity.

'Still in bits over Rita?'

He shakes his head, and he smirks. It's believable.

'Good. She was a nightmare.'

'You told me you liked her.'

He laughs a little, I think he is laughing at himself, not at what I've said. Leaning in close, I put my hand on his knee. Is this too much?

'I told you a lie.'

He is listening so closely that he could hear my thoughts. I have been where he is, I have felt what he is feeling. It is a beautiful fear, wasted on me. I must be very careful with my words. I need to say just enough that he believes we might kiss, without leading him on too much. Am I fooling myself to think that is possible?

'Did you honestly think I liked her? She stole you off me.'

Wordless, because he cannot find words for this, he smiles at me. He trusts me. He loves me. Perhaps Mother is right, perhaps the love that I have for Susannah is evil and wrong, because it has propelled me to this unfathomable cruelty. And still, I must take this further. I cannot stop until he is mine entirely, until I have exploited him beyond forgiveness. I would do anything for Susannah, anything to save my shaking relationship with Mother. I tell myself I am doing this for other people, I let myself believe it.

Hear his heart, peaceful now as the March evening. There's nobody as nice to me, there's nobody who cares about me more than he does. Right now, with the pale sun setting against him, I want to love him the right way. If not for Susannah, I would be broken hearted that I don't love him. Lucy and Martin. Martin and Lucy. This has been waited on a very long time. Let's make this weary dream come true. Suddenly, this is less about securing Susannah and more about seeing what I've missed out on. Let me just try it with him, so I can say I've made the effort to be like everybody else. My Susannah, look what you've done to me.

My hand is still on his knee, and I squeeze it, so he knows I am real. Slowly, he puts his own hand over mine, and he begins to talk. We go on talking, drifting nearer each other until the sky dims. I want to love him. I want to want this. When the trees are dark and the earth is growing damp under us, I know it is time we take this further. But what use would it be here? We need to be caught taking this further.

'I better call it a night.'

The evening is over, and I stand up. With his head at my hips, he stares up at me. It gets colder; although it felt like it for a moment, this is not Summer. Not wanting to miss a moment, he walks me home.

At the back door, the light is dying, the midges are like glitter in the air. Light from the kitchen illuminates the small square of the garden where we stand. The space between us is thick with longing, with anxiety, I see it almost spilling out of his impossibly blue eyes. Closer, I move ever closer, until I can see the pinprick blackheads on his nose, the deep thought line between his eyebrows, the serious angles of his cheeks and jaw. Desperately, my eyes dart across his face, looking for something to be attracted to, and something to be repulsed by. But I cannot see these things. I can only see my very favourite friend. Is this worth it? Is she worth it? I think of Susannah, which makes it easier. And makes it harder.

Now there is no colour in the sky, there are no birds, and as hard as I try, I can't find anything that would make this moment better than hideous. It's just his wildest dream, it's just the worst thing I've ever done, it's just a mouth on a mouth. So I put my mouth to his mouth, chaste and unmoving, hardly even pursing my lips, and after a second of surprise, he reacts. Neither of us kissing, rather, leaning our lips against each other, at last.

He moves back just enough to ask,

'What about your dad?'

'Asleep.'

'What about your mam?'

'What about my mam?'

And he kisses me, a real kiss. A piece of Martin that is new and more carnal than I thought he could be. It goes on and on, and in my head, I hear Susannah's gently whispered curses. A small part of me likes this. A part of me is intrigued to try all of him. Susannah will not sleep tonight. His stubble on my face, his affection against my leg. I will not sleep tonight. Just for a moment, I lean us into view of the kitchen, and when I feel safe that we have been seen, I push him away. Shamelessly wiping my mouth on the back of my hand, I let him start at me.

'See you at school.'

And I vanish into the awful light of the house. He walks home, thinking that tonight was so petrifying and so good that it might not have happened at all.

A tube of toothpaste is finished as I brush him off my tongue. With shivers all over, I get into bed and read Susannah's letter from today.

Lucy,

I must be insane to allow this, you really have driven me insane. This is not what love should be. We're only seventeen, it shouldn't be this com-

plicated. Why did you let everything get so complicated? How did I get tricked into allowing this? It's like I got rid of my self-worth to make room for you.

I hope we still love each other after this. I really hope I can still look at you.

Yours indefinitely,
Susannah

13

TO AVOID MOTHER AND MARTIN and the maelstrom I have stirred, I spend all of Saturday walking around Ballycove with Bernadette and then I sleepover at Joan's house. They don't seem to mind spending time with me one on one. I want to ask them all why they have been so cold with me. Instead, I let us enjoy ourselves. I am a coward, aren't I?

When Joan's mother wakes us up for Mass in the morning, I really wish she would have just let us sleep through it.

'It's nice to spend a bit of time with you.'

Joan says to me in the car. She doesn't look at me when she says it.

'Girl, we're always together.'

I know what she means by this. I can't remember the last time that she and I spent time together, just us.

'Yeah, just you're always with Susannah now. Ye have gotten really close.'

I really don't think she means anything by this. Does she? How could she know? It's just jealousy, that's all.

'Yeah, sorry, I hope it doesn't upset you.'

I ask, unsure of what else to say. If it does upset her, what am I to do?

'No, of course not. I just missed you, that's all.'

The remainder of the drive is silent. I squeeze her knee, and she laughs. Neither of us is sincere.

The sizzle of my skin is especially painful as I enter the church today. At least if I go to Mass with Joan's family, I can sit with them in the gallery, and I can skip the union of the Burkes and Nolans in the nave.

From up here, I can see the greasy scalps of everyone in Crossmore – there is my family, and all the girls and their own families. I can see the thrilling thoughts that are racing around Martin's head. I can see Maria and each of her sisters subtly looking around the church to see what people are wearing. I can see Bernadette minding her posture and tensing. A weak choir sings, and Father McDonagh has prepared a sermon on burdens. Let it begin, the weekly check-up with my guilt, when all my failings are brought before God.

Afterwards I make sure that Mother sees me leaving the church with Maria. I make sure that she sees me waving at Martin and his brothers, who keep their eyes on Maria, mainly. Small and innocent things like waving in the churchyard are perfect ways to keep Mother satisfied without really having to do anything. The kiss is done with, that's all I really needed. As long as Martin never gets another girlfriend, Mother could spend her life thinking that he and I are a couple. He already walks me to and from school and does my homework and carries my schoolbag. What else does he need to do to convince her? I can't imagine what he is going to start doing now that he has kissed me. I don't imagine it; I just leave the churchyard.

Maria walks to Susannah's house with me. I really wish that she wouldn't. Of all the girls, Maria is the pointiest, the nastiest. I don't want to be alone with her and face a barrage of questions. She won't be as subtle as Joan was in the car. But then she surprises me and asks,

'So are you not gonna tell me about your little date with Martin Burke?'

How does she know? I didn't tell anyone. He is not the type of person to tell anyone. But then again, almost the entire weekend has passed since then. If he even mentioned it to one of his brothers, the whole school could know by now. With her sprawl of sisters, every little thing that happens in Crossmore comes back to Maria. I don't even bother to ask where she heard it.

'I'd hardly call it a date.'

I try to say it in a way that would make her laugh, but she is not amused.

'I heard ye kissed. Now, I'd call that a date.'

She is desperate to hear the details of my evening with him. If I say the right things to her, I could get her back on my good side. If I say the right things to her, I won't need to say a word to anyone else. She is such a talented gossip. That one kiss seems to be the cure for everything. It's hard to know what the right thing to say is, so I just tell her,

'Let's not talk about it. I don't wanna jinx it.'

She thinks that is very cute. It's enough to stop her from asking any more. I should have known that the secret wouldn't be kept. Whatever, it's just another thing not to think about. When we arrive at Susannah's gate, we see Phil's narrow shoulders as he is bent down cleaning the lawnmower before he puts it away, his last job before he goes back up to the city. His other children are still very young, only six and nine years old. They need him to be around a lot, they need a good father. That is how he explains away his absences to Susannah, and how she justifies them to us. After all, she will be eighteen this Summer, she doesn't need him as much, they have agreed. What a great guy, she thinks, never letting herself remember how terribly he has let her down.

'Everybody deserves a second chance. It would be good for them all if he is a good father.'

The only hint that Susannah is bitter about Phil's new children is that she calls him their father, not their dad. On rare weekends, she goes to stay at his house in the city. She has her own bedroom there.

Even though it's used as a guest room most of the time and is decorated with impersonal, neutral tones, they still call it Susannah's room. Phil does everything he can to make her feel at home there, but his massive efforts make her feel more like a strange guest than family. It isn't often that she stays with him. If he isn't in Crossmore, where he is her dad and nothing else to anybody, what's the point? She can put up with his second family existing, she just can't pretend that she is happy to be their addition.

Given the mess he made, he could probably be doing more than cutting the lawn to try to make it up to her, but then again, he's only a man. It's probably easier for him to make a big fuss once every week or two rather than provide her with a steady stream of care and attention. It's easy for him to be a hero when he's not around enough to be a villain. Since I realised how little Phil actually does for the family, I have more sympathy for Catríona, I understand her temper. Neither of Susannah's parents are getting the balance right, but she always reminds me, at least they're trying. I don't know if that is meant to make me reflect on my own parents.

Maria and I stand back in the driveway and watch as Susannah says goodbye to her father, hugging him and kissing his cheek like she is a child. She still calls him Daddy; Eimear says that it makes her sound rich. He says something that makes her shout with laughter, then gets in his car, and she leans in the window to say goodbye to him once more. She is parched for his attention. As he drives down to the gate, she stays still, watching him go, still not noticing us. The car window drops, and he leans out to us. Taking my forearm, he shakes it and laughs,

'You look after my girl now!'

And with a great smile, he drives away. Maria isn't entirely sure what he means, and I am afraid that I do. Neither of us mention it as we approach Susannah on the porch.

'No sign of you in Mass.'

'Sure, was I really gonna waste my morning in there when he was home?'

Inside, she gives us tea and cherry chocolates, which her father brought her from a new chocolatier in the city. She says they have alcohol inside. Maria only takes a bite of one, because she is only allowing herself one sweet thing a week now, and because she must eat Sunday dinner. We chat about people's Mass outfits and about school tomorrow. It's nice to be here without a session happening. It's nice to be back to normal. Maria keeps probing me about Martin, and I must pretend to be too giddy to talk about it. An hour passes, and she says to me,

'Will we head away, Lucy?'

And I say,

'Oh, actually, Martin is gonna collect me. We've to water his granny's grave before dinner.'

This is a believable thing to say. We often water his granny's grave when we pass it. The closer to our friendship I keep us, the easier it all is to believe. All we did was kiss, but Maria is already completely taken with this new romance. Of course, she doesn't realise that I haven't spoken to him since he left my back step on Friday night, and that if I can help it, I won't be speaking to him any time soon. His granny's grave really is none of my concern.

As soon as Maria is gone, Susannah kisses me against the door, and everything I have been thinking about goes away. Her father, my mother, Martin, everything is gone, it's only her on me on the door, and I remember why I started this terrible lie in the first place, and I am assured that it will be worth it. Rather than talking about how she feels, she leaves a hickey on my collarbone, and I let her. It's childish, but it's a stain of her. She has made me her territory. I understand it, I like it, I don't care about how strategic I will have to be in hiding it. We need to talk about things, but we don't.

Martin doesn't collect me, of course. He hasn't come near me all weekend, because he is afraid that I regret kissing him and that if I see him, I'll tell him that. How familiar. It's for the best, because I will be using the day to make my misbehaviour up to Susannah.

We spend all day at the back of her house, going between the garden and what she calls the junk room. My house only has a junk drawer. I stand inside, at the foot of the open door, and stare out at the Spring sun as it soaks her. Like always, she is beyond beautiful. Like always, I ignore the thoughts that press on my mind. I know I am supposed to be buying time to figure myself out, but when Susannah shines this brightly, I don't care about what I am supposed to be doing.

We make love in the greenhouse, while outside the rain of late March begins to fall. Everything about me is washed away, until there is nothing left but love. This is why I am doing it, for the blinding glory of Susannah, Susannah in the Highest. What she doesn't do to me. All my guilt disappears into the condensation. My hair is damp, my skin is flushed, I don't mind how I look. Before her, I was just one of Dad's rocky fields. She came and picked all the stones from me, she made me useful and green. Afterwards she gets up to check that we haven't flattened the new strawberry runners, and she giggles. She is so bright, so colourful, I get sunstroke from looking at her.

'Have you started studying yet?'

'For what?'

I can hardly drool out a sentence. What studying does she expect me to have done?

'For the Leaving Cert, obviously. I'm meant to start over Easter.'

A lot of people started studying in September; the girls all got serious around Christmas. I haven't started. I doubt that I will start at all, when I could spend my time in the greenhouse with her instead.

'I need to do something. Daddy wants me to go to college.'

My dad wants me to go to college too. He wants me to have a big house and diamonds and everything that Susannah has. We know that wanting things is not affording them. It seems it's never enough to just want something. We don't really talk about college at home, because we know it isn't going to happen. Susannah and I don't talk much about college either, because it's just another barrier.

'Your dad was so nice to me today. Like just for a second, but he was so nice.'

'He's always nice.'

She says as she runs her finger down the plastic wall of the greenhouse, leaving a trail in the condensation. She writes her initials.

'Yeah, I think he was especially nice though, like, as if he knew something about us.'

She writes my initials many times, in a circle surrounding hers.

'Maybe he copped it because I'm always talking about you. Or maybe Catríona told him. He's grand, it's okay if he knows.'

She sits down next to me, wipes the water off her finger on my cheek, 'It would be nice to have someone on our side.'

She's right. Even if it is her father, who I seldom see, it would be nice to have him on our side. It would be nicer to have my own father on my side. Or my own mother. Something about Phil being supportive makes me sad. It's ridiculous, but sometimes I am jealous of Susannah for having a father like this. Although Dad is always home, he is just as absent as Phil. At least Susannah's father gives her all his attention when he is around. Sometimes it feels as though my father is uncomfortable around me. It's like he doesn't know how to show that he is interested in me. We don't talk about football or farming, so we don't really talk. I wonder if he would be supportive of Susannah and me. I wonder if he would be supportive of Martin and me. It might be hard for him to imagine me in love. Perhaps it makes me too grown-up for his liking. Then again, it's hard for me to imagine him in love. It's hard to imagine him as anything but a mumble at the kitchen table and the smell of the farm. In a way, he is a stranger. We don't really know each other. So why not tell him? What have I got to lose?

My breath is white in the air as I walk home. Any small heat from today is long gone. If Susannah hadn't numbed out my nerve endings, I'm sure I'd feel the cold. I think I will be numb to everything but her for the rest of my life. It might be raining, I wouldn't know, I can't feel it. Tonight, I can't even feel the guilt that normally sprawls through me like weeds. All I feel now are the places where she was. A huge smile pushes my teeth through my lips, and my cheeks stutter to stifle it. If somebody passes me now and sees me smiling to myself and they think I've gone mad, I won't care a bit. Actually, I think I'd love for somebody to pass by me now. To walk by and see the mad woman, smiling from ear to ear. Come and see the girl in love!

I am so in love. I've never felt this way before. I've never felt so comfortable. It isn't because of the girls or my family or Martin. It's her. She has given me everything. It's time I put myself aside and stop denying her. My house comes into view. Whoever is home is about to learn about the beauty of Susannah, about how ecstatic she has made me, about how I finally feel like a person.

Standing on the back step, I turn out to face the road again, out to the world, where she is. Where we were. Where my love pulses still. How light I feel. For all our time together, I've never felt this light before. Today I realised that she loves me more truly than my family does. Even after all the despicable things I have done this week, she loves through to the marrow of my bones. I never knew a person could feel anything as strongly as we feel this.

On the back step, on the edge of bliss, I realise that I am too in love to be afraid anymore. I want to set Martin free. To set myself free. To give everybody the truth that they deserve. I will tell Mother about my perfect day, and I will let her love me. I will tell Dad, and the boys. I will wake Granny and tell her, and she won't be upset. They will all love me. How could they not love me, when there is nothing left of me but love? Smell the night air. She will love me.

Mother must hear me thinking, because she knocks on the kitchen window and beckons me inside. She looks so pretty and so young. When she sees my radiance, she will be happy. How could she not be happy?

'Lucy! Come in here out of the cold!'

When she calls to me, she sounds like a singing bird. It feels like a hundred years since she last called me that way, with her voice so airy. She must know already that I am complete. She always knows everything.

'OK, Mammy!'

With a last deep breath, I take the cold night inside with me. Hanging up my coat on the hook Susannah used the last time she was allowed in the house, I catch sight of myself, pink cheeked and windswept, I am so pretty and so young. I go to her, into the kitchen, with long steps and a strong back, and I smell the night on my skin.

My arms fall around my mammy's neck like when I was a little girl. It feels so good to hug her again. Maybe I feel her hesitating a bit, but I don't need to worry about it. It must be her nerves, she is just getting used to me again. Maybe she didn't want me to hug her, because she pats my back and pushes me away, as if I shouldn't have touched her.

Looking at my red face, she flattens my curly hair and tucks it behind my ears and then pulls my jumper straight. Just like when I was a little girl. Her eyes are so deep and so full, like she is hopeful, and determined. We will be fine. Before I can't, I will tell her about my day, about how I have found myself at last.

'Martin Burke is inside.'

She gestures to the front room, and I can hear mumbled chatter from there. I won't let it distract me. Martin is often here when I'm not. He watches the football with Tadgh and talks about the farm with Dad.

'Oh yeah, that's grand. Listen, Mammy, I must tell you.'

I say, filling the kettle, ready to tell her everything.

'Go in and say hello, why don't you?'

'Sure, it's only Martin, I'll see him in a while. Is Granny gone to bed? I must tell ye something.'

I put the kettle on to boil, and she takes it off.

'There's tea inside.'

She nods to the front room again. Mother has a great talent for disguising demands as casual pieces of information. My news must wait. If she is to sit still and listen, I am to get tea from the front room and say hello to Martin. She nudges me in, and when I go, she follows me. In another life, I might think we were going to get in trouble for kissing in front of the kitchen window. At this point, I could get on my knees for Martin in front of the kitchen window and I think Mother would be alright with it.

Although there is light from the lamp and the television and the big fire, the front room is low and dim. As promised, there is Martin, sitting on the sofa, and Ciarán is on the floor, and Dad in the armchair. The television is being ignored, and they are talking about football, like I knew they would be. I've sat through this a thousand times; why must I sit through it again when I have something to say? I don't know how much they actually care about football. Martin doesn't even play it. Maybe it's just their version of small talk. Either way, they all make each other laugh, like they are friends, not fathers, neighbours, and sons. Ciarán is normally gone to bed at this hour, Dad should be heading up now too.

'Well, what are ye at?'

I ask from the doorframe.

'How are you keeping, Martin?'

Mother asks loudly from behind me, saying what she wishes I would say and herding me towards the sofa. Her hand on my shoulder pushes me down to sit next to him.

'Not bad now. Any news, Lucy?'

Isn't that a funny question? He wants to sound as polite as possible, so polite that it's like we hardly even know each other. It's just to make sure we don't seem overly familiar, but Mother has put us so close on the sofa that I might as well sit in his lap.

'Not a bit.'

I lean away from him for the tea, but Mother beats me there. She pours out my cup, she refills Martin's. We are to sit here for a while it seems.

'Lucy is just home from study with the girls. Imagine, she does study on a Sunday even! Sure, the exams won't be long coming. Then it'll be the Debs, and then I don't know what!'

Mother hoots. I realise what she is doing, and my heart deflates.

'Bit late for study, isn't it?'

Martin smiles, because he knows I've scarcely opened a book all year. If he wanted to, he could tell Mother that, and he finds it so funny.

What a nice boy, how mischievous he is, how charming.

Mother, trying to clear the room, says to Ciarán,

'School in the morning.'

And not wanting to look childish in front of Martin, he gets up and leaves without making a scene. Martin gives him a high five, because he is so lovely. Dad excuses himself as well, saying he must milk in the morning.

In a minute, it has become just me and Martin, and Mother, staring at us both, guiding our conversation. Exams, the Debs, the weather, the Debs, the news, the Debs. After a while, she says,

'I'll just make sure the small fella is gone to bed.'

She slips out of the room, thinking she has done me a wonderful favour by creating this situation, like she is my one of the girls, looking after me. I could swallow the boiling pot of tea as a distraction – why not?

'So study is going well, is it?'

Martin starts, turning to face me, waiting until he hears Mother go up the stairs. Then he whispers,

'I thought she'd kill me. I think she saw us, you know, the other night.'

What a child. He ought to just say it. He's already kissed me, what has he got to be shy about?

'I'm mortified. She's absolutely mad. You can go home, I'll tell her you're gone.'

He goes nowhere, he doesn't want to listen. He wants to talk about kissing so I'll kiss him again. Isn't he daring, looking for that in my parents' front room? Maybe he thinks that Mother actually has done us a wonderful favour, and that we really are all friends. He laughs.

'She's grand, she's only looking after you.'

That isn't a lie. In her funny, selfish way, she's doing what she thinks is best for me. It's all she ever does, even if it is to my detriment. I was so happy before, but now Martin is leaning closer to me, and he won't let me alone, I'm losing sight of my perfect day. The smell of the night is fading from my skin, the condensation has dried off my cheek. However long we have been sitting here is too long. I want to go to bed, to Susannah's letters, to sleep, and to tomorrow. I want Martin to get out of my house so I can smell the damp on my jeans from the earth of the greenhouse.

'You know, she'll probably crucify me if I don't take you to the Debs.' I fear this is an invitation. He laughs a little bit, like he's trying to make things easier. I put my brave face on and laugh with him. At him. At the whole situation. We are already going together – the whole village knows it. He doesn't need to ask me, we are just a given thing. We are best friends, we've kissed, he doesn't have a girlfriend, so what is this attempt at asking me for? A waste of words.

'I'd love to go with you, though. If you're not going with anyone else. I'd really love it.'

He is almost afraid to look at me, but then he does. He looks right at me, because Martin is not afraid of the things that he loves. He is so beautiful. He is so sincere. The softness of the moment makes me curse Rita Hegarty. For all the years I've spent saying that I don't hate Rita, I am finally willing to admit that I do hate her, passionately. If she could only have made it work with Martin, just for a few more months, then this wouldn't be happening. He would take her to the Debs, and I could go on my own, with Susannah. How embarrassing. How infuriating. Why would he do this to me? There is nothing for me to say but yes. So I say nothing. He lets a long, painful moment stretch around us, and the silence cuts through him. When he knows I am not going to say anything, he says,

'I better head.'

He lifts himself from the couch, and I feel myself spring up a little bit. I stare at the tea tray, waiting for him to go.

But he won't go. He just stands in the doorway, staring at me, waiting for something. This is a weighted moment for him. Although he should be upset with me for stringing him along, he is distracted by my hair, the way it falls around my neck. He likes it. He wants to touch it. He wishes he had made more of our evening together in the field. When he had me where he wanted me. When I was who he wanted me to be. It's clear that he isn't going to leave on his own, so I get up and walk with him to the back door.

This wretched doorstep, freshly washed. I'm inside, Martin is outside, the doorframe between us. He watches me from the night, leaning against the house, just watching, as though we love each other. As though he is putting on a great show by standing there, brooding. Objectively, he is very good looking, I know, I can see that just as well as anybody. That doesn't mean I want him on my back step, night-drenched and staring at me. Let him stare in the mirror, let him stare at another girl, stop all this.

Mother softly clears her throat. From the corner of my eye, I see that she is crouched at the foot of the stairs, waiting for me to say something to Martin. They are both staring at me, waiting.

I know who he wants me to be. Who she needs me to be. A different Lucy. A better Lucy. Who is wonderful. Who is good. Whose life is so easy. With their eyes on me, and their breathing so loud, with that version of Lucy before me, it is so easy to forget about the happiness I found in the greenhouse. When I feel any slight chance of winning a morsel of my mother back, I forget about Susannah. Martin twitches on the step. The sensor light comes on. The floorboard groans under Mother. She is nodding at me, half excited, half threatening. This is my last chance to have her back. I just need to be that other Lucy; she is so lovely. The last shred of my self-worth is caught on the night air and blown out into the yard. I become her.

'Martin.'

His shoulders drop when he hears me say his name. He turns to face me. He is so beautiful. He could be all mine. A part of me feels I have lost him, now that I have him in this strange position.

'For the Debs, will your tie match my dress?'

I ask, rubbing the door handle with my thumb, which he cannot help but stare at. I watch his throat jump as he swallows. Being this Lucy is so easy, and I play her so beautifully. There was a time I was so enamoured by the other girls when they behaved like this. I never realised how simple it is, or how sickening. A bright smile comes to Martin, and I copy it. He nods. It means the world to him. It is nothing but a cheek ache to me.

'Talk to you soon.'

I smirk and close the door. He watches until the latch clicks. His navy-blue form stands in the Flemish glass; I watch as it gets smaller. Finally, he is leaving.

Before I have time to regret it, Mother bounds towards me and takes my arms in her hands, squeezes them, and spins us around in a circle. I haven't known her this energetic since I was a little girl.

'Oh my God, Lucy! You were like something from a film! I'm so thrilled!'

A fat film of tears comes to my eyes, and I know if I blink, I will cry.

It's hard to know if she believes what has just happened is real. It gives her a little bit of hope, I suppose. Even if she doesn't believe it, she wants to. Perhaps that is enough for right now.

She makes a scene, she makes a fresh pot of tea. At last, her girl has come back to her, she has nothing to fear now, the world has found its footing once more. I wonder how well she really believes this. Surely she is just allowing herself to be deluded. Now that my plan has worked, I can feel as disgusting as I am. All the guilt I have been ignoring floods on me at once, in the form of Mother's squeezing hands. She tells me about gossip from the last few weeks, things that excited her that she chose not to share with me. It's as if nothing happened. As if she never caught me half undressed, with Susannah's teeth at my hip.

Her Lucy is back now, and I am allowed to hear these trivial things. I am so sad. I am so relieved. Mother has come back. My dignity has gone away. All it took was agreeing to one evening with Martin Burke.

In bed, I look out the window at the moonless night. Martin will be in his bed now, replaying our moment on the back step. Thinking about me as though we are finally something that could blossom. Wasn't I believable, when I looked at him like he was all I would ever see? I almost convinced myself. It could have been real. I could have been breathless.

But it was not real, because every time I blinked, I saw the green of Susannah's eyes. She comes back to me so violently. The feeling of it is like nothing else. When I think of her, even for a second, my blood stills its rushing, my body is quiet, and my thoughts are turned down. All the world halts when I think of her. It's simple. So how could anything have been real? How could I ever hope to be authentic when I am a constant lie?

How deceitful I am. This isn't who I want to be.

But how easy life would be if I just stayed low down and out of sight, with only my thoughts of her, forever. These vivid thoughts of her. Having made do with them for so long, I know they can sustain me for quite some time, and that is lucky, because when I tell her what I have agreed to, she will refuse to speak to me.

And she does. As the first bell is ringing at the school gates, when she is having her breakfast cigarette, I admit that Martin is taking me to the Debs. She is so disgusted that I am almost afraid that she will put the cigarette out on me.

'I had to say yes.'

She won't even bless me with a scowl. I keep talking, even though it's making her eyes water. If there is even a second of silence to fill, she will cry, she knows and I know. Susannah hates to be seen crying. I won't be able to ignore it. Quietly, separately, we anticipated this eventuality. It might be upsetting, but it can't be a surprise to her. This was always going to happen. Was I not born to disappoint her?

'There was nothing I could do. Mam was right there, and he wasn't gonna leave if I didn't say yes.'

My plain and unworthy hand reaches for her, but she pulls away. I would feel the same way if I were like her – proud, optimistic. Sure as the tides, Martin was always going to take me away from her, and Susannah was always going to choose a date from her horde of admirers, and we would stare at each other, and maybe have a little dance like friends, but nothing more. That's always been the way this was going to happen.

'It's not as if we could have gone together. I couldn't say no.'

That makes her look at me, but not with her usual eyes. These eyes cut through me, they want me eviscerated. It is so rare she gets mean these days, and while I hope I have not invited it, I know that I have.

'Actually, you could have said no, Lucy. Nobody would have died if you said no.'

Her voice is low and slow. This isn't the sort of anger I have seen from her before. Any anger she has previously shown me has been very heated and explosive. This is quiet and bitter. I have made her bitter. I am all wrong, and there's nothing I can do to make it better. This new rage is not something I know how to navigate. This is another part of her, again. Although I want it gone, I love it. How many more parts of her are there?

'We could have had no dates. A few of us girls could have all gone as a group.'

As if. She is one of the most beautiful girls in the school, and so is Maria, and we are all very well-liked. It wouldn't make any sense if we all went without dates. Nobody would believe it. Mother wouldn't allow it, Eimear wouldn't allow it, Bernadette wouldn't allow it. There are more boys than girls our age. It would have left them without dates. These are the politics that I have decided to concern myself with. Sometimes it's like she doesn't care about the village at all. Sometimes I wish I could forget about her and follow the pattern. There's no point in telling her all this.

We both have parts to play, and we must play them. She has to go to the Debs with a boy, and she has to be the most beautiful girl there, in the most expensive and rare dress. And I must be Martin's sweetheart and look at him like he makes the world turn, like everybody predicts.

There's nothing to be said that's worth saying. I can't give her a proper apology with all these people flooding into school. We are staying on this stale note, there is nowhere else for us to go. She accepts it. There isn't anything else to do. So she offers me a cigarette, and things soften. It's still sad, but it's better.

14

MAY 1992

THE LEAVING CERT HAS BEEN completely forgotten in our house. It's all about Martin Burke and the stupid Debs. In a way, I am glad, because my studying has been so rushed and halfhearted that I will never succeed in the exams. In another bigger, private way, I am very disappointed, because nobody cared enough to try to make me study. I suppose I didn't care enough about myself, either. Nobody cares about the outcome of my exams. It makes me feel like a very inconsequential thing. When Tadgh sat his Leaving Cert, we weren't allowed to make noise after six o'clock so that he could study and sleep without being disturbed. I always thought that was ridiculous, because his plan was to work on the farm with Dad anyway. Now that it's my turn, nobody seems as bothered. Maybe I sound spoiled. Maybe I am. The house is always noisy. Mother hasn't had my exam timetable laminated and stuck on the fridge. I don't get a treat every time she goes to the shop. In fact, she has started to serve the healthiest food she can manage, because before my education, my looks are her new priority. I need to be as pretty as possible for Martin. Perhaps she knows that looks are all I can offer him.

On the morning of my Irish oral exam, I come down to breakfast and see that Mother has magazines from the hairdresser open on the table.

'It's a shame you keep your hair so short, love. Still, I'm sure you'd manage an up-do.'

She says, feeling my jaw and cheekbones to determine which style would best suit the shape of my face while I try to eat my porridge.

Mother tells me that the Leaving Cert really isn't the most important thing that I'll do in my life, and I suppose she is right: we both know I'm not going to college, and I have never given any serious thought to a potential career. It isn't that I'm too immature or lazy to think about the future; maybe it's just that I don't have the confidence to plan one for myself. I don't know. For a few years there, I was waiting to get a vocational call, but it never came. I've started to give up on myself before I've even had the chance to start. I suppose if I end up with Susannah, we can live off her money until she inherits more, and if I end up with Martin, we can live off the farm. It's funny, I never considered myself pretty enough to be a girl who marries into a monied life, but here I am, with two lovers and two monied lives to choose from. Wouldn't it be nice if I could be a person on my own?

Maria has been studying a great deal, she has always made us aware of how competitive teaching courses are. Patricia has been studying for the Leaving Cert since before the Inter Cert, she doesn't need to worry. And there is Susannah, who will hardly read a page, but will gracefully and effortlessly ace every one of her exams. She has been threatening to fail English so she will have to repeat, either because she wants to get her mother's attention or she wants to stay a schoolgirl a little longer. I don't know which is sadder.

May heats and turns to June, and my time is split between the front seat of Martin's car and the endless green of Susannah's garden. Mother rarely gets a look at me. I think she is happy. It's hard to tell with her. I don't want to hang around the house long enough to find out. Even on my very last day of school, the most she gets from me is a quick photograph at the bottom of the stairs with the boys. I don't see the sense in any ceremony when I will have to go back to school for the exams in a week. When the photograph is taken, I feel a hesitation from her. Like she wants to give me a hug or wants to say something to sum up my lifetime. Then she comes close to me, as though she is going to kiss my cheek. Only then she falters, and instead puts a brief hand on my shoulder and doesn't meet my eyes. I don't know what else to do to please her, and so I stay out of sight.

The exams start and pass by us. Fifteen days of shrugging shoulders and being told there's nothing more we can do now. Susannah buys me sweets every day. Besides a nervous, bouncing leg at the top of the exam hall, I don't hear or see Martin once during this time, because he is doing so much last-minute revising. What a relief. He gets wound up so tightly – I'm only just realising how annoying it is.

After the first three exams, I'm over it, and most of the others seem to be over it too. The momentum ran out far too quickly, and still we have to trudge through the rest of the papers. When we finally finish, it is a great anticlimax, except for Susannah dragging me into the toilets to kiss me, because I've never let her do it in school before. After that, school is out, and we are not children anymore.

The day we shop for our Debs dresses, I'm miserable, and it's the greatest pity because we've been building up to this for years. All my life, I have known what was coming. It was primary school, then secondary school; it was Sixth Year, then the Leaving Cert; and now the Debs. Besides dying, this is the very last certain thing in my life. It's terrifying. When the Debs is over, I will have no plans at all. Nothing will be coming, nothing will be going, I will just exist until I don't. For the first time, a little part of me feels jealous of the girls that are going to college, only because they have the next four years of their lives planned. They don't need to fall into the unknown yet. I am much too young for this uncertainty, am I not?

Sorcha Kealy is driving some of us to the city, her friend Orlagh is driving the rest. Sorcha, who is so effortlessly cool, is asking us about our exams like she really cares, and she tells us why they don't matter that much and that we shouldn't be worried. We tell her about our dates and what sort of dresses we want, just like when we were fifteen in the chipper. And she tells us what people are wearing in the city and about the various necklines and colours that she thinks will suit each of us. It's so nice having an older girl with us, even now, when we're moving around eighteen and nineteen ourselves.

Orlagh and Sorcha take a seat in the dressing rooms. Having an audience is partly fun, but mostly upsetting. I looked fine at home, but now under the white shop lights, I feel I'm just exposing all my physical failings to the girls and waiting to hear why each dress looks bad on me. While looking at myself in the mirror, I can't help but think that this dress is one of my final decisions. Then, all I will have left to worry about will be Susannah, and Martin, and Mother. That could be the last thing I have control over, maybe for the rest of my life. I can hear the girls squealing, they are very impressed by the dress Joan has put on. She has very fashionable proportions. It's because of the sensible way her mother feeds her. The girls are all praise.

'Girl, you look so class.'

Normally, a comment like this would be an excuse for me to tell Susannah how good she looks, but I'm not thinking about that right now. All I can think of is how I seem to have already undergone an irreversible change. I don't feel any different to the way that I did a few months ago, and yet I am finally considered grown-up. I have to be an adult. The life that I know will morph out of shape. The girls will be far away. I will be somebody different. I am grown, and yet I have never felt so young.

Sorcha and Orlagh insist that Joan reserves the dress she has put on. I think it's red, I'm not really looking. I'm trying to see through the curtain that Susannah is changing behind, just to get a break from my severe thinking. Eimear is standing behind Joan, still in her jeans, pulling her face back and saying,

'I wish I had more hollow cheeks, you know? Sort of thinner cheeks like.'

'Don't be shallow. Am I too short for a dress with a slit?'

All I want is to be engrossed in a conversation as trivial as this. When we were younger, I had this wonderful ability to put aside my feelings and drown in what the girls were saying. Now it's not nearly as easy. Then again, when I was younger, my problems were in their infancy. They were much easier to ignore.

Today was supposed to be fun. All the girls are laughing. They are having the experience I am supposed to have. I should be enjoying myself like they are. If I put on a dress and decide on it, we will be a step closer to going home. We will be a moment closer to the end of the day, the end of the Summer. The end of this Summer will be the end of everything. The magnificent secret of Susannah and me will burn as one last glorious flame. Then Martin will bring the Autumn, extinguishing us. All the fire of my life will be nothing but a cloud of smoke, dissipating. It's a lot to think about in these small dressing rooms. I hear Maria laughing. With every passing day, my girlhood vision of happiness grows more distant and unlikely.

'Okay, obviously this dress is all wrong.'

Bernadette says, facing us. Nobody said it was a bad dress – in fact, it's the nicest dress she has put on – but she didn't get complimented immediately. To Bernadette, that is the difference between looking good and bad. But she looks lovely. They all look lovely, my girls. When Susannah comes out in her dress, she gets the immediate attention that Bernadette so desperately needed. Lilac on her warm skin, and thin straps, and a high slit. Catríona won't have any objection to any of it. I must not react. I only bite the inside of my cheeks and wonder what would happen if I announced that I was going to the Debs with Susannah, not Martin. They would probably just laugh; they might not even listen.

'Oh, that's the one, Susannah, definitely!'

Orlagh says, like she knows us all. Isn't she cool, asserting herself as one of the group?

'I thought you were going to wear green?'

I say, and she does not look at me.

'Girl, that is so stunning.'

Now that she is wearing lilac, I don't know whether I should be looking at green dresses. Wearing green was only a small thing that we said once, but I sort of thought we would stick to it. Then again, why would I expect her to be loyal to a theme when I'm not loyal to her? It might be an insult if I wore green. Still, I just thought it would be a nice secret for us. Maybe it isn't as big a deal for her as it is for me. Maybe I'm thinking about it too much, I don't know.

'Is there any colours Martin won't wear?'

Sorcha asks me.

'Probably not. He'll do whatever.'

As long as I am there next to him, Martin will go along with absolutely anything. That's a good thing, I suppose. Sorcha starts to ask more about him, saying she always thought we were so sweet, that she always knew we'd get together, and that neighbours falling in love is so romantic. I want to clarify that he isn't actually my neighbour, he's just the nearest house in the wilderness. I want to make sure that they know I am not in love with him, that he isn't my boyfriend. How degrading, how humiliating for Susannah, to have to stand here and

listen to this. Have I no respect for her at all?
'He's not that great, lads. He can actually be so annoying.'
I try to get them to relax, but it only works them up more.
'That's so cute!'
'Lads are all annoying.'
'He's a star compared to most lads.'

Suddenly, everyone is talking about Martin, and what a genuinely nice guy he is, and how stupid I have been for not getting with him sooner. There's truth to all of that. Susannah is not listening to us. I expected that she might take the chance to say something insulting about him, but she is just looking at herself in the mirror, smoothing the fabric of her dress. Her eyes are sad; the others don't notice. I ought to be buying a dress that complements her. Instead, she has to hear all about my new boyfriend and how lucky I am to have him. Tomorrow, Susannah's letter will say,

Times like that I don't feel guilty for tuning you out, because I can't stand to hear another story about that dullard who hangs off you.

Perhaps if I never knew Susannah, I would want Martin. Perhaps she is the problem. I buy a dress. It is a colour that we cannot decide on, somewhere between blue and green. Sorcha says she will do my hair if I want.

In the evening, Martin calls over, wanting to know if he can see my dress. It's just an excuse to get a look at my bedroom. He wants to see the sheets I sleep on, he wants to see the dirty laundry on the floor and the lip gloss on the dresser. Isn't he cunning? I tell him that perhaps we should go for a drive instead.

'Just so you're not tempted.'

I say quietly, without meaning to put temptation on his mind.

When I say things, he hears other things.

He drives us into Ballycove, where we take endless laps of the town. In another life, driving with him would be a dream, I would not even notice the streetlights for all the love blurring my vision. He has been talking about getting his own car for so long. It's a shame that now he has it, us driving around together is considered a date. It's a shame that I'm not the sort of girl to sing along to the radio or to pay attention to the news. I am the sort of girl to talk, and worse than that, more than that, I am the sort of girl to listen. He knows this, and so I must listen as he talks and talks and talks. He confuses my silence with interest, and I hear all about the engine capacity and the suspension and the tyres and things that I don't care about. When he starts on about cars and hurling and boyish things, he does not stop. And again I think, maybe if I never knew how interesting Susannah was, I would think Martin's car was fascinating. Maybe the problem is not that I want her, maybe it's that she is in Crossmore, wanting to be wanted by me. Although I don't want her gone, I wonder who I would be if she wasn't around.

The streetlights of Ballycove flood into the car. They colour his face orange and warm up the cold in his blue eyes. I wish our conversations wouldn't come so easily, and that the silences weren't so comfortable. I wish there were reasons for Martin to doubt that we belong together. Instead, we are effortless, and I hate it because it makes him think that we are going to make a very good couple. We would make an excellent couple. I feel bad for him. This manipulation could be considered deplorable, and I begin to think of it that way, but the orange light on his skin puts me in mind of Susannah's tanning skin, and I am convinced that anything is excusable for her. But I must wonder, how much of this is really for her?

'Did all the girls get their dresses sorted?'

He asks, as though he cares. With this, I know he is making a special effort for me, because normally he would never ask a question about the girls or their clothes. At least I know I'm not the only one faking things. If we are both pretending to be more interested than we are, why are we bothering? I look out the window and see a night rain begin.

'Yeah. Susannah looks class in hers.'

I tell him, watching as the only traffic light in Ballycove changes before us, and the green fades away. Martin might like to park up somewhere quiet. Perhaps if we do, we will feel obliged to stop talking and sit still and embrace the silence. It might be nice if we didn't talk tonight. When I think about the mess I have created for myself, it gets on top of me very quickly. It's hard to pretend that this isn't going to get more complex and upsetting every day. Yes, a little silence would be nice.

If only we had grown up somewhere else. Maybe none of this would be an issue there. I need to find a way out of Crossmore. The trouble is, without any money, my only way out is with him, or with her. It's getting harder to breathe. Martin drives faster, very fast. I think he is trying to scare some life into me. He has already done that.

It turns out that the quiet place we park up at is my driveway. This is perfect, actually. It is suitably secluded, so he feels satisfied that we have shared an intimate moment, but also, we are near enough to the house that Dad could be out with a hurley in a matter of seconds. Martin puts his hand over mine, and he looks at me with his gentle eyes. How long can I refuse him? Surely there is a long time ahead before I have to start giving in to the animal parts of him. As far as he knows, that sort of behaviour isn't in my nature – he won't want me to rush into anything. But then he kisses me, and my heart does not sink as I expect it to. In fact, it rises up, almost into my mouth, almost into his. I must wonder if that feeling is a part of me that wants this? But then, as ardent as he may be, his tongue feels like a dead weight against mine, and it makes me feel like my own perversions are cleaner than his unwashed want for me. I am lucky that we were raised so holy, because, whether or not we believe in it, it means I am expected to put an unquestioned stop to all this touching. Do I want it to stop? It might be cleansing. If everybody wants me to be with Martin, then perhaps that is what I am meant to do. I push him away from me, and I look up. In a voice that comes out condescending, I say,

'Holy God is watching.'

He laughs and shifts in his seat, because he thinks he is too eager. I really feel I could be sick. Am I supposed to tell Susannah about this? I get out of the car and don't care about the ache that I have left him with. I turn and wave to him as I go into the house. His blue heart soaring, he holds his hand up to wave back at me. He has lived for so long on gasps of my passing perfume, he will last another while on the spit I've left in his mouth. It doesn't matter that I am home late. Dad is asleep. Mother is fine as long as I am not with Susannah.

In the morning, I wake up alone. It seems so rare that I'm on my own these days. I want to make the most of it. I need to go and think all of my heavy thoughts, so I might figure them out, and they might lighten. On my own, I leave the house, and take a long walk. I only pass by one person: Tom White with a bale of hay on the front of his tractor. He salutes, I salute, and I wonder what he thinks when he sees me. Am I Dad's girl or Mother's girl or Martin's girl? I feel like Susannah's girl. I don't want to be anybody's girl; I want to be my own person. I wish I could stand up on my own. When the tractor has passed, two rabbits run out of the ditch and up the road ahead of me.

Here is a field full of cows. I stand still and watch them, and they all turn to watch me. Perhaps if I stand still long enough, they will charge for me, and I will be trampled. Then I wouldn't be stuck between Susannah and the world anymore. But the cows don't charge. They don't even move. They just look at me until they are bored of me and then they go back to eating the grass. Wouldn't it be nice to be a cow in the field? Sitting and grazing, with nothing at all to worry about. How simple it would be, to be one in a herd.

The way I have been behaving is not as clever as I once imagined. In truth, I have not behaved this way for love. I behave this way because I am a terrific coward. I grip the electric fence so I might come back to life. It brings a wonderful jolt of feeling. It goes as quickly as it comes. I didn't hate kissing Martin. All thoughts of Susannah aside, I didn't hate it. Isn't that terrible? A cow cries, and I think of Susannah, and I feel very alone on this country road.

It's hard because I am so aware of the differences between Martin and Susannah. He is the calm, she is the noise. She cannot give me the things that he can give me. He cannot give me the things that she can give me. With Susannah, I am constantly surprised that I am good enough for her. With Martin, I never doubt that I am good enough. I don't know which I should want. Do I want to be safe and secure, or do I want to be happy?

I must perk up. I must not spend the Summer alone, taking strange walks and trying to electrocute myself. Tonight we are going to Susannah's, just the girls and me. We are having a dinner party, to celebrate the end of our school days. They convinced me that it will be fun and grown-up to cook a meal for ourselves, to all sit down together, with a glass of wine, and eat and chat.

And it is fun to cook together, to once more drown myself in their frivolities. The food is served on wedding china that Catríona and Phil never used. Maria has brought strawberries and cream. She invites us all to smash up our own meringues. All our old dramas are revived tonight, and it is so sweet. Joan is reminding us of her first kiss, with Frank Brennan, outside the chipper as everybody watched through the big window. He still fancies her now, he never got over it. Everybody laughs.

'And sure then his brother was Susannah's first kiss.'

'Aw, lovely Cormac Brennan!'

'Ye could have been in-laws!'

'No, he wasn't.'

Susannah stops them.

'I had my first kiss when I was six. Big lunch, Senior Infants, in the bike sheds.'

Her face is so smug; my skin heats, and I laugh, because I can't believe she's going to expose this. I can't believe she considers me her first kiss. What adrenaline.

'With who?'

None of the girls will believe her. Is she really going to say?

'With Lucy.'

She says plainly.

'That doesn't count.'

Eimear laughs. Does she not remember kiss chase?

'Well, she was literally my first kiss, long before Cormac Brennan. It was on this cheek – I remember it so well.'

She pinches my cheek in her hand, and everyone is laughing.

'Alright, relax.'

Bernadette says, tired of how close we are. They are all tired of how close she and I are. I wonder what they think of us, if they suspect anything. They start laughing about when Sister Loretta broke up the game of kiss chase, when everyone could see her stockings in the school yard. I pretend to remember this.

I think they would like to talk about college, and all the preparations they are making for it, but they don't want to bring me down. For years, we have all been so excited to finally finish school, but now that we have finished, I wonder what it is we were rushing towards. I don't even have plans for tomorrow, never mind September, never mind the rest of my life.

When I was young, I thought that everybody in Crossmore was the same. I thought everybody liked everybody, and we all had the same opportunities. I don't think that's true anymore. Whether I was wrong before or the town has changed, it seems that some people are actually very well off, and some of us are not. It's easy to miss things like that when you're young. It gets more obvious when you can't afford to plan the future, or when you're not allowed to exist authentically. Susannah has told me many times that she can afford both of our futures. I don't know how true that is. We have very different experiences of money; I don't think either of us really knows how far that inheritance of hers would go. She tells me that if I just choose a place for us to go, she will make sure that I never have to do another thing again. Why don't I just go along with it? Even if it all goes wrong and we end up poor, back in Crossmore with nothing, at least we will have tried. Sometimes the best thing to do is the hardest.

'Lads, sorry, did ye hear about Dennis Jennings?'

Eimear asks, and everybody shakes their heads. I am so glad to be taken from my thoughts, from the familiar ache in my cheek where Susannah touched it.

'Apparently he was caught with some fella up in the city.'

'Caught doing what?'

And Eimear widens her eyes, hoping she won't have to finish spreading the rumour that a friend of theirs was caught in bed with a man. The girls understand, half of them have heard it already but don't want to let on that they knew. I sit quietly, not wanting to react in a positive or negative way. Maria is the one to speak.

'Eimear, that's a horrible thing to say. Don't be spreading that shit around, people will believe it.'

'I was only saying, relax, girl. Obviously, he's not actually gay.'

'Ugh, that's horrible. Imagine getting caught doing that.'

'Sure, what harm if he's gay? It's not like ye fancy him.'

Susannah starts. I don't know why she is doing this. Yes, it's in her character. We all know she is a liberal person from a liberal household, but this is unnecessary. All she is doing is making the girls admit they don't like gay people. Why would she make me listen to that?

'It's just not nice, Susannah. Imagine someone was saying that about one of your brothers. It's defamatory.'

Maria says, and Susannah laughs. They know that if one of Susannah's brothers was gay, she would not care. I wish she hadn't said anything. This has soured such a sweet night, possibly one of our last nights all together like this. Patricia quickly changes topic; it is clear how terribly uncomfortable she is with this conversation. Everyone keeps chatting and laughing, like all that was said meant nothing. To them, it meant nothing. And I feel just as I did when we were fifteen, eating our dinners in the chipper. I feel like an island, away from everybody. I don't want the girls to leave Crossmore, I don't want our last June to turn to our last July, and I don't want to get a day closer to being Martin's. I want to sit at this table forever, hearing the girls laugh, with Susannah's hand on my leg under the table. I want to pretend that I am no different to anyone else. But the word has been said: the girls would not accept us. Susannah gives me a look when we are clearing the plates away, a look which says, I told you so. She didn't have to tell me so – I've always known they were intolerant. I can't stop thinking that, soon, Maria is going to be a teacher. When the night ends, it feels like a part of me ends too.

I am the last one left. Martin is going to collect me. He will drop whatever he is doing to pick me up. I haven't walked anywhere in weeks. Who knew that a little kissing would make him so weak for me? When it is just Susannah and I left, and again, I find it hard to breathe. Tonight she doesn't kiss me against the door. She just looks at me, because she knows that he is coming and there's nothing she could do to get me to stay. She knows she took it too far tonight, and now we both know for sure that the girls wouldn't want us if we were honest with them. Why did she do that? When I should be furious at them, I am furious at her. Tonight I feel for the first time that our heaven may not be forever. School is over. Real life must begin, and at one time or another, we will have to embrace it.

I look at her, her face unchanged. She is so good at keeping herself together, and at keeping me together. Even when I want to be angry with her, she is such a soothing thing to look at. Even though she is cross at me, and I cannot stay, she just puts me at ease. Why doesn't Mother see how good Susannah is for me? Why do I have to want her so badly? Could I not just have been normal? In the dark hall, I want to reach my hand out to her, but then her face is lit up as Martin's car pulls onto the drive, shining reality all over my dream. Neither of us says anything, because there is nothing to say. I fear she is thinking the same as me.

She watches as I get in his car, and he smiles at me.

15

JULY 1992

THIS DAY LAST YEAR, I was in Susannah's garden, watching as she tanned, terrified by the sparkling skin of her bare torso. The sunshine made us hazy, it was good to be me. What a long year it has been. Today I'm alone in my dark bedroom with a knot in my stomach, getting ready for the damned Debs. The morning has actually been quite boring, especially for a morning that has been built up since I was a child. Sorcha has been and done my hair. It is just long enough to style up like Mother firmly suggested. Now all I can do is remove and apply my lipstick over and over, until it is time to leave. Mother keeps coming to my door, looking at me with proud and sad eyes. When Martin arrives and kisses me on the cheek, she looks so happy. It makes me feel like when I was a child, pretending to still believe in Santa Claus on Christmas morning. Martin looks so well in his suit; a lot of girls will be jealous of me. Granny gets me to twirl around in my dress. It's nice that she treats me like I'm still a child. Last year, I would have hated that, but now I am so glad of it. We stand together for a photograph, and his mother tells him to put his arm around me, and I am stunned by how small his body makes me feel, and that I like it. His funny and delayed puberty is finished: he is a man now, there is no way I can deny it.

'You look amazing.'

He says to me, in the car, when our parents are not around to hear. For me, it still feels very awkward when he compliments me like this.

For him, I think, it must feel quite natural. As he drives us to the hotel, I feel overwhelmed with disappointment. I don't want to be his date; it might be better not to be here at all. I regret this whole night before it has even started. My hair is stiff with hairspray, and my bra is too tight around my ribs. If I tell him that I'm sick maybe he would just drop me back home.

We are among the last to arrive, and I'm glad because it means there are plenty of people to distract us. If he was here with Rita, and didn't have his hand sunk into my waist, I would have been so excited to see him all dressed up. But he is here with me, right next to me, refusing to go from my side, and it makes everything different. Just as my chest tightens beyond comfort, I see Susannah, and I am saved.

She is here in her lilac dress with Jack Healey, who graduated last year. Of course she would have to bring a college boy. They are talking to Rita and her date, a boy I don't recognise – isn't that strange? Susannah is just so nice. The other girls wouldn't dream of talking to Rita unless it was going to upset her. I could have been here with the nicest girl in the village; instead, I am leading Martin on. Why am I so keen on depriving everybody of good things? If I hadn't engineered this situation, I could say it was unfair.

I knew she would be beautiful today, of course I knew, but this is unbelievable. Never in all my years of Christianity has there been talk of an angel like this. My God, she is not even walking, she floats around the room. Everybody has worn their hair up, shiny and tight, but she has left hers long and waving down her back, with small pearls threaded through. Her cheeks are glittering, and her eyelids and collarbones. And she is wearing emerald jewellery. All that emerald green, hugging her lovely earlobes and ring finger. I don't know if they're real, but I can assume that they are. For a moment, while my eyes are adjusting to her light, I forget my guilt. Everything is forgotten, all that has happened and all that is to come, it just dissolves and falls around her.

The meal isn't as bad as I had convinced myself it would be, because I forgot that we would all be seated at big tables. For some reason, I expected to be at a table for two with just Martin, trying to speak to him with my mouth full. Instead, all our friends are at a table together, and we are having fun. She sits right next to me, and I've had enough to drink that I can pretend I am here with her. And then I realise, I am here with her. Now that the photographs have been taken, there is no need for me to speak to Martin for the rest of the night. There is no point being upset or angry, not tonight, not if we can help it.

'Do you wanna be my date?'

I whisper to her, and the night starts to go differently.

Martin and I dance to one song in the slow set, and it's like he's borrowing me from her. We are just two people dancing. It's nice, actually. When we get to just be ourselves like this, to just be friends like always then I remember how much I love Martin. He is my very best friend, and although it makes things more complicated, I cannot pretend that he isn't one of my favourite people. He keeps his hands firmly on my waist and doesn't take me too close. He's too respectful to really try to touch me in front of everyone, he would rather look at me. I know this look, it's like the way Susannah looks at me. Any second now, he could tell me he loves me. He bends to speak into my ear.

'This should be our song.'

His words are hot with excitement. Years from now, he will say that tonight was the night he knew that I was the girl he wanted to spend the rest of his life with. I will say that things change. Our song, I agree and smile. I don't even know what this song is called.

Then there is the blur of Bernadette tearing across the dance floor, running to the toilets, and because Martin is so kind, he tells me I should go after her, to make sure she isn't vomiting. Bless her low tolerance, bless his heart. She doesn't vomit, just gags a little bit while I stop her hair from falling out of its bun and into the toilet.

'Danny is driving me mad.'

They look so nice together today. Danny really complements her, even if they don't get along. The bathrooms are so full of smoke I can hardly see myself in the mirror. Aisling offers me a drink from her bag, but considering all my history with Rita, I decline. Even though Rita is here with somebody else, and appears to be having a good time, I can't trust that she and her friends won't try to spike me. Anyway, I still have half a naggin in my bag, and there are plenty of other bottles being passed around the bathroom. Bernadette and I leave closer to vomiting than she was coming in.

When we get back to everybody, Martin kisses me. It's very quick, it's casual, just a way of saying hello. But Susannah sees it. She sees the smile it leaves on his face, and the tiny shine it leaves on my lips. It was so minuscule an action, and yet I felt her heart crack. I want to make it up to her.

Nobody cares when she and I dance together. I can put my hands on her, nobody minds. We are girls, we are friends, it's just what we do. We can dance slowly, together, nobody cares. Nobody notices when she looks me up and down and asks,

'Whose are you?'

And I say,

'Yours.'

And I see now why she has put up with all of this. It's because we understand each other, it's because we have this binding sort of love that is rare and good that we don't get anywhere else. So rare and so good that I cannot even make sense of it, the same way that nobody can make real sense of God or the reasons why we are alive. I think that dancing with her tonight is the reason that I am alive. If it was the other way around, and Susannah was keeping me a secret, I would put up with it too. She could take me and discard me as she pleased, I wouldn't mind.

When it's all over, and everybody is back at Susannah's after party, she drags me into her mother's bathroom, where we can get a second alone. The smell of scented toilet paper and fake tan hits me, and although I feel I might faint, I have never felt so wonderful. Our makeup has melted off, and the volume is gone from our hair. With my red eyes and her sweating hands, I feel beautiful for the first time today. Years from now, I will say that tonight was the night I knew that she was the girl I wanted to spend the rest of my life with. This is about more than her body, her tanned skin, her perfect mouth. I am in love with her blood, with her smell, with intangible things that I will never hold – her laugh, her anger, her soul.

She kisses me, and she has a thousand reasons to be upset with me, but tonight she is not upset. She just keeps saying,

'I love you, I love you, I love you, in this life and the next and the last.'

16

Lucy,

I was watching you for the whole drive, while Joan kept batting your hand away when you went to change the radio station. I felt so far away from you in the backseat. And when you turned around to whisper to us, I saw a strand of spit going from your teeth to your lips, and it was like a perfect gossamer cobweb, and I wanted to be caught in it. That's dramatic, isn't it? You've made me so dramatic.

Sometimes when I leave after walking you home, I stand at Martin's gate and look up at his bedroom window, and I can see all the wicked thoughts he has in there, floating in the air. I know you have been worshipped in there, even if you never go in. He's in love with you, and I know what loving you can do to a person. Where you are involved, right and wrong go to Hell, and all that's left is senseless longing. His head must be filthy. Like today, in the car, when you were listening to Joan, you pressed your front tooth down between your thumb and nail, into all the dirt under your nail, it was so rank, the dirt probably touched your teeth, and all I could think was that I wanted to suck on your dirty thumb. That's the sort of thing I think now, Lucy, and I get the release of you; imagine how unclean his thoughts are. I hate every piece of him. It makes me so angry that he thinks he has even a scrap of you. This might be one of those letters I write but don't give you, I dunno.

S xxx

THESE DAYS ALL ANYONE WANTS to talk about is what is going to happen next, so much so that nobody cares about what's happening now. All Susannah wants to do is run away, and all Martin wants to do is settle down, and I realise that I've only ever thought of ways to keep everyone happy, so I have no idea what I want. What I do know is that I can't stay at home for much longer. Mother is dying to get rid of me. I must find a place to go before she finds one for me.

I'm in Martin's kitchen. I'm with him most days, just for an hour, so we have been seen together. Being in his company has become so loaded. Now that he thinks I am almost his girlfriend, it's like I am no longer his friend. The more comfortable he gets, the worse it is, because he has started to put his arm around me, to hold my hand, and to kiss me without waiting to be invited. A part of me really hates that this isn't enough for me. Maybe he thinks I'm a prude, or maybe he thinks I'm playing some sort of flirty game where I like to deny him. Whatever, I care less and less about what he thinks. It was so stupid of me to think that just the chance of a relationship would satisfy him. He's eighteen years old, he is touch-starved, he is love-starved. It will only be so long before he can wait no more. Soon brushing my hand against his will not be enough. He will come looking for more, or he will get tired of waiting and he will go from me. I don't want either.

'I don't know what to do. Take the farm or chance going to college.'

He is looking so deeply into his tea that he might fall into the cup. This is his biggest dilemma, and he has been talking about it all Summer. Now our exam results are impending, decisions must be made. He will do very well, he is bound to. I might do alright, it doesn't matter. Whether he chooses to stay on the farm or go to the city won't make a difference, because either way, he will have his family and their land to fall back on. Really, the question he's asking is: do I stay on my parents' land, or do I rent my own for a while?

'Will anyone mind if you go? I mean, if it goes wrong, you'll still have everything waiting here for you. Nothing would really change.'

I want to sound harsh. I want him to realise that this isn't a real problem. Mine are real problems, nobody else's. He looks illuminated, as if I have been helpful and not mean. He puts a hand on my cheek and lets my hair fall on his fingers. It feels so invasive.

'You're so amazing, I don't tell you often enough.'

It's all he ever tells me. He deserves all the love in the world, he is wasting his wonderful heart on me. I smile, my face stiff as glass, and he kisses me quickly, because we're in his mother's kitchen. I could count on one hand the number of times I've let him kiss me properly. He must think I am afraid to be touched. Perhaps I ought to put a bit more care into helping him make this decision, because whatever path he chooses, there's a chance that I'll be taking it with him. I only needed him to get to the end of the school year, but here we are, halfway through the Summer, together. Who is to say I will be brave enough to finish this in the Autumn? After he kisses me, I feel that I have more than met my quota of duties for the day, and so I let myself go home, resigning myself to the possibility of life as his lover, thinking of him as a very kind and patient backup plan.

A few hours later, by her gate, Susannah is exhibiting herself as a much better and less feasible option. I can have her, she says, but it has to be all of her, and it has to be honest, and it has to be now. She tells me that we cannot live in secret anymore.

'You know I'm leaving Crossmore. I won't keep asking you to come with me, Lucy. One day I'll just go without you.'

Each new piece of the moon washes another wave of impatience over her. I can't blame her, she's put her life on hold for me, and I almost wish that she hadn't. If only things were the way they were last

Summer, when she did not know all the ways that I loved her. I would be no closer to freedom, but she would be so much further from this nightmare.

'There are so many people in the real world, Lucy. Not everybody is your mother. Not everybody wants to get married off and live on a farm. People would love you the way you are, we just need to find those people.'

That is all true. It's so sweet, and so exciting, but I cannot pretend that to gain all that acceptance I wouldn't lose all that I have now. The village, and all our girls, our families – everything we grew up with but each other would be gone. I would have to leave them all behind. Sometimes you just know when somebody isn't going to understand. If it wasn't for Susannah, I might not understand this either. At the very best, the most important relationships I have would be strained and bent out of shape. Could she make up for the loss of all that? I am afraid that if we go away together, I might find that her heaven-sent love is not enough for me.

'I'll look after you, and you'll look after me. I'd never be safer with anyone else.'

And she's right, she's always right, but is it not terrifying? Jesus, would she not shut up with her hypnosis?

'We don't have to talk about it right now.'

Like always, I prove myself to be her greatest disappointment. The life she wants for us seems like science fiction.

'Please, Lucy.'

Susannah's family is already long gone and disintegrated, and she doesn't need to worry about money, and she is dying to leave Crossmore. The truth is, Susannah has already lost all that I am afraid to lose.

'We won't be saved.'

There would be no safety nets, no second chances, no Heaven. And in her perfect voice she tells me,

'I'll save you.'

There is nothing to say. Rather than disappoint her further, I put my arms around her shoulders, and let her take what she will from it. I feel her chest rising, filling with breath to talk again – darling, please stop talking.

'Can we just be happy for a few days then and pretend you're not afraid to want me?'

I bring her nearer to me, I put my head against hers, so she cannot look at me. Her question goes unanswered, although she knows what I would say. And because she still loves me too much to leave me, she lets me stay quiet, she lets us carry on for a while as if nothing needs to change. I am allowed to be afraid, and she continues to make herself more difficult to refuse. Maybe if she had to make a choice like this, she would understand my hesitation.

As I am pulled in two very different directions, a sweltering July blurs the days into the nights, the air is clouded with the dust of fertiliser, and I keep life as close to simple as I can. For a little while, it really is bliss. We live with our eyes closed, Susannah and her money, Martin and his land, and me, without the confidence or ability to do anything on my own. Autumn is looming, the pressure is mounting, and I draw closer to breaking every day. And so I ignore the Autumn and the questions and reality. And for a short while, my life is an endless Summer night.

17

AUGUST 1992

A WEEK HAS PASSED SINCE Susannah's eighteenth birthday. The second day in August – is that not the loveliest day of the year? Today she is coming home from Eimear's house, where Deirdre fed her a bigger dinner than she has had in a long time. Thick, salty chunks of boiled ham and a heap of shredded cabbage and more potatoes than could fit on her plate. Nobody said anything as she wolfed the food down, they were all silenced by her enormous appetite, and their pity for it. Since all Ms O'Neill ever taught us was how to make **meringue**, Susannah has almost no ability in the kitchen. If not for doting mothers like Deirdre, she might not get her hands on proper food at all.

Before they even sat down, Deirdre had started making a commotion about how she had accidentally made too much food and that they would be eating the same dinner for days to use it all up. Again, nobody said a word about how unlikely it was that Deirdre's meticulously eyeballed measurements would go wrong. To her husband and children, it was very obvious what she was getting at. Deirdre knew she had seven dinners to make, and she made nine so that Susannah would have to take something away with her.

'Oh, Susannah! You'd never take a plate home with you?'

Susannah tried to deny her offer, but Deirdre insisted.

'You'll have to, love, I couldn't put this all to waste. We'll be eating it for a week!'

Susannah really didn't notice what was going on – because Deirdre has always been so kind and high-pitched, it just seems like the sweet sort of thing that she would do. Susannah comes home with two lunchboxes of food, never once thinking that they are an act of charity, because she is very well able to take care of herself.

At home, while putting the lunchboxes in the fridge, she notices a folded note on the kitchen island in her mother's curled writing.

Susannah,

Dear, I have gone away for a while, with a good friend of mine, Patrick. If necessary, I can be contacted at his house (045-72656).

I won't be home again. Know that I'm very proud of you, and you have been wonderful all your life. As usual, your father will be around if you want anything.

Catríona

At first this letter doesn't mean much to Susannah, she just thinks it means her father will be around for a few days. Getting over that brief excitement, she goes back to taking a moulded head of cauliflower out of the fridge to make space for Deirdre's dinner. It is only after reading the letter for a second time that she registers what it really means. Catríona is gone.

And she is struck with an awful rush of questions, like who is Patrick, and what area code is 045? The letter is the fullest explanation and the nearest thing to goodbye she gets, because she is too proud and too afraid to call the number. She is sure that, sooner or later, Patrick will get bored of Catríona, and she will be forced to come home. Catríona has had boyfriends in the past, and eventually, they all dump her back on the porch of Croft Hall. But she has never left so suddenly before. It's difficult to predict how long this trip will last.

That night, when Susannah goes to bed, there is a new silence in the house. For the first time, she realises just how big the rooms are, and she is cold. She wonders if she should phone one of her brothers, or me, but she doesn't get out of bed to do it. There, in the empty dark, she takes a breath and accepts that if her mother doesn't come home to her again, mine might be the only love she has left.

Although she has had countless spells of loneliness, this one is the worst, because it has no end. Usually, she knows that she only needs to make it through the weekend, a fortnight at the very most. But this could last forever. When she wakes up, she will phone her father, who will say that he cannot talk and will call her back when he gets a chance. He hasn't visited for the last two weekends.

Before any of us knows what has happened, a crack has already appeared in Susannah. She puts on the engagement ring that her mother left behind, and in her grand bedroom, she walks to the window to watch the light pass through the diamond and shatter into a rainbow, and her sigh echoes. She opens the window wide to smoke and then laughs at herself, because there is nobody around to get angry at her for smoking. And still she ashes onto the windowsill, suddenly uninterested in misbehaving. Three days pass before she considers looking for help.

If Susannah calls my house and Mother answers, the phone gets disconnected. She knows this, and so she doesn't bother calling me. Instead, she calls Maria, and very vaguely explains what has happened, because she isn't sure what else to do. Then, in my hallway, the telephone rings, and it is Maria, who does not waste time with formalities.

'Catríona is gone.'

'Are we having a party?'

'No, she's gone. She's after leaving a note, like she completely left.'

There's nothing to do but go to Susannah's house. We all squeeze into Maria's car and find Susannah sitting on her porch, waiting, but not for us. If she wasn't so stuck, she wouldn't have wanted any of the girls to come. Since our dinner party, she has started to distance herself from them. Today she must take the help she is given. When she sees us coming up the drive, she lights a cigarette. We sit down with her and fall into her silence. It's difficult to know how to start. How do you begin a conversation about abandonment so soon after it has happened? I wonder if we should phone the Guards, but I don't suggest it, because it might worry her. It's difficult to know how serious this situation is. The only thing that isn't difficult is that I know I am allowed to put an arm around her and put a kiss on her head and let her rest on my shoulder. The girls won't think twice about it. After some coaxing, she shows us the letter. It produces more questions than answers.

'So has she sort of left you the house?' Eimear asks. What a daring question.

'She won't be gone forever. I'm just minding it, I suppose. She'll be back.'

Susannah doesn't look at us when she answers, she just rubs the diamond on the ring. We sit on the porch with her until the sun disappears behind the fuchsia bushes. I lie to the girls and tell them that Martin will come over and take Susannah and me for 99s. What's one more lie? They need to go now and stop crowding her. When they leave, I take Susannah to bed and lie next to her until she falls asleep.

I don't tell Mother what happened, but she finds out quite quickly. It would be short-sighted of me to be surprised.

'She just packed up and left! She wanted for nothing, and she left them. Imagine!'

She is telling Granny this in the kitchen, knowing I can hear but decidedly not talking to me. This is one of her many small ways of telling me that she has always been right about Susannah and the O'Sheas.

'Disgraceful.'

Granny says. If I were any good at all, I would remind Mother that Phil left a long time before Catríona did, but that might just further hurt my cause.

'Sure, is it any surprise? She was never a mother to those children. It's no wonder they ended up the way they did.'

It's hard to disagree with that. I don't want to stand up for Catríona, but I don't want Mother talking about her either. It seems that she is taking genuine pleasure in Susannah's desertion. For all the hateful things that Mother has done, this is the first time I have truly felt hate for her.

Phil doesn't make it down to Crossmore until two o'clock on Sunday, about the time he would normally be packing up to leave again. It was a busy week, which turned into a busy weekend. He couldn't have planned for this, Susannah assures me, as we watch him pull into the driveway.

Getting out of the car, he bends down to touch his palm to the grass, unshorn and wild. Dandelions and weeds have sprouted all over in his three-week absence. Looking from the grass to the house, he says to himself,

'Can't say I'm surprised.'

There is something like regret in his voice, but it is too distant to name. Susannah meets him in the hallway, and he tells her how sorry he is, as though Catríona has died, as though he didn't leave just as abruptly years ago.

He steps into Catríona's bedroom on his own. I wonder if I should follow him in and talk to him. It seems like such an adult thing to do. I would like to confront him, and ask him what his plan is to look after Susannah. I would like to ask him why it has taken him so long to come down, and how he is going to fix everything. Of course, all I actually do is politely mumble along with his small talk. Perhaps he would feel more comfortable if I wasn't here.

Before he leaves, he asks Susannah to go back to the city with him, and she refuses. Then he tells her that she has no choice but to come back with him, and still she refuses.

'This is my home, Daddy. I'm not going.'

With a kiss pressed hard into her forehead, he gets back into his car, leaving the lawn long, and he drives back to the city. The whole visit lasted half an hour.

Although I sleep over most nights, there are times when I have to go home. It's hard to know whether she wants me to stay or go. When I am around, she clings to me like she is afraid I will float away. But when it comes time to leave, she hardly says goodbye.

The days of her decomposition are plain and slow. Dark, dim Summer evenings. Hot air, and not a slice of sun in the sky. Any minute, it could rain, and she might come to life again. It's awful, but I wonder if this will slow her down a little bit. Perhaps she will forget about leaving Crossmore for a while. Perhaps I have been given some extra time to work things out. The girls seem to think that this is a good thing. They are always there, drinking and laughing and making light of the situation, while Susannah floats around, smoking and making them tea in unwashed mugs. Inside, the house is hot and musky from weeks of unopened windows, and a fine dust has fallen on everything. It has almost fallen on her. Deirdre's bacon has turned black in the fridge, and a great white fur has formed on the cabbage.

The fun seems to stop whenever I come over. The girls are annoyed that I keep interrupting their good time. I just don't think that all this drinking is what Susannah needs right now. They shouldn't be taking advantage of her situation just for the sake of a free house. We are all old enough to get served, can't they just go to the pub?

This afternoon, I hear thumping music as I walk up Susannah's drive. Maria cuts it off as soon as she sees me. They all stop talking and stare at me in the doorway. I feel like a teacher who has caught them smoking.

'Do ye ever get off the session, girls?'

I ask them, while I pick up the empty cans on the coffee table. Perhaps I am being a killjoy.

'It's the Summer holidays, Lucy. What else are we supposed to do?'

Joan asks, while putting out whatever she was smoking. It's embarrassing that they think I'm so rigid. It's embarrassing that they are disrespecting Susannah like this.

'Where's Susannah?'

'Dunno.'

Why don't they know where she is? As I go to check the back garden, they turn the music back up. I hear Eimear snickering as I go, Why are they being like this? Do they not like me all of a sudden? I go out into the sweet-smelling death of Summer and see Susannah settled beneath a fuchsia hedge where the sun cannot reach. There on the marshy grass, among the soft bugs and curling, light-starved buttercups, she is lying down, letting the earth give under her. She will stay here until the very last hint of light has left the sky, considering her options. When the rest of the garden is as dark as her corner, she will go in, and one of the girls will roll her a joint. It appears that when Catríona left home, she took Susannah's pulse with her. I wouldn't have expected this. I always thought that she would function fine without her mother. She and I both need our mothers, it seems. I wonder if she understands my position a little better now.

'Seems like good craic in there.'

I say to her, and she sits up. Perhaps I am seeing what I want to see, but she doesn't look happy.

'Yeah, they're loving it.'

'Are you? I can ask them to go if you want.'
Rather than answering me, she kisses me. Rather than panicking, I allow it for a second. It's nice to see some life in her. The girls can't see us from the living room anyway. I would like to clean the house for her and make her dinner and watch the television with her for the night. I would like to take care of her, the way she takes care of me. When I stop kissing her, she gets up and goes into the house without a word. Perhaps she doesn't want to be taken care of. Obediently, I follow her. I feel so out of place among the girls today. It's like being fifteen again. Maria calls out to Susannah, offering to pour her a drink.

'No, you're grand. Make one for yourself though.'

Susannah says, coming into the room. When Maria sees me come in behind Susannah, she puts the bottle down.

'Actually, I think it's time we head off.'

She looks me up and down as she talks. Maria has never treated me like this before. She is usually such a nice girl. Have I done something to upset her? There are some mumblings from the other girls, who are gathering their things to leave. Susannah doesn't try to stop them. She just goes into the kitchen, so she doesn't have to watch them leaving. It doesn't take long before they are calling out their goodbyes, promising they will be back at the same time tomorrow, and hurrying out the door. I wonder what they will do with the rest of their afternoon. I wonder why they don't want me around.

'You put them on edge.'

Susannah calls to me from the kitchen. I didn't know that about myself. I wonder if I have always put them on edge, or if it's just since they started their unending session. Does it even matter? They will come around to me again, I'm sure.

Martin asks about Susannah all the time. When he asks about her, I almost cry. Not just because she is sad and her mother has left her, but because there is nothing I can do to make her feel better. Unless I can find Catríona, wherever she has gone, and drag her back down to Croft Hall. Sometimes hours go by while I imagine searching the country for her, and all the things I would say if I found her.

When Martin picks me up in the morning, all I talk about is how the girls are behaving. It's nice to purge all my bad feelings about them. Being with him is so different to being with the girls. He is calming and gentle. He doesn't judge. While I am ranting about Maria, he holds my hand.

'She's so lucky to have you, Lucy, you're such a good friend.'

Oh, won't he stop? Why is he so good to me? Why can I not enjoy my time with him anymore? I want so terribly to go back to Susannah's. To put a hand on her neck and check for a rhythm. Instead, I am sitting in the garden with Martin. Once again, my back is against the house, his against the tree. It must all be very confusing for him, that I would kiss him and then not do a thing more about it. This evening, he wanted to take me for a drive or to the pub, but all I want to do is sit in view of my parents, on our cursed land, like a child. For a minute, with the birds singing and the rough wall on my back, I do feel like a child. Selfishly, I let myself forget what is happening in Susannah's big house, and all that has happened between us. Just for a second, I can exist without thinking, and it is so sweet. It is relief. It is the breath after tears, it is the sun on my skin. A moment of calm. And then he reaches for my hand and pulls me towards him.

I am too tired to fight it. I need my friend. Rather than do what is fair, I get up, and I sit right next to him and let him hold me still. This kindness is so cruel. I love him, even as he ruins the only peace I've known in weeks.

She stinks of cigarettes; it's so strong that I can't even romanticise it, she just smells like she doesn't care about herself. I think of her paper-thin lungs filling with smoke and browning, it's terrible. During this time of melancholy, she writes me many, many letters. Not all of them are meant for me – there are some for the girls, one for Ms O'Neill, countless for her parents – but they are all written in my name. There are stacks of them in her room, and she keeps writing more. Although I have glanced over them, she only ever gives me one.

Lucy,
Please tell Joan to stop bringing me sandwiches, it is such a waste. The bread tastes like meat, the meat tastes like water, water tastes of bone. Soon I expect I will taste of nothing but clotted blood and ash. Will you still put your mouth to me so feverishly then, when I have fully decayed?
Yours

I take her to bed. I put my mouth to her. She has soured. There are layers of dirt on my Susannah, and I love her. I will love her till her bones brown. I am taken over with relief when I see her chest rise and feel her quietly shaking: there is something in her still. The breath she lets out is so weighted, louder than the rushing of all the water in the ocean, it brings new dimensions to me. She is not numb. I could bring her back to life.

I draw a bath, so that I can keep a hand on her heart, so that she can wash away some of the last few weeks. Her head lays against my chest, the ends of our hair are black wet, like vines stuck to us.

'The letter she left...'

She starts, and I wait minutes before she revisits her sentence.

'It was like a legal letter, wasn't it? Not something for a daughter.'

I don't know what to say to make it better because it's true. All I can think to do is kiss the back of her head, the hair there thin from the weight of the water.

'It's so embarrassing. Why didn't she want to stick around with me?'

She asks so quietly that I'm not sure she is asking me. She speaks it into the bath water.

'Lucy, please tell me you're nearly ready to leave. I can't manage much longer here.'

Oh, she would be gone. If not for me, she would already have left Crossmore and saved herself.

I will never be ready. I will keep her waiting forever, and she will wait, because she loves me. I am evil, I have said this. The guilt lies between each of my ribs, it has a tighter hold on me than she does, it grows all over my body like mould. If she leaves it up to me, we won't ever leave Crossmore. We will die here, shrivelled up by fear, separate from one another.

'Love you.'

'Love you more.'

She turns the tap with her toe and lets more hot water in.

18

THE SUN IS GOING DOWN. I am running out of time. Very soon, I will have to decide whether I am brave enough to be with her. To be with her is a sin, to be without her is a tragedy.

Since I have known her, Susannah has been a flame in bloom. She took me from ash and made me human. I fear if she spends one more day in the garden, her flame will dwindle, and to ash I will return. She cannot wait any longer for me to be brave. If I don't choose her, she will not wait around. I know this, I know this, I know. And still a naive part of me thinks that since we have made it this far, we will make it forever. If we existed for even a second, we could exist eternally. That might be too romantic to be true. She has existed without me before, she could do it again. Doesn't she realise that I may never be ready to bloom like her? Doesn't she feel me shaking with fear? What I need is her help. All she gives me is pressure. Oh, this fatal, impending freedom, which will give her all she has ever wanted and snatch away all I have ever needed. I used to think that she was just a bruise, a nice sort of pain that would fade away to nothing. That was all wrong.

If I choose Susannah, I will be left motherless. I have seen what being motherless can do to a person. Surely Susannah wouldn't want me to go through what she has been going through. If my brothers and father were to deny me, distant as they are, I could not cope. If the girls were to go from me – and they would go – I could not live. The girls who raised me, and whom I raised. After everything, they would not hesitate to disappear. Even with the soil that we grew from still under our fingernails and the same wind burning our cheeks, they would not wait a heartbeat. They would just go, and with them, my soul would go too.

It's overwhelming. Susannah pushes me so gently I could fall to my death. I wish I would.

I want to be with her. She is the first and last thing that I want, but she is not the only thing. And there are so many more things that she wants, and so many more things that she deserves, but I am the only thing that she has left. That keeps coming back to me – if not for me, who does she have? My God, all this love has broken my heart. It's just too much to decide. All I want is to go back to a time before I knew there was anything around me, back to our tiny sheltered world, when all I had to worry about was looking nice and getting to school on time. I would sacrifice my whole life just to relive last September.

At home, wheels have started turning ferociously fast, and Mother is anxious for me to commit myself to Martin and for him to take me out of Crossmore, far away from Susannah O'Shea. Every day she reveals herself to be appallingly old fashioned.

'I heard Jim McNamara's girl is getting married on Saturday.'

She says to Granny, knowing that I am listening. She goes on,

'What was her name again? Nina? Niamh!'

Granny replies,

'That poor girl – and what she put her parents through!'

'Well, it just goes to show it's never too late to turn your life around. Sometimes all it takes is the right man.'

It's like they rehearsed the whole conversation. Their light accents float around me like a lovely, familiar song. It's hard to listen to, but so nice to hear, and I close my eyes and let them talk while I sit at the table, and I think of Niamh McNamara.

Then they stop talking, and I feel them looking at me. When I open my eyes, there is Martin at the back door. I wish he would ask before coming over. Now I must leave Susannah alone for the evening without warning.

He has come to take me away again, down to another field, for another evening of sitting under the perfect country sky. It's hard, because I would love to let Martin look after me tonight if it wasn't going to be so romantic. I'd rather be in the damp shadows of Susannah's garden, catching a cold, with my hand near hers. Instead, he drives me away from the farm, to sit on the gate of a field that belongs to another family. The late sun has made everything pink. When the sky looks like this, it's hard to believe that the Summer is ever going to end. That end is rushing towards us. And still Crossmore will be stunning. I hate that he has brought me here, my sour heart is ruining the lovely field.

'It's so nice, isn't it? I always took it for granted when I was small.'

He says, and looks at me. I don't know why he is making small talk with me, it's not as if we are strangers. Why does he get like this? He keeps looking out to the field that he thinks is so nice, rather than at me. He is not himself, he is nervous. All I ever do is make him nervous.

'Sure, where else would you want to be?'

I say, just so that I have said something, although I mean it. Where else is nicer than Crossmore in the Summer? I sit on the gate; he leans up against it from the other side. My hands are next to his head. I don't know why, I can't explain it, but something makes me reach out and put my hand through his hair. I just want to show him we are together, I want to feel close to him, close to the ground, because he is my friend, and I have felt so out of control lately. There is the deep thought line in his forehead. What has he been thinking about? Is it me that has been troubling him? I realise too late how he will interpret my hand in his hair, and I know that I might as well be stroking an animal I've tamed. It settles him, just for a second. I didn't realise just how nervous he was until he exhaled and I felt his breath rush against my thigh. The hedge at the edge of the field is coated in the rust-and-soil colours of new blackberries. I would like to jump off the gate and pick one; instead, I just look at them. I think he might want to ask me to concentrate on him, and not the hedge. Perhaps he will go and pick one for me. Instead he looks up at me.

'I'd say I'm going to college, Lucy. I got my course.'

The way he says it, it's like he's telling me that someone has died, like it's heavy news to deliver. Martin is going to college. Perhaps I will be without him for a while. Oh dear.

'I told your dad I'm going.'

It sounds like he is telling me this through water, his voice so far away and unintelligible. It's like he doesn't want to say it, like he doesn't want to go. And I understand it. Leaving is so hard. Even when there's nothing here, it's so hard to go. I only half hear him until he says,

'Are you coming with me?'

This I hear. This I feel, like a sharp stabbing in my chest. I almost fall backwards off the gate. I almost say yes. He puts his hand on mine, and I can't bring myself to look at him.

Okay, alright, get down off the gate and just talk to him. So I get down off the gate. He stands on one side, and I stand on the other. I look at him; his hand stays on mine. Now that he has offered, I don't know how I can refuse. He won't wait before asking my parents, there won't be time for an excuse. I don't even know which college he is talking about. Where is he asking me to go? The way he looks at me now, it's exactly how Susannah looks at me. Exactly the same, only I cannot feel it. My God, my heart, what I wouldn't give to love this man. The way he loves me is so beautiful. He can see that he has made a big offer, and that he has scared me.

'Just think about it, love.'

It's all that I can think about, even when he tries to change the subject. I spend the whole evening pretending to listen. If I had been with Susannah tonight, he couldn't have asked me to move away with him. Maybe he would have asked tomorrow, but I could have had one more night without it. I should be spending all my nights with Susannah, not hanging around Martin and his car. My mind is racing, because I cannot think of a single way that I could get out of this. To Mother, to Dad, to everybody, there isn't any reason why I shouldn't go away with Martin. I have one perfect reason, and I cannot give her to them. I need a cigarette, but Martin does not smoke.

When he leaves me at my back step, he takes a letter out of his pocket and gives it to me, and I hate how easily he has intruded on mine and Susannah's secret language. He thinks it is a very thoughtful way to reach me, because he's seen me writing so many letters. And I suppose it is thoughtful. Maybe he only wrote it because he thought he wouldn't have the nerve to ask me to my face. When saying goodnight, he kisses me very softly, like he loves me too much to leave a mark on me. I let him kiss me, of course I do. And then he goes, and I am alone at the back door.

Lucy,
I want you to come away with me. We need a chance to be together, just us. You deserve a fresh start, somewhere new, where you aren't stifled. A place that deserves you.
I'll talk to your parents – they will want you to come with me.
Lucy, my love, we need to stop pretending that we weren't made for each other.
Martin

If I were another girl, in another life, this offer would be irresistible. If he gets to my parents, then I will have no choice but to be that girl and make that other life my life. How sweet it would all be if I could just make it work with him. Martin comes with plenty of land, good land, without rocks. I could do a lot worse. He treats me so well, he would give me the world. Susannah would give me the world. I don't need to convince myself that I love her. I don't need to convince anybody but myself that I love Martin. This is hateful. If everybody loved me as much as they claim to, I don't think I would be in this position, back and forth between them like a pendulum, always stuck between her and everything else in the world. I am so sick I could scream.

The last of August is peeling off my shoulders, revealing softer skin for the Autumn to destroy. It seems cruel that the Summer should leave me in a way as physical as this. There is a mess of clothes so large on the landing of Croft Hall that I cannot see the carpet, that I cannot stand near Susannah. On Thursday, Phil is taking her to Paris to celebrate her wonderful exam results. I don't think he knows how many points she got in her Leaving Cert. It's just a grappling attempt to compensate for her mother's new absence, and to distract from his countless ongoing absences. She is piecing outfits together. Even in her Irish clothing, she is sure that she could be the best-dressed woman in Paris. In the long mirror she has pulled into the hall, she holds a blouse to her body, then drops it on the ground again without much enthusiasm. She is still ghostly, but packing a suitcase has given her a greater sense of purpose than I have been able to. Leaning over the clothes, not wanting to step on all her precious pieces, not wanting to ruin this pleasant interruption in her gloomy mood, I hand her the letter from Martin.

When she has read it, her hands move to crumple it into a ball, but something stops her. Perhaps she thinks I love the letter and want it saved. Perhaps she realises that she is not the only person who wants me. It is dropped to the floor, and suddenly, there is life in her once more. All it took was a scrap of paper in Martin's handwriting. The ghostliness goes from her. The colour rushes back to her face, her irises are eaten up by her pupils – she wants his blood. Merciless Susannah, I have missed you.

'He can forget it. I'm sick of him. I'm sick of Crossmore. You're the only good thing here, and you're miserable. We need to just go.'

Ah, this refrain.

'Go where, Susannah? And how?'

Stepping on her clothes, she comes close to me, she takes my hands. It's supposed to be sweet, but I feel her clammy fingers. I feel their grip. It's desperate.

'Wherever you want! Dublin, or London, even America, I don't care – I can afford it now, let's just go!'

Frustrated, she puts a hand to my collar, perhaps trying to calm herself with my pulse, perhaps willing herself not to choke me. If I deny her this, I will lose her. I would sooner face the Devil than lose her. When I am without her, I feel nothing but sadness, I do nothing but look at the clock and wait for her to come back. When she looks at me, a simple look, I am newly stunned by the ways that she can look. Sweet Susannah, where I am a burnt-out star, you are the sun. All I want is to tell her the ways I adore her, and yet I know that to do anything but have this argument would be insulting. Her arms come around my shoulders.

'Imagine, a big city where nobody knows us. We could get a flat and our own jobs, and we wouldn't have to be a secret anymore. Just you and me. Why not? Just tell me why not.'

Wet-eyed, she is so full of hope, and yet absolutely hopeless. Not allowing me a chance to say no, she carries on.

'We could do anything if it's just you and me.'

Although it sounds unlikely, Susannah is never wrong. She ought to know that I am never brave. I am actively missing my chance, I am watching as everything slips away from me. Taking all the good in the world and all the light in my life, I pack it up tight and throw it away. I lift her arms off me. She is a sun too hot to enjoy.

'I can't.'

'You can! You can, because I can, and I can only do it if you can.'

Already her fingerprints have disappeared from my collar, gone fast, like smears of the day moon. I am so tired of disappointing her, of justifying this.

'Susannah, I can't go through this again. What about the girls, and Mam and Dad, and my brothers? I don't want to lose them. You already lost your family, don't make me lose mine.'

Perhaps that was too cruel. Perhaps she will respond to cruelty. She doesn't remind me that I have already lost the girls. They haven't been on my side in weeks. It is too sad to think about. Susannah is the only one of them left who wants me around. I might be the person that she wants, but – at least right now – I am not the person that she needs. I repeat this again and again until the words are not words, they are like a Communion prayer committed to memory. All those prayers that I still cannot understand.

'If you'd lose them over this, then maybe you never had them at all.'

We could have this argument for the rest of our lives. This circle of dissatisfaction is unbreaking and ever growing. I fear that all our glimmering chances are gone. It is not the heat of her love that I feel, it is the flames of our reckoning. Let me breathe a minute.

A childish part of me is sad enough to think that we could carry on. If we are clever, and very determined, we could make this work, and we would not be reduced to a bleak memory. The rest of my life could be something to look forward to, if she was only willing to bend to the point of breaking.

SUNBURN

Turning back to her clothes, she lets her words hang in the air, hoping I will have the courage to say something worth hearing. And although I want to say something to make this better, all I can do is stare at her reflection in the long mirror. There is her acne, exposed, a litter of spots clinging to her jaw. Susannah, I would be a yellow spot on your jaw, I would be a moth in the wardrobe or a stain on your clothes, let me be anything as long as I am your special, secret thing. I haven't changed at all. Even after everything, I am just a subordinate friend who is obsessed with her. This is not what she wants to hear.

Rolling her perfect eyes, to stop them from watering further, she gets back to packing her suitcase, taking a dress from the floor. I must be stupid to think we could end up happy, as though I have never made her sad. When everything is this fragile, it's easy to convince myself that all the hideous ways I behave are for her. That everything I have done since I was fifteen has been for her. Like this awful thing I am about to say is for her.

'I just need Mother to think that Martin and I are moving in the right direction.'

I begin, and her face drops. She scoffs. If I had only written this in a letter, it might sound different. Those romantic letters which have kept her sedated and believing that I am worth the pain I cause. Speaking the words is not the same, I don't have a hope of convincing her. Outside, the evening is falling into the night, I can feel the last of the sun's heat around us as it slowly drops below the horizon. Soon all the light will be gone, and I will be left with nothing but the burning, suffocating heat of an August night.

'I'm not sharing you with him anymore. It's now or never, Lucy.'

Even fading, it is too hot, her feelings are too hot. She nears me, she stands before me. I look everywhere but at her. In the mirror, I see her matted hair, tied up. I focus on the tangles. She raises a hand to touch me, but she cannot bring herself to do it. My chest feels cavernous, as though she is retreating from all the space that she takes up inside me. Her hand falls back down. If she would only touch me, if we could only share a thought, then she would know all my agony. She only breathes on me. All the heat of August around us, all the cold of her breath, and my body aching where she will not touch it. This is when I should kiss her and fan the flames of our quiet shame. This is when I should bring her back into my darkness.

'I think we could make it work, Susannah, if we just make a plan. It will just take two or three months, but when I'm settled in the city, I promise I'll finish with Martin. And you could come up then, and we could just, like, you know, be together. You and me, together.'

It all sounds so unlikely that I can hardly get the words out. She tries to say something, she tries to sigh, but I have used up all her patience. Instead, she turns around to her clothes again and tries on a top. I steal a look at her blessed stomach, bare for a moment in the mirror. When she is dressed and sees that I am staring, she glares at me. That is her body, gone from me. She is no longer mine to look at.

There is a grumbling outside, an engine revs, and she knows without looking that it is Martin, come to take me away from her. Our time is almost up; she knows I will get in his car.

Something has changed. We are not the people that we used to be. Sometime over the last year, we grew in different directions. To look at her would ruin me, and still, for one brave and guiltless second, I turn to look at her. All of her. And I see that her sunlight is still blooming. With or without me, she will go on blooming, she will always be a glorious thing. I would rather lose everything than lose her. I realise this too late, and she says to me,

'I'm fairly sick of your plans, Lucy. Do you not think I deserve a little better? Why don't you try this one without me.'

That is her heart, gone from me. That is my final breath of air, my induction to a life without Susannah O'Shea. I feel my soul is damned to Hell.

That's it. There's nothing else to say. What a simple end to such a complicated story. I run out of the house, I leave my beating heart on her porch. Just for a second, I stare at the setting sun and feel her watching me from the window. By the time she gets back from Paris, I will be in the city. When I get in the car with tears in my eyes, Martin asks me why I'm crying. I have to laugh, and smile, and say,

'I'm just gonna miss everyone so much!'

Without any respect for the sanctity of her garden, where I fell in love and where I am leaving all my love, he leans over and kisses me. The engine revs once more, the horn beeps, and Martin tears out of the gate. I turn to see the tiny blur of her in the window, fading away. Too late I realise that she has been the Summer of my life. What a slow and painful death this shall be.

Now, as he speeds through the backroads, I realise that I have absolutely nothing left but Martin. Everybody else has fallen away, it feels they are growing more distant by the minute. How long will it take for the girls to forget what my house smells like, for Granny to forget the sound of my laugh? How long will it take for Mother to heal from me? The only one left is Martin, and I have no choice but to be dragged up to the city behind him, and hope that he doesn't get tired of me when we arrive.

19

JUNE 1994

IT ALL SEEMS SO LONG ago now. When Martin dropped me home that day, Mother had already started gutting my bedroom, as though it had never been mine. Expecting I would challenge her, Mother said,

'You might as well go with him, Lucy. There's nothing here for you anymore.'

Somehow, she made it sound like advice, although I knew it was a warning. She will never know all the ways that she was right. It felt like it was all decided without me, and suddenly, I was glad. If I had spent another moment in Crossmore, I might have lost my mind.

It was not difficult saying goodbye to the girls after all. I promised to visit home after a month, and they promised to come to Dublin for Halloween. They might have meant it, I did not. The deposit was paid on the flat, the car boot was bursting with our bags, the tank was filled with petrol. The day we left, as Susannah had her picture taken outside a museum in Paris, Mother became a small dotty shape in the wing mirror, and I hated her with every molecule of my body. That was the last time I was home. I hardly think of Susannah anymore now. Only at bedtime, and in the mornings, and on hot days, when I wonder what she is wearing.

Besides Martin, and Mother's voice in the telephone, I don't have any connections to Crossmore. I haven't heard a word from any of the girls since the week I left. Things fall apart when you grow up.

Our flat is small: the kitchen is the living room, and the bedroom is a little box off that with dark maroon walls. The last people who lived here left a lot of throws and sheets behind, which saved us from buying a duvet but also means the bed can never really be made properly. If I'd had a choice, I would have bought us all new bedding. We are saving up for a coffee table now; maybe after that we will get new bedding. Isn't my life plain now? The bathroom is so small that I can sit on the toilet and put my feet in the shower at the same time. We buy the same scented toilet paper that used to be in Catríona's bathroom. I always thought my house in Crossmore was small – maybe that was just because there were three generations living there. That house is enormous compared to this flat. The size doesn't matter so much when all we do is sleep in it.

Every morning, Martin brings a cup of tea into bed for me, and says, 'Morning, love.'

Then I get kissed, and he lies next to me. From the outside, it would seem that everything has fallen into place.

On our first night here, I was so afraid to get into bed with Martin, because I didn't know what he would expect from me. Sex was never something we discussed, because he didn't want to scare me off, and I didn't want to put ideas in his head. But the flat only has one bed, it could not be avoided forever. Perhaps back in Crossmore, perhaps if we were still teenagers, then I could have been coyer. But when we got to the city, we were suddenly a big age, neither of us even nineteen. Secretly, I planned to make him sleep on the couch that first night, but then the flat was surprisingly cold, and I felt so lonely that I couldn't have slept alone. When he got into the bed, I clung to him so tightly, like a little sister might. The way I shivered must have made him feel wonderful, so big and brave. And I admit that, even now, I feel safer when he puts his arm around me. It was silly, because we could have gotten in the car that night and been in Crossmore before the morning. But I had never been so far from the village, and I needed to smell the farm on him before it wore off. I didn't expect to miss that smell so much. When I told him that, he laughed and squeezed my shoulders and told me that it was no sort of smell to miss.

After only a week here, I got a job in a café. Considering my CV was essentially empty, I was very proud of myself. It's nice to fill the days while Martin is at college. The owner's niece, Geraldine, was my first friend in the city. She is French. When we first met, I wanted to ask her if she had seen Susannah in Paris. Martin got a job at a pub in town. When we got our first payslips, we celebrated with a bottle of prosecco from the supermarket, and he made love to me with such exuberance that I almost felt it. If I had kept up my celibacy any longer, he might have proposed to me to break it. It seemed then that having sex with him would be easier than marrying him. Now I'm not sure. It isn't anything like the sex I've had before. That's not a bad thing, it's just not as enjoyable. It's more like a favour that I don't really mind doing for him. It's complicated. I don't like it, but it does make me feel close to him. The very first time it happened, he told me,

'I've actually never done this.'

He was almost afraid to see me naked. Perhaps he didn't want to shine a light on his fantasy, in case I wouldn't be what he had hoped. I was trying to be another person, the sort who could be with Martin in a real way, and so I had to ease both our nerves. To make him feel better, I said,

'I've never slept with a boy before.'

He took that to mean I was a virgin too, and that there was nothing to live up to. Unaware of the standard of excellence that Susannah had set, we stumbled through the first few times together. It was all very painful. He is yet to reach Susannah's heights.

Tonight he comes home smelling of sweat and the pub, and unshowered, he makes space for himself inside me. In the half-dark, I look to the ceiling and make out the faces of salvation in the damp. Mother, Maria, Deirdre, darlings, if you ever cared about me at all, won't you come and take me away from this place? Maria Kealy, Ave Maria, please, is this the path you meant to put me on? Please, tell me how it came to this. Why did I have to turn my back on myself? My mind wanders so far when Martin is doing what he must do.

When he finishes, he gathers me up and holds me very close to him, and tells me,

'I love you.'

That is my absolution. It's fine. When he has gone to sleep, I cry. It's only a reflex. It's only my watering eyes. I really don't mean it – in fact, I hardly even notice it. I really don't mind having sex with him, I just don't like it. Even sleeping, he holds me tightly. His blood recirculates, his head clears, he is my man, as I know him, as I have always known him. Something in the tightness of his grip is soothing. The awful longing can be forgotten again until tomorrow night, when a long day of work will bring the beast back.

Except for those moments, I adore Martin. The complexities of my feelings have simmered. I know that I love him, that's enough. To categorise my love as romantic or platonic – or strategic – would be an unnecessary pain. There are few people who know me for who I really am: only Geraldine and the friends she has given me. They are subtle, patient people, they are not rushing me to figure myself out.

The most alluring of these friends is Evelyn Smith. I have become something of a pet to her, and I am so glad, because without a guiding hand I am no good. Sometimes she is so quick with solutions that it feels as though she has lived my entire life already. She is like how Maria used to be, keeping me on my path, only she has let me choose my own.

When I first met her, I felt myself let go of a breath I had been holding since I left Crossmore. All night I listened while she dropped pieces of her life for me to pick up – like that she used to live in America, and that she has her own apartment, and that she sells pottery, and that she could save me. Walking home that night, I hung off Martin, and knowing that I was drunk, he picked me up and spun me around. Nobody noticed, nobody cared.

'Did you meet Evelyn? Isn't she amazing?'

And he said, not half as drunk as me,

'She's Geraldine's friend, yeah? She's grand, bit quare.'

That word is not used in the city, not the same way it is used in Crossmore. It's nice hearing words from home, even if they are unkind. Things like that make me miss the country so much.

We are in the middle of another sparkling Summer. The long days put a hunger in me. This evening, in work, Geraldine brings me into the walk-in fridge. She wants help lifting some boxes. As we kneel on the cold floor, I feel her looking at me. This happens now and again, more often since I told her I used to have a girlfriend. It's like she is trying to create tension; she feels the hunger of deep Summer too. These days I am really trying to be a new, less self-involved person, so I ignore her mostly. But oh, this tension. Today, for the first time in a long time, I follow my bad instincts, and as she goes to pull out the boxes, I lean closer to her, I look the way she has been looking. Have I imagined the tension? Does she feel the cold clouds of my breath fall on her? Suddenly, she stops, and looks at me over her shoulder, her face nearer to mine than it has been before. This close up, I can see each crack in her lips. It only lasts a moment, a serious moment, but I think she could kiss me. This feeling is unmistakable, and I lean closer, looking from her cracked lips to her eyes. Then she stops, straightens her back so she is far from me again. How close we drifted, how quickly I abandoned my good behaviour.

'Just checking something.'

What she was checking, I know, was how I would react to having her so near. My heart sinks, because I liked it. It has been some time since I felt that sort of magnetism. Long ago, when I realised I could not fully fall in love with Martin, I decided never to fall in love again. Something as small as Geraldine leaning towards me could spark a fire in a person as fragile as I am. My life is sufficiently confusing without adding more feelings to it.

After work, I am glad to leave. I go straight to Evelyn's, unsure whether to let her know what did not happen in the walk-in fridge. Since she knows how unresponsive I am in my relationship, it might be nice to say that I felt an urge today. When I arrive, her living room is already clouded with warm white smoke. She puts a pipe in my hand as soon as I come through the door. This will make me talkative to an impolite degree. We sit on the sofa, I let her talk about her day, about work and the date she has planned for Saturday night. She is just as close to Geraldine as I am, perhaps it wouldn't be tactful to let her know what I felt today. There is no need for me to decide what to do, because she asks me,

'Who do you fancy right now?'

It makes me laugh. Aren't we a bit old for this? It's obvious that she is only asking on behalf of Geraldine. They must have planned this all out. Do we ever really grow out of girlhood?

'Obviously don't say Martin! Don't worry, I won't tell.'

She giggles, she is rarely this sweet. She doesn't stop.

'And obviously, it can't be a boy.'

Why doesn't she just ask me to say Geraldine? Evelyn is twenty-five years old, she should not be playing these games. But it's funny. I'm stoned, and I like these games. I can play too. If she's teasing me, I will tease her. So I won't say Geraldine. Who is a girl that I fancy?

'Susannah O'Shea.'

Oh dear. I've shocked myself. Suddenly, I feel too high. Why do I always let myself go too far? I want to open the windows and feel cold air on me. What have I said? Her eyes widen, and she laughs. Of course, she was not expecting this. How do I smooth this over?

'And who is Susannah O'Shea? Why have I never heard of her?'

Why not be honest? It is exhausting to haul secrets around all the time. Secrets that nobody is asking me to keep. Why do I weigh myself down so voluntarily? The way that people react to me is out of my control, I know this. Why not just tell the truth, and see what happens?

'That's my ex from school. Remember, I told you a bit about her.'

'You hardly still fancy her.'

A pause. I have come this far.

'I do.'

It's strange to talk about her. It's strange that I considered her a lethal secret for so long. Nobody in Dublin even knows Susannah. And what is Evelyn going to say? She has known me long enough, her chance to judge me is gone.

'Girl, you need to get over her.'

She says, like it's all cool. Like it doesn't go very deep at all. If I don't want it to go deep, it doesn't have to. I could leave it all behind. I could.

'I can't. I'll never get over her, you know?'

And she does know. At one time or another, everybody falls irreparably in love. Nobody ever really gets over it. As I am searching for more to say, Evelyn asks,

'Does Martin know about her?'

Must we bring Martin into this? No matter how mature I think I am, the same teenage problems seem to follow me. Perhaps they were adult problems that I faced young. If she only knew how badly I need Martin, how many cans of lemonade he bought me in school, or how many times he left the boys to walk me home. To Evelyn, he is only an inconvenient thing that stops me from being myself. But I am the inconvenient thing. I am my own biggest obstacle. I always have been.

'No, definitely not. My mother found out by accident, but nobody else ever knew. That was kind of the problem.'

And Evelyn sighs; she must empathise. Perhaps she has a difficult family too. It all reminds me of the last sad day that Susannah and I had together, on her landing. When she stood holding her hand up and not touching me. When she asked me to try this one without her. This is the thought that comes to me when I am trying to sleep at night, when I am on my own too long. Why don't you try this one without me? Why don't you stop breathing, Lucy? Why don't you see how well you get on without water or air or me?

'Do you still have proper feelings for her?'

'A bit.'

It's been so long since I've seen her, I don't know if I could honestly say I still want her, although I know undeniably that I still love her. Lovely Evelyn looks at me with pity. If I could only make this kinder.

'You should get onto her.'

Isn't she good? Isn't she encouraging? Shall I tell Evelyn all the ways that I failed Susannah? About my grotesque heart, and the wrong ways that it beats? I clench my jaw to stop from speaking too honestly or thinking too deeply.

Even saying Susannah's name feels unfair. She isn't my thing to talk about. Now she is free, I should let her stay free.

'I couldn't talk to her. It was all so sinful, it's better to just forget it.'

'Girl, there's no such thing as sin.'

Laughing, she trivialises all I have lived through, and I let her laugh.

I am the meaning of sin, I don't need her to define it for me. Let me bring us back to the virtue of Susannah before she gets me discussing indoctrination.

'I wouldn't be able to speak to her, I wouldn't have the nerve.'

And all-knowing Evelyn says,

'Sure, write her a letter. You don't even have to post it, just write it and get it all off your chest.'

Illuminated Evelyn. I take a sheet of paper from the ream on her desk, careful not to touch the computer in case I break it. The letter practically writes itself. All the while, Evelyn continues to speak, and I let her. She never judges my motives, she only wants me to be happy. That's what a good friend does, I think. Since Evelyn has let me exist as myself, I have a new love for existing.

'So you obviously don't fancy anyone else?'

She begins, trying to redirect the conversation to Geraldine. I shrug, pretending I am keeping a secret back. Perhaps I do like Geraldine. There is enough to think of before I start thinking of that. Evelyn gets up to peer over my shoulder as I write.

S,

I hope you're well. I'm really sorry for writing this letter, because I know you don't want to hear from me, but I don't have the self-control to stop myself from bothering you. I miss you a lot. There's a hedge of foxgloves near my flat that makes me think of you. I'm sorry for all the things I do and all the things I didn't do. I really hope you are well.

I've been in Dublin the last two years. It's better than home, and still I miss home so much. I'm always thinking about Crossmore, about us, and how there was a time that you would get ready to see me. You used to make an effort because you wanted to impress me. I was always endlessly impressed by you.

There isn't anything left of me but the useless blood my heart keeps circulating. You can have all of it, if you want. I have no use for it now. I hope the sun is shining very brightly on you. I think of you every day. Still yours,
L

Knowing it is not her business, and knowing I will not stop her, Evelyn takes the letter from me and reads it plainly. To anybody but Susannah, it might seem too morbid to be considered romantic; I can tell this is true by the way Evelyn raises her eyebrows. Perhaps it is clear now that I have more than a few unresolved feelings for Susannah. The letter is put in an envelope, just for the sake of privacy. Then, only because I have been smoking, I address it to Croft Hall and put it in Evelyn's handbag.

'Throw it in the postbox if you're passing. Don't hassle yourself, though, if you can't find a stamp.'

It's up to Evelyn now, not me. I am not really sending her a letter. I am not reaching out. Croft Hall is probably empty now anyway. A part of me hopes that Susannah is far away from Crossmore. Another part of me hopes that she is still sinking into the marsh of her garden, the same as when she loved me. I want her to read the letter, and I don't. I want her to be reminded of me, but not all the ways that I broke her heart. Perhaps she could read it many years from now, when I have changed so much that I cannot even locate myself.

I get home to Martin when my eyes brighten up. He doesn't like me getting high without him. He says it's because he doesn't like me walking home alone like that, but I wonder if it's because he's jealous of me having fun without him. He has left dinner for me. There were days when I used to complain about rationing three pork chops between seven people. Now I could probably make three pork chops last a fortnight. Even when I had nothing, I was spoilt. When Martin cooks, everything is boiled in one pot. It's a taste of home.

'Not bad, ha?'

He says, stopping to kiss my cheek as he darts around getting ready for work. The smell of his aftershave when he passes makes me feel safe, it makes me feel like a child. The potatoes are hard in the middle, the broccoli is limp. He must work on his timing. Still I eat every morsel. I don't ever want to appear unappreciative. Why did I bother coming home if he is going out to work? While I am licking my knife clean, he shouts from the bedroom that I missed a call from Maria Kealy; my heart skips a beat. A part of me hopes that he is lying.

Before today, I was doing really well. I had more or less moved on with my life. Susannah was just a fleeting agony that I was learning to repress. Now I feel the way I did the day I left Crossmore. Tonight I find myself looking for her scent in the air, her touch in the pillowcase. It's a strain to find meaning where there is none. It's such a teenaged thing to do, why can I not stop doing it? Not everything is a symbol. Sometimes the world is plain and obvious. Sometimes the things I feel and the things I want don't matter.

In the morning, I return Maria's call. When I first got to the city, the girls and I talked a lot. Then it became less and less, until we stopped altogether. They are always too busy to speak. I am busy too. Now the dial tone fills me with butterflies. Please, let me hear my sister's voice once more. It rings and rings, and I know that Maria is not going to take my call, and that nobody is going to call me back. Sometimes I wonder if Martin lies about these missed calls so I don't feel forgotten about. I shouldn't bother embarrassing myself, but I leave a message on the answering machine.

A week comes and goes, and another, and as predicted, I don't hear from Maria. Weeks keep coming until a month passes, and I am left with a lead weight in my stomach. All I can think of is the letter I sent to a house Susannah isn't even in. It's hard not be demolished by the thought of her, because I live in a body that has loved her and I see with eyes that have witnessed her. She is part of my muscles, my tissue, she is unforgettable. Presumably, if she ever remembers me, it is only when she catches a perfume that is vaguely familiar, and it takes her hours to recognise it as mine. I bet she laughs because she hasn't thought of me in a long time and then puts my memory away again, folded up in a drawer in the back of her mind.

If only I wasn't a perpetual teenager, I might get used to being without her. I might have listened when she told me that she wouldn't be satisfied to stay a secret forever. The earth deserves to know her, she is too bright to hide. Heaven and Hell should know her. We should all be versed in the joys and sorrows of her. I did this to myself. I was selfish. I was not proud enough.

20

AUGUST 1994

I WISH I COULD GO back a few weeks, to before I was pulled backwards. Thinking of her has cut me in half. It is bothering everybody. Even Martin is beginning to lose a little of his infinite patience.

At last we have saved up enough to buy our coffee table. Standing in the furniture shop, we weigh up two options. Isn't this a grown-up way to spend our Sunday morning? We don't go to Mass in the city. We found that without being dragged there, we had no desire to go. It's been nice to sleep in and do what we want with our Sundays. Martin felt guilty about this at first, but now I think he likes sleeping in too.

Both tables are probably bigger than we have space for, but I'm sick of leaving our tea on the floor while we watch television. I can't cope with him knocking over one more mug. It was charming the first two or three times, but now I am worried that he has stained the carpet so deeply that we won't get our deposit back. Then, where do I think I'm going that I would need that deposit back?

We are getting an expensive coffee table, so that it will last. Putting aside a few pounds each week has been a nice project. It has given us a point to get to, although now we are here, it's not as rewarding as I had hoped. Stupidly, I had expected that this might fix the void inside me, but it turns out coffee tables don't do that. It was just another way of getting through the weeks. After this, we should have to save up for something extravagantly expensive, and really make it last. Susannah would just buy a coffee table, no saving, no consideration. Perhaps she would miss out on the satisfaction of earning something, but at least she wouldn't spend months putting her faith in something dull. She would know about an antique dealer, she would get something impossibly cool.

'It's just, that one is so low, we might as well keep putting stuff on the floor.'

Martin says, pointing at one of our two options, and I realise I have missed all his list of positives and negatives because I was thinking about her. I huff, only because I am annoyed at myself, but he takes it the wrong way.

'Sure, I'm only being honest.'

And he goes on to talk about the next table. Look at his forearms, permanently tanned from years on the farm. Look at his hands, rough from the work. One day, when we go back to Crossmore, will this table come with us? We are going home eventually. When he takes the farm over from his father, or when he finishes college; whenever Martin says so, we are going home. And this table could come with us. Suddenly, I realise what a contract a coffee table is. It isn't just the money, it's everything. We might have this table until we die. Buying furniture is just another thing holding us together. So perhaps we should buy more. Or perhaps we shouldn't even buy this.

'It's such an investment.'

I'm speaking more to myself than to him.

'The table?'

Why have I chosen this moment to start thinking?

'Yeah, the table, yeah. Are we really sure? Should we wait another bit?'

And I see his eyes widen for a second, as though we aren't talking about a coffee table, but marriage or children or our wills.

'Don't worry, it's only a table.'

He laughs and puts an arm around me, like this is a relaxing and casual situation to be in. He wouldn't care if we were talking about children. They will come. In time, we will have to have all these conversations, and he is not afraid of them.

He chooses the low-down coffee table, because he thinks that I like it better. He pays the man, he carries it out to the car, he drives us home. I stay at his side the whole time, like we are a nice young couple excited to be starting a life together. I suppose we are. I'm not unhappy. Everyone believes what we project. When we get home, I won't let him put his feet on the table, or his dinner plate. I won't let him lean me over it. I won't even let him put his mug of tea on it. I just think we need to keep it nice for a while, just in case we decide to return it and split up and never speak to each other again. Even though he is annoyed, he lets me get away with it like always, because Martin cannot get cross at me, even when I make him cross. I can't imagine how he is happy, but look how he smiles.

Every day my thoughts grow heavier. I was stupid to think I could make friends and buy furniture and forget her. Before that letter, before Maria's missed call, Susannah only passed through my mind once a day. Now she is inescapable. The thought of her is weighted, and scented, and heated. She is the drip of the tap that keeps me awake at night, the roar of traffic that wakes me up in the morning. Have I so little emotional capability that I am welcoming this familiar ache back? I feel like I am a teenager again.

And I remember years ago, when Eimear told us that to get over somebody, you must get under somebody else. I remember thinking she was crass, but probably right. Let's find out if she was right.

At work, I watch Geraldine as she ices the éclairs, and I let her catch me. She could be the thing that I get under. All it takes is a few long looks for her to invite me over after work. The roof of my mouth aches. In her bedroom, she leans close to me, like she's done before, and because I am tired of dying, I lean close to her.

'Don't make a habit of this.'

She says, her accent thick in her throat. What a beautiful respite she is, such a welcome interruption to getting stoned and sighing. I take everything she offers me: a glisten of hair on her abdomen, a slew of whispered curses. I can't say if she does this differently to Irish girls, but she does it differently to the one that I've had. The change is therapeutic, it's so wonderful to get a break from Martin's body. And although it makes me churn for Susannah's old way of loving, I am so glad to be shown something new. To have feelings of attraction that are totally separate to Martin or Susannah. I have never had something like that. Afterwards Geraldine lights a thin cigarette and lies on her back, offering me the box. She isn't looking to be held or loved, and I'm so glad because I wouldn't know how.

Only when I am leaving, I realise what I have done. How has it taken me until now to realise that I have just cheated on Martin? After everything, how could I have done that to him? It really is like being a teenager again, having no regard for anybody but myself. My God, won't the city please just swallow me up, so I don't have to worry about this? Won't a bus just sweep me under its wheels? Maybe Susannah would hear about it, wherever she is.

When I get home, my key is sticky in the lock. I am so glad Martin isn't home. I think if I had to face him now, I would be sick. The sink is full of dishes to be washed, there is post is piled on the welcome mat. A letter from the college and a payslip from the pub, both with 'Martin Burke' typed in bold letters, a series of leaflets and menus, and then one cream envelope, with 'Lucy Nolan' handwritten in bronze glittering ink, and I know this hand better than my own. I tear it open.

Hello heartbreak,

I hated to read that you've been sad, although I've been hoping that you would be.

Karma.

It's unsigned, there is no need. Nobody else would send me a letter like this. Nobody else would be thrilled by my sadness. I am nobody else's heartbreak. It's possibly the worst reply I can imagine, and still it puts ripples in my heartbeat. It's a reply. It's Susannah O' Shea. SOS. My soul has been saved.

How predictable we are; she knew I would smell the paper, because I knew she would spray her perfume on it. This is a far greater, deeper rush than anything I felt this evening with Geraldine.

S,

I am more than sad, I can hardly breathe. However sad you want me to be, I promise I am sadder. Let me be the thing that fulfils your hopes. Let me do whatever it takes to earn some good karma.

I'll be here, gathering dust, waiting for your reply.

L

I don't even think as I write it. When it is finished, I know for sure that I'll never get over her for the rest of my life. Her letter goes into the drawer next to my bed, where all her letters from our schooldays hide. This small exchange has brought my pulse back. Just hearing from her has made me feel so excited, so driven, so romantic. I want her here now, so I can cook her dinner and listen to her talk. I want the life I have with Martin, but with her. When I was younger, I could never understand how Mother was happy, but suddenly, I understand it. I want the reward of making us a home. I want us to be a family, in a place that we love with people that we love. The domesticity that once seemed like a prison is now a bliss to aspire to.

The ugliness, the perfection of this long day. The way I used Geraldine is an unwelcome joy. The way I am using Martin is a necessary evil. And this letter – I could talk forever about all the good and bad contained in this letter. There is nothing to do but ring Mother, and hope that she might tell me something dreadfully plain, so that my heartbeat might slow and I might sleep tonight.

After we speak, and she gets her fill of my nice, normal life, I put myself to bed and push myself into a thoughtless sleep. The night is cold. Our thin windowpanes let the clean air in. That must mean that they let the dirty air out. In the middle of the night, I am stirred from my half-sleep by Martin tumbling through the flat. He has been at the lock-in at work and quickly fills our room with the smell of drink. I sit up and try to rub my dry eyes awake, and I see him trip as he tries to take off his jeans. He so rarely gets this drunk.

'Do you want a hand?'

I ask, and get out of bed with the blanket wrapped around me. He shushes me and collapses onto the mattress. The thought line in his forehead is deeper now than it used to be. The blanket falls to the floor, and I untie his shoes and pull off his jeans.

'That's my girl.'

He says, his voice like velvet, and he moves away from me to reach into the drawer and take out my cigarettes. For a second, I forget that her letter is even there, and I am filled with panic as he reaches around for the box. In his current state, he wouldn't be able to read the letter if he found it. He can't even sit up to keep the ash from falling on his cheek, and I am afraid that this will end in me cleaning his sick off the bathroom floor. Normally, Martin wouldn't smoke.

'Whatever you want, Lucy. Just tell me whatever you want, and I'll suss it.'

This is as close to heartfelt emotion as he ever gets. This is his way of telling me that he can see I am dissatisfied, and that he wants to change it. Right now there's no point in lying to him. It won't make him feel any better. He won't remember tomorrow, I don't think. He reaches for my hand and squeezes it tight, and he smiles. Martin is content. He is on the brink of our forever, and so I put the cigarette out and let him fall asleep.

21

SEPTEMBER 1994

THE END OF SUMMER SLOWS things down. So much so that I don't even feel the centre of gravity changing. Susannah has reasserted herself as the focal point of my life, her letters coming more and more frequently. Sometimes Martin collects the post, and he holds Susannah's writing in his hands, unaware. I have always written letters; he would never think they were worth opening, he doesn't even ask who they're from. It reaches the stage where I think she must be sending one every day. Not in response to anything, but releasing everything she has held in for the last two years. Each is slightly less savage than the last.

I learn that she isn't in Crossmore anymore. She has gone to London, to live with her brother Damien. She let me send five letters to Croft Hall before telling me that her aunt isn't going to forward them anymore. She hasn't said which aunt took over the house, but it must mean that Catríona never came home.

This morning, before I go to work, Martin and I are on the sofa watching the television. He has skipped his first lecture to spend time with me. This reminds me of our sleepy Saturdays at home on Mother's sofa. The only difference is that this morning he is not afraid to pull my legs across his lap and rest his warm coffee on my knees. Any minute, this nice silence could be interrupted by the blessed post falling through the letterbox, or by Martin's want for me.

'Do you wanna call into the pub when you're done work?'

It's nice when he asks this. It makes me feel so grown-up. I wonder when feeling grown-up will stop being a novelty to me. I will meet him in the pub, and we will talk, and I will build a house of cards on the tacky surface of the bar.

Before this, I have a day of Geraldine's lingering eyes to endure. Things really are no different between us. There was always a thick tension in the air, she has always been quiet and intense. The evening we spent together in August was not our last. We often go home together, and neither of us mentions it the next day. What I originally believed to be a mutual, brief end to our separate and insurmountable problems has been proved otherwise. When Evelyn found out how many times I have slept with Geraldine, she came close to slapping me. Apparently, Geraldine is much more sensitive than she lets on. Apparently, she has told Evelyn privately that our evenings together mean a great deal to her. Soon I will regret being so cavalier with a heart as gentle as hers, so Evelyn says. I ought to feel guilty, but I don't. The feelings I have for her only exist as long as I am in her bed. When I leave, they disappear, both the good and the bad. It's cruel, but my history has proven that I am cruel – cruellest of all to those I make love to. Given time and proper attention, perhaps Geraldine would show me her sensitive side, and my impressionable heart would probably give way to it. But Susannah keeps on sending her letters, and so I don't have proper time or attention to give. This small link to her makes everything I do day to day feel inconsequential and imaginary; those letters are reality, nothing else.

Those letters are enchanting. They so easily make me forget the arch in Geraldine's back and all her unknown gentleness. For a while, Susannah was writing to me on pearlescent paper. Once just on the back of a long pharmacy receipt. Today I got a postcard which read,

Lucy,

I'm trying not to miss you. It's weird writing to you again. I want to really enjoy myself while I'm away, but I can't stop thinking back to when I was home. When I was in it, last summer seemed so important. It seemed almost like a dream. Now I think back to it and I mostly remember crying.

When writing my name, she takes her time, I can tell by the languid stutter of the ink. It is such a treat. The first time I saw it, I nearly cried. To see my name in her handwriting awakened something in me. It made me sad and happy at once.

She suggests I get an email address, and a computer, because soon she will be leaving London. Her original plan was to holiday in Mexico with Damien for a fortnight, but now they are planning to travel all across South America, her trip funded by the remainder of the inheritance that she once wanted to spend on me. It's miserable, but a part of me feels that if she wants me to stay in touch, it will be like I am leaving London with her. Although I did try to work out how long I would need to go without food to save for a computer, Evelyn told me I would starve before I could afford one. She told me just to use hers. There was a computer in my school, I'm sure we were supposed to have classes on how to use it, but we were never trusted. The classroom stayed locked. There's every chance that room was empty; if the school wouldn't turn the heating on for half the Winter, I can't imagine they had a budget for an unused computer.

Sitting at Evelyn's desk, I feel suddenly illiterate, barely able to type my own name. I have to write everything out on paper first, because I am so slow at typing that by the time I finish a sentence, I forget what I wanted to say. I loathe emails. The terrible, pixelated text missing the loops of her handwriting. The screen missing her perfume. I cannot touch paper that she has touched. I cannot get any real trace of her. I must remind myself that without the emails, I would only be a stack of letters in a desk drawer in London. The emails take me with her as she goes all the way to Tijuana. Living less than eight hours from Crossmore has left me feeling like a part of me has died; how is she taking herself across the miles of the Americas and into that heat without crumbling to dust?

Every few days, I get a new email. Something to let me know that she has made another new friend, had another lover, or done another spectacular thing. She likes to reiterate that everyone thinks she is pretty and nobody minds when she sleeps with women. It's heartbreaking, it's enraging, it fills me with regret and sends me straight to Geraldine's bedroom to be distracted.

Lucy

A few nights ago, we were invited to take ayahuasca at the beach. I think I was the only one who could handle it without having a panic attack. I felt the hot sand burning all the sadness off me, at last.

'She probably spent half the time puking, I've heard that stuff is lethal.'

Evelyn tells me, with her mouth full of food. I wish she wouldn't read over my shoulder. She wants me to see that all I am to Susannah is a taste of something familiar while she trips. She doesn't see that I don't mind that.

It's so nice to get a break from London. Everybody here loves the colour of my hair. I wish you could taste the coffee and the fruit here, I wish I could tell you how wonderful the lovers are. The sun ripens everything just right. It's the best I've ever had.

Am I stupid to wonder what she looks like now? I should be upset by what she is saying, but all I can think of is her sitting at her window, typing, or writing in a café or by a pool. Maybe she's put a little weight on, maybe she has cut her hair. Yes, I am stupid to wonder.

I tried it with a man. Julian. He is very broad, and he carries my bags for me. He lets me drive his truck. I would never have slept with a guy if I were still with you. I'm so glad I got to try it out. Maybe I'll keep doing it. Would you hate that?
Susannah

Hideous. I leave Evelyn's house and do not allow one thought to emerge the whole walk home. Julian might give her everything I could not. Let him. I come through my front door to the ringing telephone. It is Mother, looking to gossip. With such a great distance between us, we find it easy to forget the heinous parts of each other. We can just talk, untouched by her prejudice or my perversion. It's nice to feel like we are ourselves, even briefly. Even falsely. She tells me how the postman scratched the side of the car, we are both annoyed, and we both laugh. I love this phone call, this funny lie that takes me away from my sad life.

When we hang up, I am tremendously alone in the flat. I wish I was in Crossmore, to have seen the postman scratch the car myself, welcome to cling to Mother's side. I wish I had more than a pair of fizzling childhood romances. I wish I had been more to Mother than a mess to clean up. And ferociously, I regret whatever queer bump in my gestation knocked me off course, leaving me here, alone in Dublin. There has never been a moment when my heart wasn't breaking from Mother's absence. When I was young, Granny used to call me a changeling. It seemed like a joke back then. It doesn't anymore.

I need to purge all the hatred of Susannah's last email. It would be very easy to revel in the negativity. To let it sustain me. For a little while, I did, but I am too fragile for that today. I could go to Geraldine's and let her take it all away. How nice that would be.

Instead, I go down to Martin in the pub. It's like he knows I'm about to walk through the door. As though he smelled me in the air. He's only an animal, after all. A pint is poured for me; he begins to talk about something while he wanders around tidying up, and I listen. I fully absorb myself in what he is saying, because he makes little things so interesting. What a wonderful distraction he is. Great road maps of veins bulge from his arms as he lifts a tray of glasses from the dishwasher. Look at that bruise on his bicep. That is from my thumb, digging into his skin while he had sex with me. That bruise is my name on him. Something about it makes my skin crawl. His boss passes by and pats him on the back.

'Alright, bud?'

Martin says while nodding at an old man. Everybody here really likes him. He knows everyone's drinks, he can break up fights, he knows how to chat. Martin was made to be loved and shared around. Whenever I catch his eye, he winks at me, and a man at the bar says,

'He's mad about you.'

His boss lets him go home early. Walking in the city with him is nice, because he will look after us both while I enjoy the spectacle of the lights and shop windows. By habit, I hold onto his arm as we go. All of these habits are what make things so difficult. He pays for me on the bus, and he lets me sit while he stands. Only because he has been on his feet at work, I let him take the seat, and although I know it will add another breeze to the hurricane, I sit on his lap. I am stunned when he says into my hair, on a bus full of people,

'When are we gonna get married?'

He doesn't expect me to reply. I think he only said it to shock me, or excite me. All he has done is give me a good reason to leave him. I must go, or we really will end up married. At home, when he is in the shower, I try to think of a way to end our relationship without the world falling apart. When I cannot think of anything, I write my letter and pretend that I am excited for the day that he proposes.

S

A lady came into the café today, her daughter had your name, and she kept calling it. It was like my thoughts were being broadcast. It's been so long since I've heard anyone call your name. It's been so long since you were mine, I feel I don't have any claim to you anymore. The curve of your shoulders, the colour of your eyes, the sound of your sighing. These are distant things I have remembered and misremembered so many times that I no longer have a truth for them. It has been so long, and still I could have died today when that woman said your name.

The lovers here are not as you describe them in South America. Here they come with a lot of strings attached. Maybe I've just chosen the wrong ones. I suppose I come with a lot of strings attached too.

Tonight Martin asked me when we are going to get married. I am still thinking about ending things.

L

When it is done, I regret each word written. Tomorrow I will type it out and send it, and she will be disappointed to read that I still don't have the courage to leave Martin.

The time between days grows longer. This year, there isn't much romance in the burnt colours of the leaves or the trees they leave naked. This year, they are just dying things. The cold mornings don't thaw out, the air bites at me all day. But then, among the decay, there are brilliant flashes of light: nights walking in the city with Martin, when I am grateful to have him as my best friend; mornings at Evelyn's house, when everybody has cleared out and we can talk about the night before; the pale brown of Geraldine's eyes as she stares me down in work. These small things help my days pass far easier. They keep me from thinking of Susannah. But then I am reminded with a letter that she is more than a flash of light. She is the sun, she always has been.

Lucy,

We were in a chapel today in Guadalajara. It's the first time I've been in a chapel since leaving Ireland. The Virgin Mary here is a tanned brunette, isn't that funny? She was always blonde at home. It doesn't seem fair that the women here should look at the face of Mary and see themselves, when I never saw myself in her. There are no Marys that look remotely like you. If Mary looks different in every country, that must mean there is no true face for her, so she must not be real. Don't you think? Lately I've thought about how easy life would be if I were to give up on God and the whole thing.

Being there reminded me of school Mass and the smell of dust that was always in the chapel. Do you miss things like that? Do you still talk to the girls? It's been so long since I heard from any of them, probably because, after you left, I told Maria I liked a girl. Not you, just a girl. She was so nice about it, but I could tell I freaked her out. I think she wanted to be okay with it, but she just wasn't. I remember all I wanted was to talk to you about it, but I couldn't, because you were gone. Isn't it funny that ye were my whole world, and now we struggle to even speak to each other? I told Maria that I was in love, actually, but that was a long time ago.

That statue of the Virgin was like Maria, with her brown hair and bright face. Only Maria is no virgin. She is a horrible tramp. Maybe Mary was the same. I just don't care anymore, I hope she's happy, wher-

ever she is now.
It's so hot here all the time, it's like a heatwave that never stops.
Still yours,
Susannah

How could I focus on anything when she sends letters like this? When she says she is still mine? How must it have felt for her, to let go of God, and the guilt, and everything that burdens us? She just dropped it in that chapel and left Mexico unafraid of the Lord. I cannot imagine how terrifying or liberating that must have felt. All it took was some brunette hair.

If I could only write back to her and tell her that I have given up on God too, and on Mother, and Crossmore, and everything that kept us apart. As much as I have given up on those things, I haven't let them go, because for every way they are deplorable there is a way they are beautiful. I have an unshakeable faith in them all. I don't know if there is anything to be done about it.

Tonight Martin is standing in the doorway of our bedroom, his evening eyes heavy from looking at me. It's obvious what he wants, but I don't invite him to come near. Instead, I lie on my side, facing away from him and his body, which is aching to be known. Even when I deny him, he is loyal. There are plenty of women down in the pub who would gladly take him home, and yet he is glad to spend the night in our touchless bed. I could withhold my body forever, and still I don't think he would leave. It's as though he has an unshakeable faith in me.

22

JANUARY 1995

Sunflower,
You keep impressing me with your stories, where are you now? I wish I could have seen you in Colombia. Why don't you come to Dublin next? Why don't we go to Crossmore? Sometimes I think I ought to go back there and talk to the girls and my mother and everyone.
I don't mind where you go next, or where you've been before, as long as when you read this, you stop and you're with me. I don't care if that's selfish, I am selfish, you must know that by now.
Yours in depth,
Lucy

WE SHOULD GET HOME NOW before it gets rowdy, but everybody likes to dawdle around outside the pub. The last few weeks have been an endless string of nights out. There's really nothing else to do, since I am not going home for Christmas. Evelyn's wonderful mother invited us all over for Christmas dinner. She reminds me of Eimear's mother. I was so glad, because Martin has gone home this year, and I was sick at the thought of spending Christmas Day on my own. It didn't seem sensible to go home. I couldn't face Mother, especially after learning that Susannah came out to Maria. Although he wanted to stay with me, I insisted Martin went home to his mother. He needed to get back to the farm for a week and get back to himself.

'You'll break your mother's heart if I go down and you don't.'

He told me. How little he knows. I have already broken Mother's heart, we got over it. Reluctantly, he left me in the city on Christmas Eve and promised to be back before the New Year. I asked him not to rush. This break from him has been very strange. We have not spent a day apart since we were eighteen. Christmas went by in a nice blur.

Outside the pub, Geraldine offers me her jacket. I hate this gesture, but I hate the cold more, so I take it. She is only another person to use. It's such a dark night, there's not even the hint of a star in the hateful city sky. When Róisín's cigarette will not catch, I take it from her and light it inside Geraldine's jacket, where I am struck by the smell of her soap. I hate the cigarette going from my lips to Róisín's, and her winking at me when she says thanks. I hate the way that Geraldine looks at me in her jacket. It seems my New Year is going to be full of hate. We really ought to go home.

I haven't been at the flat much, only once to check the post, when I received a photograph from Susannah. A physical, glossy photograph, which I brought in my handbag tonight. How embarrassing. Having it with me is so sickeningly comforting.

On New Year's Day, I wake up in the spare room, the warm blonde of Geraldine's body lying on me. Carefully, I lift her off me and sneak out of bed with my handbag, past everyone dozing on the couches. There is light chat happening, people are beginning to stir. I could just leave now and not say a word to anyone. In the bathroom, I take the photograph out of my bag, and under the noise of the fan, I whisper the note on the back to myself: *Because you were wondering how I look...*

As soon as I see her there, I don't hear my waking friends or the fan or my conscience. I hear the humming of the desert and her laughter. Even in Ireland, on the first day in January, I feel the sun of Peru beating on me. I feel like it's only been a few hours since I last saw her. Suddenly, I wish I was drunk again. Perhaps if I ask, some of the girls would come day drinking with me to get my mind off this photograph. Look at the colours of her. Look at all the colours of her world. There is not one shade of me. She looks so happy.

She is standing on a porch, under the arch of the canopy, propping a dark wood door open with one hand, kicking one foot to the camera.

Julian took this one of me. I'm waiting for Damien and Deirdre to bring back our dinner. Imagine weather this hot in the winter.

Her hair is so much lighter and longer than it used to be. She is tanned and looks shorter than she is. The sole of her bare foot is stained with orange dust, she might not wear shoes at all anymore. That filthy Julian, with his filthy camera, taking this perfect picture.

There were lizards running around the porch, I don't think you can see them in the picture, but one ran over my foot. They used to freak me out, but I don't even notice now.

We won't have any internet in the jungle. I'll send letters when I get a chance.

S

Julian, the world granted you a wonderful favour. How he must have felt to look up at her there, framed by the canopy and arch of the door, lit up by the porch light and the late purple sun, with lizards running round her feet. How I must look, half-dressed in the ensuite, staring at this photograph. If she knew. If anyone knew.

Martin's return from Crossmore is nearing. I don't want to walk back to the flat this morning, not in the snow. Could I lie in bed with Geraldine all day, not speaking? I go back in and wake her with a kiss, and hope she will treat me as well as she did last night. Briefly, I am stopped by the smell of sweat in her hair; only briefly. Later Martin will tell me I'm getting a bit old for sleepovers. He might tell me I owe him a New Year's kiss. Evelyn will tell me the reason I'm not happy is because I keep giving myself to people that I don't care about.

'So what's happening with Martin?'

Meadhbh asks me from her bed on the sofa as Geraldine and I creep into the living room. Nobody asks about what we did last night, or this morning. Isn't Meadhbh funny to ask such a complicated question so early in the morning?

The windows need to be opened now, last night needs to leave our bodies. I will make us breakfast and put the stereo on and hope that we can all have fresh starts this morning. Evelyn is in the kitchen with the fridge open, wrapping a little sheet of acid in tinfoil and putting it in the egg tray. When we first met, I really thought all her money came from selling her pottery. It isn't my place to call her out. We just won't have eggs, I'm sure there are enough rashers to go around.

When Meadhbh mentions Martin, I see Geraldine perking up and listening. I think she wants to hear that I'm unhappy with him. Maybe she thinks I could leave him for her. That's not likely, considering I couldn't even leave him for the love of my life. I tell Meadhbh through the serving hatch,

'I have no idea. He keeps mentioning marriage, but he's not even finished college. We haven't even had sex in so long. I don't know what's happening.'

As her eyes widen, I realise that she only meant to ask what is happening with Martin over the next few days. As in, when is he coming back from Crossmore. Evelyn laughs while she washes her hands. Why would I assume that Meadhbh woke up dying to hear about my drama? This is not breakfast talk. So far everything about 1995 has been embarrassing.

'Go away.'

Meadhbh laughs and gets off the sofa to join us in the kitchen. Maybe she thinks I will tell her more if we are closer. Maybe she's right. The rashers start to hiss in the pan, and she lights a cigarette for me. I have started now, I might as well go on.

'He's coming home today. I'm afraid he's after asking Dad if he can propose to me. It's really weird, I miss him but I'm dreading seeing him.'

'Yeah, and what about your one?'

Evelyn asks. It's sad that I don't even consider that she might be talking about Geraldine. By now Meadhbh must have some small idea about Susannah, because I mention her fleetingly but intensely, as though she were dead and I have not mourned her loss. It is a little like that. I ash the cigarette into the sink and realise too late that it is full of dishes. Evelyn does not react.

'It's complicated.'

I laugh.

'Actually, no, it's not complicated. I was in love with her, and I ruined it. That's all.'

'Is she back home with Martin now?'

'Peruvian Amazonia, last I heard, but that was a while ago. It's harder to talk when she's so remote.'

I ash in the sink again. Meadhbh is surprised, and she would like to ask me what I've heard about Peru, but won't. Now that we are talking about her, I realise that Susannah and I were only together for one year. One small, very full year. Maybe even less than a year. It felt like a lifetime. Yes, I definitely need to move on. I press the rashers into the pan, and they spit on my arm.

'So you talk to her?'

Meadhbh asks, and Evelyn leaves the kitchen to go and sit with Geraldine, who can probably half hear what I am saying.

'When I can. I don't think she misses Ireland at all. Am I pathetic?'

Meadhbh shakes her head. It is so strange to be understood. Even when they don't approve of what I'm doing, they don't judge.

Going home, I'm struck with the fear, and I can't help but think of what Martin has said and heard in Crossmore, and of all the things he will want to do and say when he gets home. The flat is empty and cold when I get back. Although I see there is a few days of post on the floor, I can't bring myself to check it yet, just in case there is something from her. Instead, I stand in our tiny shower until the water runs cold. The wallpaper in the bedroom is yellowing; I'm afraid it's from my cigarettes. They are so bad for me, I know that, and still I light one and smoke it and further yellow the walls and my teeth and my lungs. In the kitchen, I wrap myself up in our mass of blankets while the kettle boils, and as I suspected, I find her letter in the pile of post.

L,

I was outside most of the day, I caught the sun. I know you like me best like that, sun rusted. Do you remember the day you iced my sunburn in my kitchen? I'm sucking an ice cube now, and it made me think of you.

It's very easy, trudging through the jungle. After trudging through a year with you, everything is easy.

I have a lot of important things to do tonight and tomorrow. I better go and do them. Merry christmas and happy new year. I hope '95 is less of a fuck up for you than the last few.

All my love,

S

The kettle boils, the steam is lifting the paint away from the wall. This flat will be dust by the time we are finished with it. I hate it. There isn't one thing in my life that I'm not sick of. The flat, Martin, the letters, my ugly feelings. I feel as though I am nothing but a lesson for other people to learn, a necessary heartbreak before they know true happiness. This is no way to live. I am not bringing this into the new year with me.

I will send Martin back to Rita, I will finish with Geraldine, and I will write a final letter to Susannah, perhaps with enough conviction that she comes back to me, perhaps not. Either way, this living death must end.

Susannah,

There is a constant humming within me, beyond my heartbeat, a feeling of permanent dissatisfaction. It is the void which you used to fill. For a while, I thought that writing to you would help me move on, but it has only made the void greater. You waited so long for me, I wonder, are you still waiting? Because I cannot let you go.

It feels as though I never left Crossmore. I am still just a teenager, there in the rocky fields, where you are the brightest thing, the hottest thing, the only thing. I hope you know that you were never just a phase or a passing thrill. You were everything, you still are. I am not being romantic, I am being honest. I have not grown since I left you. Please, I think I need you to grow.

I've been smoking a lot recently. The smell always reminds me of you. For the second when the flame lights the joint, you are with me. Then the flame goes, and I am left with only embers of you to breathe. I cannot live on your embers anymore. If you want me, I'm yours, if not, let me know now, so I might learn to live without you.

I'll go to South America, or you could come here, or we could go to the Otherworld or to Hell, or we could go home, to Crossmore, where I left my heart. Just tell me the place, and I'll meet you there.

Susannah, you are Heaven made flesh, you have been the greatest fire of my life. It's not good enough, I know, but for every time I made you feel inadequate, I have died a hundred deaths. I'll love you until the earth finishes. Just tell me, yes or no.

Yours forever,
Lucy

Martin bursts through the door, I hurry to hide the paper. He is heavy with bags from home, his skin is brighter, he is swollen from all the feeding. There is a lot to make right with him too. Hugging the cold off him, I catch the scent of his mother's house, and there is the hint of country air left on his jumper. I breathe it deeply. I want to wear his clothes so I smell of it. It's nice to feel him again, to have my shadow back. But I must not let this confuse me. This is only a hug from one friend to another, I'm just a little lonely. He is not what I want, and I will tell him that and then remain unfeeling until Susannah tells me what to feel.

He has presents from my family, and his family, and biscuit tins filled with Granny's baking, and so many stories. I put it all on the coffee table, and he kisses me like he was dying without me, like he is looking for something he left behind. The cigarette taste from my mouth does not deter him, he has missed me. We have a lot to catch up on.

A part of him seems far away, like he doesn't know me. He must be homesick. Perhaps now that he has been back there without me, he doesn't see me as a thing from Crossmore anymore. Perhaps he is upset that I didn't go home with him. Perhaps he's just tired from the drive. Sitting on the sofa, he tells me all sorts of things that make me wish that I had gone home too. Ronan Breen had a party, and all the boys were there, and all the girls were there.

'They didn't stop talking about you. Everybody had something to say.'

He says, his voice without inflection. He must be very tired. My girls, do I even want to hear about my girls, or will it break my heart? But I want to know everything about them. What they are doing, who they are seeing, their weight, their haircuts, their clothes. I want to know if they miss me at all, or if my leaving was a great alleviation they didn't realise they needed. If they had been saying lovely things about me, they might have returned my phone calls, they might have come to visit. He tells me that his father has lost weight, that Danny O'Neill got a girl pregnant in the Summer and Bernadette left him, that Rita Hegarty is engaged. Oh dear. Talk like this would normally have me craving the village, where things are slower and life is easier. I must remind myself that life in the village was never easy.

He looks at me, long and quiet. Regardless of what nasty comments the girls might have made about me in Crossmore, he loves me, and although he is trying, looking at me now, he can't find a reason to stop. I have hypnotised this man into submission. I hope I have not damaged his confidence; I hope it is just love, and he isn't as afraid to leave as I have been. Like always, I am sick with guilt. Pulling me near him, he kisses my head and tells me softly about everyone at home. It's like he never left. If I close my eyes now, I might never open them again. I close them.

In the evening, he takes himself from the sofa and carries me to bed. I don't open my eyes once. I love him.

When I wake up in the morning, the bed is empty. He must work double shifts this week to make up for all the time he missed over Christmas. They might still be drinking from last night when he arrives to mop the floor. I hope he'll have a drink with them. With my free morning, I can get rid of my last letter. This can't wait until she is out of the jungle. It must be taken from me now. On my way to Evelyn's, a small rain begins to fall, and I wonder when last Susannah saw the rain. When last did she stand in the ocean or hear my name? When will these thoughts dim and leave me?

Evelyn opens her door in a t-shirt, and points to her bedroom and whispers,

'Don't wake her.'

I don't know who Evelyn went to bed with, I don't have the patience to find out. Leaving my jacket at the door, I cross her dark living room to sit at her desk. Like a sister, like a mother, she ties my hair into a ponytail while I wait for the computer to come alive. I feel guilty for intruding on Evelyn's morning, on whoever she has in her bedroom. The frenzy of me, bursting through her door, pulling a mad proclamation from my bag to send to a girl who could not possibly love me anymore. Evelyn squeezes my shoulder and goes to fill the kettle. Whoever is sleeping in Evelyn's room must be exhausted, because not even the screeching of the dial up wakes her. She must not be terribly important either, because Evelyn could have told me to come back later.

'Don't feel like you have to watch.'

I whisper. But Evelyn does not go back to bed. Instead, she lights the last of a blunt left in the ashtray and opens the curtains and makes the coffee. When finally I can see my emails, I am presented with something unnerving. A little alert, an email received, waiting to be read. It takes from my momentum, but I read it before I begin the long task of typing out my letter.

Lucy,

You are my deepest wound, you always will be. I thought I was healing from you, with the distance and the heat, but I'm not. I can't get over you

unless you go away.

Recently, I've had my heart newly broken. It's so much different to what happened between us. I don't even have the same heart anymore, you wouldn't love me if you knew me now. Knowing all the ways you think of us just makes everything hurt worse. I can't bear to hear it anymore.

Don't contact me again, or you'll shatter me beyond repair.

Forever,

Susannah

It's dated from two nights ago. The email was sitting here in the computer on New Year's Eve, when I was one door away with Geraldine. Just as I was clawing my way back to her, she sends me my own death certificate. I feel myself fall backwards, into the grave I dug in my garden so many years ago. It was dug to keep good love away.

Her heart is newly broken. Somebody else has had her heart to break. It wasn't just me and her. It will never be us again. That's it. Over. She has said the word, and it is so.

I do what she asks. I leave her alone, knowing I won't ever get over her, no matter how much silence passes between us. I drink the coffee, I smoke the blunt. Evelyn goes back to bed, and I go home. Now my world has ended, the rebuilding must begin.

23

FEBRUARY 1995

WITHOUT SUSANNAH TO RUN TO, my plan to be a better person quickly fades from view. I am too afraid to stop Martin from loving me, I'm too lonely to stop Geraldine from loving me. Yes, it's wrong, yes, I know, but if I can't have the one that I want, I'm going to make the best of the ones that I have. My guilt has gone away, I don't care about anything anymore. Hate me if you want to hate me, I'd love the attention. Let me be delivered to the Devil and wait in Hell for a second Harrowing. All I'm doing is trying to love people. All I need is the right kind of love back.

Every evening, I ring Mother, and my throat tightens as I wait for her to answer the phone. We have the same conversation every time, I can almost predict the lilts in her voice when she is talking. Neither of us ever has much gossip, but still we go through it. We talk about Granny, the farm, the town, and then Martin. She wants to know about his job, when he is moving home, and if he ever mentions the future. He must have said something at Christmas. All she wants is to hear that I'm committed to him, nothing else about me. I miss her as my mother, when she cared about every facet of me; these days she is only a matchmaker or a familiar older woman I talk to.

Still, it's nice to hear her voice. I like the distraction, and Mother likes to hear about the city. When she was young, she visited a handful of times, and certain landmarks still stick out in her head – the stone walls of the university, the statues on the main street, obscure cafés and bars that she walked past or spent a few hours in, places that belong to her because they only exist in her memory. The pub she visited at sixteen, on a street I can never find though it is in the same tiny city as me. She likes to tell me all about these places as though I don't live here – what the facades are like, the smells of the streets, the dark wood of the bars – and she asks what they are now. Though I always promise to find out, I can never tell her for sure.

I try not to let her hear me smoking while we talk. But she is my mother, she always knows when I am doing something I shouldn't be. Paranoid, I drop the box of cigarettes into the drawer by my bed and get a glimpse of the last letter I wrote to Susannah, all the words that never made their way to her. The photograph of her on the porch. All she has sent me, right before my eyes, and Mother's voice in my ear. It makes me wince, it scares me. I close the drawer tight, just in case Mother can sense it through the phone. Perhaps I'll take those things to Evelyn's and burn them. Perhaps I'll keep them forever.

There was a bomb scare in Derry that wasn't reported on the news. Somebody told Martin about it at work, and as I am telling Mother, an ambulance races past my window. The way it screams is unignorable, even all the way down in Crossmore, where it deafens her. Instinctually, I bless myself, and she does the same. A silly habit that could mean life or death.

'You'd hear so many ambulances here, Mam. I hardly notice them now.'

'Gosh, you'd never get them here.'

It's something for us to laugh at. I've never even seen the inside of an ambulance; we are quietly glad that suffering belongs to others.

'Nobody dead at home?'

A stupid question, a little joke. I am not expecting to hear a name, but she says,

'Ah, only Catríona O'Shea there.'

It's old news, she doesn't say it with any tone of importance. There is a deaf second as we both realise what she has said. She is biting her tongue, I can almost hear her teeth cutting through her tastebuds. Catríona O'Shea, who left in 1992, who made Susannah motherless, who I haven't heard a word about since, dead. Oh, Mother, who have you dragged up from the dirt?

'When did she die?'

'I didn't think you knew her.'

She stutters across her words, trying to buy another minute.

'Of course, I knew her. You know who she is, Mam.'

'Oh yes, she was belonging to one of your friends, I just don't know. Somebody's auntie or something.'

Who knows what will happen if I say her name. I don't think I've mentioned her to Mother since she caught us tangled up in my bedsheet as teenagers. When was the last time I said her name out loud? Those blessed syllables, do I dare?

'Susannah's mother. You know who she is, Mam, she walked out on the family.'

And she pretends to remember.

'Oh yes, that was her! Well, you'd never hear about them anymore, they're all more or less gone. Catríona's sister is living in the house, I think.'

Should I care about the house? They've always been gone. The whole family was always gone, it was always just Susannah, there on her own. How alone she must be now.

'What happened to her?'

'Breast cancer. I think by the time they found it she was half gone already.'

I couldn't bless myself enough. I need to go home.

'Well, they were all home for the funeral, of course. The brothers are sort of hippies, I think. I didn't see them with years.'

The funeral has happened already. She never said a word. Nobody said a word.

'When was she buried?'

I ask, and Mother hates me for asking, she hates herself more for mentioning it.

'God, I don't know. Early in January.'

I breathe deeply, twice. I'm lost for words.

'I think Martin is looking for the phone, Mam. I'll ring you after.'

I hear her trying to stop me, to catch me before I fall back into who I used to be, but I have already fallen. I cut her off. May I never lift the phone to her again.

Catríona O'Shea, dead and gone. At last. All she ever wanted was to disappear, now she has gone beyond finding. Susannah already mourned her mother once, when she was eighteen and abandoned, spending half the Summer lying in the bog of her unkempt garden. I wonder if the funeral was any comfort since Susannah denounced God. Did she finish her grieving all those years ago? Or is she falling to a deeper depth, into a new and harsher world with even less of a mother? If I could only have her with me, even for a second. If I could only be there without hurting her and make her a little less lonely. What I wouldn't give. When she said her heart was newly broken, I never expected this.

She never said her mother was sick. Did she even know? Why did nobody tell me? Are they really so afraid of us? A little love, a great love, is that such a threat? Maria, Eimear, Joan – those names that I once said like prayers are now just noises I no longer hear. Those old sisters of mine have done all they can to separate themselves from me, as though we never meant anything to each other. Could nobody have spared two minutes to phone me and tell me Catríona was gone? And

Mother, with her mouth shut tight, terrified that if I went home to the mourners, her nightmare would come back to life.

I get in the shower, the smallest place in the flat, and still it is impossibly big, and expanding. All this time later, all the distance between us, all the worlds that keep her from me, and still I have shattered just by saying her name to Mother. The water is scalding, caustic, endless, and scrubbing my skin, I know that it would take an entire ocean to wash her off me.

Dripping wet, I leave the shower and walk naked across the bedroom. Martin has come home; he looks at me from the bed. He glances up at me, not caring that I am undressed. He has never looked at me this way. Like I am a normal thing that does not startle him. Any old girl off the street, soaking the carpet. Whatever has him so quiet must be serious if he can keep a steady hand when I am wet and naked before him. I know I've lost some weight since the new year, but not enough to merit this look. I'm in such shock now that he could pull me onto the bed and I wouldn't even feel it.

Martin, won't you look at me like you always do? Let me be your sweetheart, just for a minute, give me a bit of your steady ground. Remind me that you and I are a sure thing, as certain as the sunset. Martin, tell me that you are where I belong, or I'll go back to Crossmore right now. Stop me from going back to her, stop her sunlight from burning through me. Stop me from disappointing her. Look after me the way you always have. Martin just look, your girl is here.

He ashes his cigarette onto the floor.

A cigarette. My box on the bed. The drawer pulled open.

'Martin, darling.'

I get a glance, and then he's back to looking out the window. No matter what I give him now, all I will get is apathy. The nearest he comes to me is with his eyes, falling on the spot where my hair is dripping on the carpet, darkening the weave.

'I love you, Martin.'

I say, and I mean every letter. I sit next to him on the bed, every part of me laid out before him. My skin, my sorrow, my soul, all there to be taken. I have never been so earnest with him. He sighs, I close the drawer. It's too late, he has seen what I keep in there, he has seen the place I keep her. The letters that spell out all the ways that she hates me, and all the ways that he is not enough. Those letters, wet with all the blood from my heart. He has seen them. If I had stepped out of the shower a minute earlier, if I had left my cigarettes on the bed, if I had any control over my wild and eager heart, this might have been avoided.

I wish I wouldn't cry, although I do. Not only for tonight, but for all the years I have spent away from Crossmore. For all the seasons of Susannah that I have missed. For her loss, for my loss. For his tender punishment of my body, the sin and its penance, and for my unrelenting attempts to straighten the curve. I cry out for this rigid life that has killed us.

'When I was home at Christmas and everybody was talking about you. Do you know what they were saying?'

My heart slows. I shake my head and pretend there is nothing to know.

'They were all telling me that you used ride Susannah O'Shea. Maria Kealy was after telling everyone. Imagine that. People were telling me that about my own girlfriend. Imagine how stupid I looked. Ye all laughing behind my back for years.'

My heart stops. They all know. Susannah only confessed a small and anonymous feeling to Maria, and look, it has become this. The raw and painful longing I have felt all my life is scattered around Crossmore. They all know. He knows. His eyes are watered, they were never so blue. He is trying to keep his voice hard, but he cannot.

'I should have known, like. The way you carry on, and all them girls you hang around with. Since I came back, I've been trying to convince myself that everything was grand. It actually was grand, until I seen that.'

And he nods over to the drawer, where the letters are. I don't want to ask how much he has read. He is trying to find words that would hurt me the way that I have hurt him. It's clear in the way he sucks on the cigarette that he is humiliated. He ought to tell me that he could have been the one engaged to Rita, and that he only broke up with her because he wanted me; he ought to let me know all the ways I wasted his time. But his world was only just torn to pieces, it will take a while before he can say all the terrible things that I deserve to hear.

Part of me is so nervous that I could faint, because he could do anything. He could throw me out now, naked, with nothing. He could ruin me. The other part of me doesn't care what he does, because the worst has just happened. I wait for him to do what he wants. And he sees me, ready to take whatever I am given.

Finally, because he loves me so deeply that he cannot stop himself, he gives me what I need. He pulls me into his arms, he covers my nakedness and doesn't complain as I soak his clothes. He kisses my head, and with his voice as soft as moss, he says,

'It's alright.'

Already my ache is eased, I can breathe; he is saving me from himself. I never loved a man more. We have become emotional people.

'I'm really sorry, Martin.'

'I know.'

'For everything. I wish it was different, I wish I was different.'

There is a soft silence. I feel his heart breaking, I feel him thinking, and he hugs me tighter.

'I don't. Then you wouldn't be my Lucy.'

He doesn't let me apologise anymore. There is nothing to be sorry for, there is nothing to forgive. It isn't my fault. In the morning, or in a year, when he has had some time to adjust, there might be hatred. But tonight, he is my Martin, as I have always known him. As I love him and need him. Even with all I have done, he bends to be the man that I need. He loves me like he has always loved me, because I have always been this way. All along, a part of him has known that he has just been something for me to lean on. Now I have woken him up from his dreaming, and he sees the girl that he adores so fiercely is different than he thought. And still he lets me cry on him and holds me like I am important. Still he loves me. He is still Martin. I am still Lucy.

'I can go to Evelyn's, it's okay.'

He sighs, full of feeling, and says,

'Not tonight, love.'

He pulls the blanket over us and takes his last chance at holding me before I am gone forever.

24

MARCH 1995

CROSSMORE IS AS IT ALWAYS was: a wild and overgrown place where hearts swell and burst the most violently. We feel deeply here. No matter how far I go, I am soaked from the earth and dusted from the pollen, and I will always carry these deep feelings. So will Martin, so will Susannah, so will the others. And although we go far to escape them, at one time or another, we must return to Crossmore. To the roots of ourselves.

It is so strange to be home. I only told Mother that I was coming last night. It will be so surreal to be in the house again. As soon as I stepped off the bus, I started making my way to Susannah's house. This is why I'm here. I need to get to her house before my nerve wears off. A part of me is afraid to look around as I walk, because I don't want to be seen. I like the feeling of putting that part of myself away and ignoring it.

Walking through the morning, down Susannah's road, I feel myself become who I was. I am on my own path. At last, I am nearing the place where I belong. All the time I spent trying to find myself, I was being somebody that I am not. I was born perfect, and every step I took brought me further from that. Now every day I am closer to being that girl again. I want to be that girl here. I want the full version of myself to exist under the pale skies of Crossmore. I want to feel blessed by the serenity of the wasteland again.

It really does feel so good to be back. A few houses have been repainted, there are some new flowers growing in the hedges, but besides that, nothing has changed. It's so lovely to walk on this road again. To smell the country air, to see the fat, bright fuchsias, so unlike the thin ones in the city. I don't know where in the world Susannah is now, but I must deliver this letter. I might be delivering it to nobody, but at least it will be gone from me. I just want her to know all those things that I couldn't tell her before. If she knows them, I might know some peace.

When this weight is lifted from me, I will be able to face Mother. Something has shifted in me lately, and at last I am ready to tell her that Martin and I are finished. That I have been staying at Evelyn's house. That I am gay. I've been saying that a lot recently. I've settled into it now. It feels nice. I used to think it would always feel like an inconvenience, or at best, a numbness. But it feels good. I like it more and more. And even if this feeling fades when I see Mother, and I am terrified again, I will still have to tell her so that Martin can tell his family. He has been so gracious.

I'll tell her everything. And if she wants me to go, I will go back to the city. And if she wants me to stay, I will stay a while. I will be okay either way. If this is the last breath of Crossmore air I ever get, I will be okay. If I have to say goodbye to the village, I will be okay eventually. My sweet wasteland, all you ever really did was hold me back.

There are the towering, untrimmed tree branches. There is her gate, unlocked. The drive is empty. The lawn is cut close. The interior may have been gutted by now.

Standing at her door, I don't feel the way that I used to. There is no guilt, no fear. I don't care if anybody sees me here, looking for the love of my life. I want to be seen here. I want the world to see me with her. I want them all to see me setting myself free. I put the letter through the door. I knock. I walk away.

Inside, it falls on the carpet. Before I'm off the porch, the door opens.

And here is Susannah, a flame in the doorway. I am winded. She holds the letter in her hand as though she knew I was coming.

'Lucy.'

She says softly. I have to squint to see her.

'You're back.'

ACKNOWLEDGEMENTS

I would like to extend a huge thank you to my agent, Hannah, for taking a chance on me and for the time she has dedicated to getting my novel where it is. Likewise, thank you to all of the team at Northbank Talent Management for all their hard work.

I would also like to thank my editor, Jenna, for her enthusiasm and efforts, and all of the team at VERVE for their time and energy.

All of your hard work is so appreciated, thank you.

Reading Group Questions

1. *Sunburn* depicts the excitement of first love alongside the trials of coming of age as a queer person in a very specific setting. Do you think that Lucy and Susannah's relationship would have unfolded differently in another place?
2. How is Lucy's sense of self affected by her environment, in Crossmore and then in Dublin?
3. To what extent is the dynamic between Lucy and Martin complicated by social expectations?
4. The novel deals with complex and seemingly unhealthy mother-daughter relationships. Discuss this, and consider the impact of these relationships on Lucy and Susannah, and their relationship.
5. To what point is Lucy her own obstacle? Do you think she can or should be judged for struggling to choose between her relationship with Susannah and the stability of her teenage life in Crossmore?
6. Discuss the portrayal of teenage female friendship in the novel.
7. How does this depiction of growing up queer in a small Irish town in the 90s compare with other imaginings of 90s queerness in literature?
8. Lucy maintains that she loves Crossmore throughout the novel, despite her complex personal experience there. Why do you think this is?
9. What's next for Lucy and Susannah? Do you think their love is sustainable or do they – especially Lucy – view each other through the rose-tinted lenses of first love?